This book is a work of fiction. All characters and events portrayed in this book are fictional, and any resemblance to any real people or incidents is purely coincidental.

THE HERO

W. Somerset Maugham 1874-1965

Cover Painting:

"The Prodigal Son in Modern Life: The Departure" by James Jacques Joseph Tissot, 1882.

Cover Design Copyright © 2008 by Vera Nazarian

ISBN-13: 978-1-60762-005-1
ISBN-10: 1-60762-005-7

Original Publication: 1901

Reprint Trade Paperback Edition

November 2008

A Publication of
Norilana Books
P. O. Box 2188
Winnetka, CA 91396
www.norilana.com

Printed in the United States of America

The Hero

Norilana Books
Classics

www.norilana.com

"Rule, Britannia!
Britannia, rule the waves;
Britons never will be slaves."
"Alfred": a Masque.
By James Thomson.

"O Sophonisba, Sophonisba, O!"
"Sophonisba": a Tragedy.
By the same Author.

To
Miss Julia Maugham

The Hero

W. Somerset Maugham

I

Colonel Parsons sat by the window in the dining-room to catch the last glimmer of the fading day, looking through his *Standard* to make sure that he had overlooked no part of it. Finally, with a little sigh, he folded it up, and taking off his spectacles, put them in their case.

"Have you finished the paper?" asked his wife.

"Yes, I think I've read it all. There's nothing in it."

He looked out of window at the well-kept drive that led to the house, and at the trim laurel bushes which separated the front garden from the village green. His eyes rested, with a happy smile, upon the triumphal arch which decorated the gate for the home-coming of his son, expected the next day from South Africa. Mrs. Parsons knitted diligently at a sock for her husband, working with quick and clever fingers. He watched the rapid glint of the needles.

"You'll try your eyes if you go on much longer with this light, my dear."

"Oh, I don't require to see," replied his wife, with a gentle, affectionate smile. But she stopped, rather tired, and laying the sock on the table, smoothed it out with her hand.

"I shouldn't mind if you made it a bit higher in the leg than the last pair."

"How high would you like it?"

She went to the window so that the Colonel might show the exact length he desired; and when he had made up his mind, sat down again quietly on her chair by the fireside, with hands crossed on her lap, waiting placidly for the maid to bring the lamp.

Mrs. Parsons was a tall woman of fifty-five, carrying herself with a certain diffidence, as though a little ashamed of her stature, greater than the Colonel's; it had seemed to her through life that those extra inches savoured, after a fashion, of disrespect. She knew it was her duty spiritually to look up to her husband, yet physically she was always forced to look down. And eager to prevent even the remotest suspicion of wrong-doing, she had taken care to be so submissive in her behaviour as to leave no doubt that she recognised the obligation of respectful obedience enjoined by the Bible, and confirmed by her own conscience. Mrs. Parsons was the gentlest of creatures, and the most kind-hearted; she looked upon her husband with great and unalterable affection, admiring intensely both his head and his heart. He was her type of the upright man, walking in the ways of the Lord. You saw in the placid, smooth brow of the Colonel's wife, in her calm eyes, even in the severe arrangement of the hair, parted in the middle and drawn back, that her character was frank, simple, and straightforward. She was a woman to whom evil had never offered the smallest attraction; she was merely aware of its existence theoretically. To her the only way of life had been that which led to God; the others had been non-existent. Duty had one hand only, and only one finger; and that finger had always pointed definitely in one direction. Yet Mrs. Parsons had a firm mouth, and a chin square enough to add another impression. As she sat motionless, hands crossed, watching her husband with loving eyes, you might have divined that, however kind-hearted, she was not indulgent, neither lenient to her own faults nor to those of others; perfectly unassuming, but with a sense of duty, a feeling of the absolute rightness of some deeds and of the absolute wrongness of others, which would be, even to those she loved best in the world, utterly unsparing.

"Here's a telegraph boy!" said Colonel Parsons suddenly. "Jamie can't have arrived yet!"

"Oh, Richmond!"

Mrs. Parsons sprang from her chair, and a colour brightened her pale cheeks. Her heart beat painfully, and tears of eager expectation filled her eyes.

"It's probably only from William, to say the ship is signalled," said the Colonel, to quieten her; but his own voice trembled with anxiety.

"Nothing can have happened, Richmond, can it?" said Mrs. Parsons, her cheeks blanching again at the idea.

"No, no! Of course not! How silly you are!" The telegram was brought in by the servant. "I can't see without a light," said the Colonel.

"Oh, give it me; I can see quite well."

Mrs. Parsons took it to the window, and with trembling hand tore it open.

"*Arriving to-night; 7.25.*—JAMIE."

Mrs. Parson looked for one moment at her husband, and then, unable to restrain herself, sank on a chair, and hiding her face with her hands, burst into tears.

"Come, come, Frances," said the Colonel, trying to smile, but half choked with his own emotion, "don't cry! You ought to laugh when you know the boy's coming home."

He patted her on the shoulder, and she took his hand, holding it for comfort. With the other, the Colonel loudly blew his nose. At last Mrs Parsons dried her eyes.

"Oh, I thank God that it's all over! He's coming home. I hope we shall never have to endure again that anxiety. It makes me tremble still when I think how we used to long for the paper to come, and dread it; how we used to look all through the list of casualties, fearing to see the boy's name."

"Well, well, it's all over now," said the Colonel cheerily, blowing his nose again. "How pleased Mary will be!"

It was characteristic of him that almost his first thought was of the pleasure this earlier arrival would cause to Mary Clibborn, the girl to whom, for five years, his son had been engaged.

"Yes," said Mrs. Parson, "but she'll be dreadfully disappointed not to be here; she's gone to the Polsons in Tunbridge Wells, and she won't be home till after supper."

"That is a pity. I'm afraid it's too late to go and meet him; it's nearly seven already."

"Oh, yes; and it's damp this evening. I don't think you ought to go out."

Then Mrs. Parsons roused herself to household matters.

"There's the supper to think of, Richmond," she said; "we've only the rest of the cold mutton, and there's not time to cook one of to-morrow's chickens."

They had invited three or four friends to dinner on the following day to celebrate the return of their son, and Mrs. Parsons had laid in for the occasion a store of solid things.

"Well, we might try and get some chops. I expect Howe is open still."

"Yes, I'll send Betty out. And we can have a blanc-mange for a sweet."

Mrs. Parsons went to give the necessary orders, and the Colonel walked up to his son's room to see, for the hundredth time, that everything was in order. They had discussed for days the question whether the young soldier should be given the best spare bedroom or that which he had used from his boyhood. It was wonderful the thought they expended in preparing everything as they fancied he would like it; no detail slipped their memory, and they arranged and rearranged so that he should find nothing altered in his absence. They attempted to satisfy in this manner the eager longing of their hearts; it made them both a little happier to know that they were actually doing something for their son. No pain in love is so hard to bear as that which comes from the impossibility of doing any service for the well-beloved, and no service is so repulsive that love cannot make it delightful and easy. They had not seen him for five years, their only child; for he had gone from Sandhurst straight to India, and thence, on the outbreak of war, to the Cape. No one knew how much the lonely parents had felt the long separation, how eagerly they awaited his letters, how often they read them.

* * *

But it was more than parental affection which caused the passionate interest they took in Jamie's career. They looked to him to restore the good name which his father had lost. Four generations of Parsons had been in the army, and had borne themselves with honour to their family and with credit to themselves. It was a fine record that Colonel Parsons inherited of brave men and good soldiers; and he, the truest, bravest, most honourable of them all, had dragged the name through the dust; had been forced from the service under a storm of obloquy, disgraced, dishonoured, ruined.

Colonel Parsons had done the greater portion of his service creditably enough. He had always put his God before the War Office, but the result had not been objectionable; he looked upon his men with fatherly affection, and the regiment, under his command, was almost a model of propriety and seemliness. His influence was invariably for good, and his subordinates knew that in him they had always a trusty friend; few men had gained more love. He was a mild, even-tempered fellow, and in no circumstance of life forgot to love his neighbour as himself; he never allowed it to slip his memory that even the lowest caste native had an immortal soul, and before God equal rights with him. Colonel Parsons was a man whose piety was so unaggressive, so good-humoured, so simple, that none could resist it; ribaldry and blasphemy were instinctively hushed in his presence, and even the most hardened ruffian was softened by his contact.

But a couple of years before he would naturally have been put on half-pay under the age limit, a little expedition was arranged against some unruly hill-tribes, and Colonel Parsons was given the command. He took the enemy by surprise, finding them at the foot of the hills, and cut off, by means of flanking bodies, their retreat through the two passes behind. He placed his guns on a line of hillocks to the right, and held the tribesmen in the hollow of his hand. He could have massacred them all, but nothing was farther from his thoughts. He summoned them to surrender, and towards evening the headmen came in and agreed to give up their rifles next day; the night was cold, and dark, and stormy. The good Colonel was delighted with the success both of his stratagem and of his humanity. He had not shed a single drop of blood.

"Treat them well," he said, "and they'll treat you better."

He acted like a gentleman and a Christian; but the enemy were neither. He never dreamed that he was being completely overreached, that the natives were using the delay he had unsuspectingly granted to send over the hills urgent messages for help. Through the night armed men had been coming stealthily, silently, from all sides; and in the early morning, before dawn, his flanking parties were attacked. Colonel Parsons, rather astonished, sent them help, and thinking himself still superior in numbers to the rebellious tribesmen, attacked their main body. They wanted nothing better. Falling back slowly, they drew him into the mountain defiles until he found himself entrapped. His little force was surrounded. Five hours were passed in almost blind confusion; men were shot down like flies by an enemy they could not see; and when, by desperate fighting, they managed to cut their way out, fifty were killed and over a hundred more were wounded.

Colonel Parsons escaped with only the remnants of the fine force he had commanded, and they were nerveless, broken, almost panic-stricken. He was obliged to retreat. The Colonel was a brave man; he did what he could to prevent the march from becoming a disorderly rout. He gathered his men together, put courage into them, risked his life a dozen times; but nothing could disguise the fact that his failure was disastrous. It was a small affair and was hushed up, but the consequences were not to be forgotten. The hill-tribes, emboldened by their success, became more venturesome, more unruly. A disturbance which might have been settled without difficulty now required a large force to put it down, and ten times more lives were lost.

Colonel Parsons was required to send in his papers, and left India a broken man.... He came back to England, and settled in his father's house at Little Primpton. His agony continued, and looking into the future, he saw only hideous despair, unavailing regret. For months he could bear to see no one, imagining always that he was pointed out as the man whose folly had cost so many lives. When he heard people laugh he thought it was in scorn of him; when he saw compassion in their eyes he could scarcely restrain his tears. He was indeed utterly broken. He walked in his garden, away from the eyes of his fellows, up and down, continually turning over in his mind the events of that terrible week. And he could not console himself by thinking that any other course would have led to just as bad results. His error was too plain; he could put his finger exactly on the point of his failure and say, "O God! why did I do it?" And as he walked restlessly, unmindful of heat and cold, the tears ran down his thin cheeks, painful and scalding. He would not take his wife's comfort.

"You acted for the best, Richmond," she said.

"Yes, dear; I acted for the best. When I got those fellows hemmed in I could have killed them all. But I'm not a butcher; I couldn't have them shot down in cold blood. That's not war; that's murder. What should I have said to my Maker when He asked me to account for those many souls? I spared them; I imagined they'd understand; but they thought it was weakness. I couldn't know they were preparing a trap for me. And now my name is shameful. I shall never hold up my head again."

"You acted rightly in the sight of God, Richmond."

"I think and trust I acted as a Christian, Frances."

"If you have pleased God, you need not mind the opinion of man."

"Oh, it's not that they called me a fool and a coward—I could have borne that. I did what I thought was right. I thought it my duty to save the lives of my men and to spare the enemy; and the result was that ten times more lives have been lost than if I had struck boldly and mercilessly. There are widows and orphans in England who must curse me because I am the cause that their husbands are dead, and that their fathers are rotting on the hills of India. If I had acted like a savage, like a brute-beast, like a butcher, all those men would have been alive to-day. I was merciful, and I was met with treachery; I was long-suffering, and they thought me weak; I was forgiving, and they laughed at me."

Mrs. Parsons put her hand on her husband's shoulder.

"You must try to forget it, Richmond," she said. "It's over, and it can't be helped now. You acted like a God-fearing man; your conscience is clear of evil intent. What is the judgment of man beside the judgment of God? If you have received insult and humiliation at the hands of man, God will repay you a hundredfold, for you acted as his servant. And I believe in you, Richmond; and I'm proud of what you did."

"I have always tried to act like a Christian and a gentleman, Frances."

At night he would continually dream of those days of confusion and mortal anxiety. He would imagine he was again making that horrible retreat, cheering his men, doing all he could to retrieve the disaster; but aware that ruin only awaited him, conscious that the most ignorant sepoy in his command thought him incapable and mad. He saw the look in the eyes of the officers under him, their bitter contempt, their anger because he forced them to retire before the enemy; and because, instead of honour and glory, they had earned only ridicule. His limbs shook and he sweated with agony as he recalled the interview with his chief: "You're only fit to be a damned missionary," and the last contemptuous words, "I shan't want you any more. You can send in your papers."

But human sorrow is like water in an earthen pot. Little by little Colonel Parsons forgot his misery; he had turned it over in his mind so often that at last he grew confused. It became then only a deep wound partly healed, scarring over; and he began to take an interest in the affairs of the life surrounding him. He could read his paper without every word stabbing him by some chance association; and there is nothing like the daily and thorough perusal of a newspaper for dulling a man's brain. He pottered about his garden gossiping with the gardener; made little alterations in the house—bricks and mortar are like an anodyne; he collected stamps; played bezique with his wife; and finally, in his mild, gentle way, found peace of mind.

But when James passed brilliantly out of Sandhurst, the thought seized him that the good name which he valued so highly might be retrieved. Colonel Parsons had shrunk from telling the youth anything of the catastrophe which had driven him from the service; but now he forced himself to give an exact account thereof. His wife sat by, listening with pain in her eyes, for she knew what torture it was to revive that half-forgotten story.

"I thought you had better hear it from me than from a stranger," the Colonel said when he had finished. "I entered the army with the reputation of my father behind me; my reputation can only harm you. Men will nudge one another and say, 'There's the son of old Parsons, who bungled the affair against the Madda Khels.' You must show them that you're of good stuff. I acted for the best, and my conscience is at ease. I think I did my duty; but if you can distinguish yourself—if you can make them forget—I think I shall die a little happier."

The commanding officer of Jamie's regiment was an old friend of the Colonel's, and wrote to him after a while to say that he thought well of the boy. He had already distinguished himself in a frontier skirmish, and presently, for gallantry in some other little expedition, his name was mentioned in despatches. Colonel Parsons regained entirely his old cheerfulness; Jamie's courage and manifest knowledge of his business made him feel that at last he could again look the world frankly in the face. Then came the Boer War; for the parents at Little Primpton and for Mary Clibborn days of fearful anxiety, of gnawing pain—all the greater because each, for the other's sake, tried to conceal it; and at last the announcement in the paper that James Parsons had been severely wounded while attempting to save the life of a brother officer, and was recommended for the Victoria Cross.

II

The Parsons sat again in their dining-room, counting the minutes which must pass before Jamie's arrival. The table was laid simply, for all their habits were simple; and the blanc-mange prepared for the morrow's festivities stood, uncompromising and stiff as a dissenting minister, in the middle of the table. I wish someone would write an invective upon that most detestable of all the national dishes, pallid, chilly, glutinous, unpleasant to look upon, insipid in the mouth. It is a preparation which seems to mark a transition stage in culture; just as the South Sea Islanders, with the advance of civilisation, forsook putrid whale for roast missionary, the great English middle classes complained that tarts and plum-puddings were too substantial, more suited to the robust digestions of a past generation. In the blanc-mange, on the other hand, they found almost an appearance of distinction; its name, at least, suggested French cookery; it was possible to the plainest cook, and it required no mastication.

"I shall have to tell Betty to make a jelly for dinner to-morrow," said Mrs. Parsons.

"Yes," replied the Colonel; and after a pause: "Don't you think we ought to let Mary know that Jamie has come back? She'd like to see him to-night."

"I've sent over already."

It was understood that James, having got his Company, would marry Mary Clibborn almost at once. His father and mother had been delighted when he announced the engagement. They had ever tried to shield him from all knowledge of evil—no easy matter when a boy has been to a public school and to Sandhurst—holding the approved opinion that ignorance is synonymous with virtue; and they could imagine no better safeguard for his innocence in the multi-coloured life of India than betrothal with a pure, sweet English girl. They looked upon Mary Clibborn already as a daughter, and she, in Jamie's absence, had been their only solace. They loved her gentleness, her goodness, her simple piety, and congratulated themselves on the fact that with her their son could not fail to lead a happy and a godly life.

Mary, during those five years, had come to see them every day; her own mother and father were rather worldly people, and she felt less happy with them than with Colonel Parsons and his wife. The trio talked continually of the absent soldier, always reading to one another his letters. They laughed together over his jokes, mildly, as befitted persons for whom a sense of humour might conceivably be a Satanic snare, and trembled together at his dangers. Mary's affection was free from anything so degrading as passion, and she felt no bashfulness in reading Jamie's love-letters to his parents; she was too frank to suspect that there might be in them anything for her eyes alone, and too candid to feel any delicacy.

But a lumbering fly rolled in at the gate, and the good people, happy at last, sprang to the door.

"Jamie!"

Trembling with joy, they brought him in and sat him down; they knew no words to express their delight, and stood looking at him open-mouthed, smiling.

"Well, here you are! We were surprised to get your telegram. When did you land?"

When they found their tongues, it was only to say commonplace things such as they might have spoken to a casual friend who had come from London for the day. They were so used to controlling themselves, that when their emotion was overpowering they were at a loss to express it.

"Would you like to go upstairs and wash your hands?"

They both accompanied him.

"You see it's all just as it was. We thought you'd like your old room. If you want anything you can ring the bell."

They left him, and going downstairs, sat opposite one another by the fire. The dining-room was furnished with a saddle-bag suite; and Colonel Parsons sat in the "gentleman's chair," which had arms, while Mrs. Parsons sat in the "lady's chair," which had none; nor did either dream, under any circumstances, of using the other's seat. They were a little overcome.

"How thin he is!" said Mrs. Parsons.

"We must feed him up," answered the Colonel.

And then, till the soldier came, they remained in silence. Mrs. Parsons rang the bell for the chops as soon as he appeared, and they sat down; but James ate alone. His people were too happy to do anything but watch him.

"I have had tea made," said Mrs. Parsons, "but you can have some claret, if you prefer it."

Five years' absence had not dulled Jamie's memory of his father's wine, and he chose the tea.

"I think a strong cup of tea will do you most good," said his mother, and she poured it out for him as when he was a boy, with plenty of milk and sugar.

His tastes had never been much consulted; things had been done, in the kindest manner possible, solely for his good. James detested sweetness.

"No sugar, please, mother," he said, as she dived into the sugar-basin.

"Nonsense, Jamie," answered Mrs. Parsons, with her good-humoured, indulgent smile. "Sugar's good for you." And she put in two big lumps.

"You don't ask after Mary," said Colonel Parsons.

"How is she?" said James. "Where is she?"

"If you wait a little she'll be here."

Then Mrs. Parsons broke in.

"I don't know what we should have done without her; she's been so good and kind to us, and such a comfort. We're simply devoted to her, aren't we, Richmond?"

"She's the nicest girl I've ever seen."

"And she's so good. She works among the poor like a professional nurse. We told you that she lived with us for six months while Colonel and Mrs. Clibborn went abroad. She was never put out at anything, but was always smiling and cheerful. She has the sweetest character."

The good people thought they were delighting their son by these eulogies. He looked at them gravely.

"I'm glad you like her," he said.

Supper was finished, and Mrs. Parsons went out of the room for a moment. James took out his case and offered a cigar to his father.

"I don't smoke, Jamie," replied the Colonel.

James lit up. The old man looked at him with a start, but said nothing; he withdrew his chair a little and tried to look unconcerned. When Mrs. Parsons returned, the room was full of smoke; she gave a cry of surprise.

"James!" she said, in a tone of reproach. "Your father objects to smoking."

"It doesn't matter just this once," said the Colonel, good-humouredly.

But James threw his cigar into the fire, with a laugh.

"I quite forgot; I'm so sorry."

"You never told us you'd started smoking," observed Mrs. Parsons, almost with disapprobation, "Would you like the windows open to let the smell out, Richmond?"

There was a ring at the door, and Mary's voice was heard.

"Has Captain Parsons arrived?"

"There she is, Jamie!" said the Colonel, "Rush out to her, my boy!"

But James contented himself with rising to his feet; he turned quite pale, and a singular expression came over his grave face.

Mary entered.

"I ran round as soon as I got your note," she said. "Well, Jamie!"

She stopped, smiling, and a blush brightened her healthy cheeks. Her eyes glistened with happiness, and for a moment, strong as she was, Mary thought she must burst into tears.

"Aren't you going to kiss her, Jamie?" said the father. "You needn't be bashful before us."

James went up to her, and taking her hands, kissed the cheek she offered.

The impression that Mary Clibborn gave was of absolute healthiness, moral and physical. Her appearance was not distinguished, but she was well set up, with strong hands and solid feet; you knew at once that a ten-mile walk invigorated rather than tired her; her arms were muscular and energetic. She was in no way striking; a typical, country-bred girl, with a fine digestion and an excellent conscience; if not very pretty, obviously good. Her face showed a happy mingling of strength and cheerfulness; her blue eyes were guileless and frank; her hair even was rather pretty, arranged in the simplest manner; her skin was tanned by wind and weather. The elements were friendly, and she enjoyed a long walk in a gale, with the rain beating against her cheeks. She was dressed simply and without adornment, as befitted her character.

"I am sorry I wasn't at home when you arrived, Jamie," she said; "but the Polsons asked me to go and play golf at Tunbridge Wells. I went round in bogy, Colonel Parsons."

"Did you, my dear? That's very good."

The Colonel and his wife looked at her with affectionate satisfaction.

"I'm going to take off my hat."

She gave James to put in the hall her sailor hat and her rough tweed cloak. She wore a bicycling skirt and heavy, square-toed boots.

"Say you're glad to see us, Jamie!" she cried, laughing.

Her voice was rather loud, clear and strong, perhaps wanting variety of inflection. She sat by Jamie's side, and broke into a cheerful, rather humorous, account of the day's excursion.

"How silent you are, Jamie!" she cried at last.

"You haven't given me a chance to get a word in yet," he said, smiling gravely.

They all laughed, ready to be pleased at the smallest joke, and banter was the only form of humour they knew.

"Are you tired?" asked Mary, her cheerful eyes softening.

"A little."

"Well, I won't worry you to-night; but to-morrow you must be put through your paces."

"Mary will stand no nonsense," said the Colonel, laughing gently. "We all have to do as she tells us. She'll turn you round her little finger."

"Will she?" said James, glancing down at the solid boots, which the short bicycle skirt rather obtrusively exposed to view.

"Don't frighten him the moment he comes home," cried Mary. "As a matter of fact, I shan't be able to come to-morrow morning; I've got my district-visiting to do, and I don't think Jamie is strong enough to go with me yet. Does your wound hurt you still, Jamie?"

"No," he said, "I can't use my arm much, though. It'll be all right soon."

"You must tell us about the great event to-morrow," said Mary, referring to the deed which had won him the decoration. "You've put us all out by coming sooner than you were expected."

"Have I? I'm sorry."

"Didn't you notice anything when you drove in this evening?"

"No, it was quite dark."

"Good heavens! Why, we've put up a triumphal arch, and there was going to be a great celebration. All the school children were coming to welcome you."

"I'm very glad I missed it," said James, laughing. "I should have hated it."

"Oh, I don't know that you have missed it yet. We must see."

Then Mary rose to go.

"Well, at all events, we're all coming to dinner to-morrow at one."

They went to the door to let her out, and the elder couple smiled again with pleasure when James and Mary exchanged a brotherly and sisterly kiss.

* * *

At last James found himself alone in his room; he gave a sigh of relief—a sigh which was almost a groan of pain. He took out his pipe unconsciously and filled it; but then, remembering where he was, put it down. He knew his father's sensitiveness of smell. If he began to smoke there would quickly be a knock at the door, and the inquiry: "There's such a smell of burning in the house; there's nothing on fire in your room, is there, Jamie?"

He began to walk up and down, and then in exhaustion sank on a chair. He opened the window and looked into the night. He could see nothing. The sky was dark with unmoving clouds, but the fresh air blew gratefully against his face, laden with the scent of the vernal country; a light rain was falling noiselessly, and the earth seemed languid and weary, accepting the moisture with little shuddering gasps of relief.

After an event which has been long expected, there is always something in the nature of reaction. James had looked forward to this meeting, partly with terror, partly with eagerness; and now that it was over, his brain, confused and weary, would not help him to order his thoughts. He clenched his hands, trying to force himself to think clearly; he knew he must decide upon some course at once, and a terrible indecision paralysed his ideas. He loved his people so tenderly, he was so anxious to make them happy, and yet—and yet! If he loved one better than the other it was perhaps his father, because of the pitiful weakness, because of the fragility which seemed to call for a protective gentleness. The old man had altered little in the five years. James could not remember him other than thin and bent and frail, with long wisps of silvery hair brushed over the crown to conceal his baldness, with the cheeks hollow and wrinkled, and a white moustache ineffectually concealing the weak, good-natured mouth. Ever since James could recollect his father had appeared old and worn as now; and there had always been that gentle look in the blue eyes, that manner which was almost painful in its diffidence. Colonel Parsons was a man who made people love him by a modesty which seemed to claim nothing. He was like a child compelling sympathy on account of its utter helplessness, so unsuited to the wear and tear of life that he aroused his fellows' instincts of protection.

And James knew besides what a bitter humiliation it was to his father that he had been forced to leave the service. He remembered, like a deadly, incurable pain suffered by a friend, the occasion on which the old soldier had told him the cause of his disgrace, a sweat of agony standing on his brow. The scene had eaten into Jamie's mind alongside of that other when he had first watched a man die, livid with pain, his eyes glazed and sightless. He had grown callous to such events since then.

Colonel Parsons had come to grief on account of the very kindness of heart, on account of the exquisite humanity which endeared him to the most casual acquaintance. James swore that he would do anything to save him from needless suffering. Nor did he forget his mother, for through the harder manner he saw her gentleness and tender love. He knew that he was all in the world to both of them, that in his hands lay their happiness and their misery. Their love made them feel every act of his with a force out of reason to the circumstance. He had seen in their letters, piercing through the assumed cheerfulness, a mortal anxiety when he was in danger, an anguish of mind that seemed hardly bearable. They had gone through so much for his sake; they deprived themselves of luxury, so that, in the various expenses of his regiment, he should not need to economise. All his life they had surrounded him with loving care. And what their hearts were set upon now was that he should marry Mary Clibborn quickly.

James turned from the window and put his head between his hands, swaying to and fro.

"Oh, I can't," he groaned; "I can't!"

III

In the morning, after breakfast, James went for a walk. He wanted to think out clearly what he had better do, feeling that he must make up his mind at once. Hesitation would be fatal, and yet to speak immediately seemed so cruel, so brutally callous.

Wishing to be absolutely alone, he wandered through the garden to a little wood of beech-trees, which in his boyhood had been a favourite haunt. The day was fresh and sweet after the happy rain of April, the sky so clear that it affected one like a very beautiful action.

James stood still when he came into the wood, inhaling the odour of moist soil, the voluptuous scents of our mother, the Earth, gravid with silent life. For a moment he was intoxicated by the paradise of verdure. The beech-trees rose very tall, with their delicate branches singularly black amid the young leaves of the spring, tender and vivid. The eye could not pierce the intricate greenery; it was more delicate than the summer rain, subtler than the mists of the sunset. It was a scene to drive away all thought of the sadness of life, of the bitterness. Its exquisite fresh purity made James feel pure also, and like a little child he wandered over the undulating earth, broken by the tortuous courses of the streamlets of winter.

The ground was soft, covered with brown dead leaves, and he tried to see the rabbit rustling among them, or the hasty springing of a squirrel. The long branches of the briar entangled his feet; and here and there, in sheltered corners, blossomed the primrose and the violet He listened to the chant of the birds, so joyous that it seemed impossible they sang in a world of sorrow. Hidden among the leaves, aloft in the beeches, the linnet sang with full-throated melody, and the blackbird and the thrush. In the distance a cuckoo called its mysterious note, and far away, like an echo, a fellow-bird called back.

All Nature was rejoicing in the delight of the sunshine; all Nature was rejoicing, and his heart alone was heavy as lead. He stood by a fir-tree, which rose far above the others, immensely tall, like the mast of a solitary ship; it was straight as a life without reproach, but cheerless, cold, and silent. His life, too, was without reproach, thought James—without reproach till now.... He had loved Mary Clibborn. But was it love, or was it merely affection, habit, esteem? She was the only girl he knew, and they had grown up together. When he came from school for his holidays, or later from Sandhurst, on leave, Mary was his constant friend, without whom he would have been miserably dull. She was masculine enough to enter into his boyish games, and even their thoughts were common. There were so few people in Little Primpton that those who lived there saw one another continually; and though Tunbridge Wells was only four miles away, the distance effectually prevented very close intimacy with its inhabitants. It was natural, then, that James should only look forward to an existence in which Mary took part; without that pleasant companionship the road seemed long and dreary. When he was appointed to a regiment in India, and his heart softened at the prospect of the first long parting from all he cared for, it was the separation from Mary that seemed hardest to bear.

"I don't know what I shall do without you, Mary," he said.

"You will forget all about us when you've been in India a month."

But her lips twitched, and he noticed that she found difficulty in speaking quite firmly. She hesitated a moment, and spoke again.

"It's different for us," she said, "Those who go forget, but those who stay—remember. We shall be always doing the same things to remind us of you. Oh, you won't forget me, Jamie?"

The last words slipped out against the girl's intention.

"Mary!" he cried.

And then he put his arms round her, and Mary rested her face on his shoulder and began to cry. He kissed her, trying to stop her tears; he pressed her to his heart. He really thought he loved her then with all his strength.

"Mary," he whispered, "Mary, do you care for me? Will you marry me?"

Then quickly he explained that it would make it so much better for both if they became engaged.

"I shan't be able to marry you for a long time; but will you wait for me, Mary?"

She began to smile through her tears.

"I would wait for you to the end of my life."

During the first two years in India the tie had been to James entirely pleasurable; and if, among the manifold experiences of his new life, he bore Mary's absence with greater equanimity than he had thought possible, he was always glad to receive her letters, with their delicate aroma of the English country; and it pleased him to think that his future was comfortably settled. The engagement was a sort of ballast, and he felt that he could compass his journey without fear and without disturbance. James did not ask himself whether his passion was very ardent, for his whole education had led him to believe that passion was hardly moral. The proper and decent basis of marriage was similarity of station, and the good, solid qualities which might be supposed endurable. From his youth, the wisdom of the world had been instilled into him through many proverbs, showing the advisability of caution, the transitoriness of beauty and desire; and, on the other hand, the lasting merit of honesty, virtue, domesticity, and good temper....

But we all know that Nature is a goddess with no sense of decency, for whom the proprieties are simply non-existent; men and women in her eyes have but one point of interest, and she walks abroad, with her fashioning fingers, setting in order the only work she cares for. All the rest is subsidiary, and she is callous to suffering and to death, indifferent to the Ten Commandments and even to the code of Good Society.

James at last made the acquaintance of a certain Mrs. Pritchard-Wallace, the wife of a man in a native regiment, a little, dark-hatred person, with an olive skin and big brown eyes—rather common, but excessively pretty. She was the daughter of a riding-master by a Portuguese woman from Goa, and it had been something of a scandal when Pritchard-Wallace, who was an excellent fellow, had married her against the advice of all the regimental ladies. But if those charitable persons had not ceased to look upon her with doubtful eyes, her wit and her good looks for others counterbalanced every disadvantage; and she did not fail to have a little court of subalterns and the like hanging perpetually about her skirts. At first Mrs. Wallace merely amused James. Her absolute frivolity, her cynical tongue, her light-heartedness, were a relief after the rather puritanical atmosphere in which he had passed his youth; he was astonished to hear the gay contempt which she poured upon all the things that he had held most sacred—things like the Tower of London and the British Constitution. Prejudices and cherished beliefs were dissipated before her sharp-tongued raillery; she was a woman with almost a witty way of seeing the world, with a peculiarly feminine gift for putting old things in a new, absurd light. To Mrs. Wallace, James seemed a miracle of ingenuousness, and she laughed at him continually; then she began to like him, and took him about with her, at which he was much flattered.

James had been brought up in the belief that women were fashioned of different clay from men, less gross, less earthly; he thought not only that they were pious, sweet and innocent, ignorant entirely of disagreeable things, but that it was man's first duty to protect them from all knowledge of the realities of life. To him they were an ethereal blending of milk-and-water with high principles; it had never occurred to him that they were flesh and blood, and sense, and fire and nerves—especially nerves. Most topics, of course, could not be broached in their presence; in fact, almost the only safe subject of conversation was the weather.

But Mrs. Pritchard-Wallace prided herself on frankness, which is less common in pretty women than in plain; and she had no hesitation in discussing with James matters that he had never heard discussed before. She was hugely amused at the embarrassment which made him hesitate and falter, trying to find polite ways of expressing the things which his whole training had taught him to keep rigidly to himself. Then sometimes, from pure devilry, Mrs. Wallace told stories on purpose to shock him; and revelled in his forced, polite smile, and in his strong look of disapproval.

"What a funny boy you are!" she said. "But you must take care, you know; you have all the makings of a perfect prig."

"D'you think so?"

"You must try to be less moral. The moral young man is rather funny for a change, but he palls after a time."

"If I bore you, you have only to say so, and I won't bother you again."

"And moral young men shouldn't get cross; it's very bad manners," she answered, smiling.

Before he knew what had happened, James found himself madly in love with Mrs. Wallace. But what a different passion was this, resembling not at all that pallid flame which alone he had experienced! How could he recognise the gentle mingling of friendship and of common-sense which he called love in that destroying violence which troubled his days like a fever? He dreamed of the woman at night; he seemed only to live when he was with her. The mention of her name made his heart beat, and meeting her he trembled and turned cold. By her side he found nothing to say; he was like wax in her hands, without will or strength. The touch of her fingers sent the blood rushing through his veins insanely; and understanding his condition, she took pleasure in touching him, to watch the little shiver of desire that convulsed his frame. In a very self-restrained man love works ruinously; and it burnt James now, this invisible, unconscious fire, till he was consumed utterly—till he was mad with passion. And then suddenly, at some chance word, he knew what had happened; he knew that he was in love with the wife of his good friend, Pritchard-Wallace; and he thought of Mary Clibborn.

There was no hesitation now, nor doubt; James had only been in danger because he was unaware of it. He never thought of treachery to his friend or to Mary; he was horror-stricken, hating himself. He looked over the brink of the precipice at the deadly sin, and recoiled, shuddering. He bitterly reproached himself, taking for granted that some error of his had led to the catastrophe. But his duty was obvious; he knew he must kill the sinful love, whatever pain it cost him; he must crush it as he would some noxious vermin.

James made up his mind never to see Mrs. Wallace again; and he thought that God was on his side helping him, since, with her husband, she was leaving in a month for England. He applied for leave. He could get away for a few weeks, and on his return Mrs. Wallace would be gone. He managed to avoid her for several days, but at last she came across him by chance, and he could not escape.

"I didn't know you were so fond of hide-and-seek," she said, "I think it's rather a stupid game."

"I don't understand," replied James, growing pale.

"Why have you been dodging round corners to avoid me as if I were a dun, and inventing the feeblest excuses not to come to me?"

James stood for a moment, not knowing what to answer; his knees trembled, and he sweated with the agony of his love. It was an angry, furious passion, that made him feel he could almost seize the woman by the throat and strangle her.

"Did you know that I am engaged to be married?" he asked at length.

"I've never known a sub who wasn't. It's the most objectionable of all their vicious habits. What then?" She looked at him, smiling; she knew very well the power of her dark eyes, fringed with long lashes. "Don't be silly," she added. "Come and see me, and bring her photograph, and you shall talk to me for two hours about her. Will you come?"

"It's very kind of you. I don't think I can."

"Why not? You're really very rude."

"I'm extremely busy."

"Nonsense! You must come. Don't look as if I were asking you to do something quite horrible. I shall expect you to tea."

She bound him by his word, and James was forced to go. When he showed the photograph, Mrs. Pritchard-Wallace looked at it with a curious expression. It was the work of a country photographer, awkward and ungainly, with the head stiffly poised, and the eyes hard and fixed; the general impression was ungraceful and devoid of charm, Mrs. Wallace noticed the country fashion of her clothes.

"It's extraordinary that subalterns should always get engaged to the same sort of girl."

James flushed, "It's not a very good one of her."

"They always photograph badly," murmured Mrs. Wallace.

"She's the best girl in the world. You can't think how good, and kind, and simple she is; she reminds me always of an English breeze."

"I don't like east winds myself," said Mrs. Wallace. "But I can see she has all sorts of admirable qualities."

"D'you know why I came to see you to-day?"

"Because I forced you," said Mrs. Wallace, laughing.

"I came to say good-bye; I've got a month's leave."

"Oh, but I shall be gone by the time you come back."

"I know. It is for that reason."

Mrs. Wallace looked at him quickly, hesitated, then glanced away.

"Is it so bad as that?"

"Oh, don't you understand?" cried James, breaking suddenly from his reserve. "I must tell you. I shall never see you again, and it can't matter. I love you with all my heart and soul. I didn't know what love was till I met you. God help me, it was only friendship I had for Mary! This is so different. Oh, I hate myself! I can't help it; the mere touch of your hand sends me mad with passion. I daren't see you again—I'm not a blackguard. I know it's quite hopeless. And I've given my word to Mary."

The look of her eyes, the sound of her voice, sent half his fine intentions flying before the wind. He lost command over himself—but only for a moment; the old habits were strong.

"I beg your pardon! I oughtn't to have spoken. Don't be angry with me for what I've said. I couldn't help it. You thought me a fool because I ran away from you. It was all I could do. I couldn't help loving you. You understand now, don't you? I know that you will never wish to see me again, and it's better for both of us. Good-bye."

He stretched out his hand.

"I didn't know it was so bad as that," she said, looking at him with kindly eyes.

"Didn't you see me tremble when the hem of your dress touched me by accident? Didn't you hear that I couldn't speak; the words were dried up in my throat?" He sank into a chair weakly; but then immediately gathering himself together, sprang up. "Good-bye," he said. "Let me go quickly."

She gave him her hand, and then, partly in kindness, partly in malice, bent forward and kissed his lips. James gave a cry, a sob; now he lost command over himself entirely. He took her in his arms roughly, and kissed her mouth, her eyes, her hair—so passionately that Mrs. Wallace was frightened. She tried to free herself; but he only held her closer, madly kissing her lips.

"Take care," she said. "What are you doing? Let me go!" And she pushed him away.

She was a cautious woman, who never allowed flirtation to go beyond certain decorous lengths, and she was used to a milder form of philandering.

"You've disarranged my hair, you silly boy!" She went to the glass to put it in order, and when she turned back found that James had gone. "What an odd creature!" she muttered.

To Mrs. Pritchard-Wallace the affair was but an incident, such as might have been the love of Phædra had she flourished in an age when the art of living consists in not taking things too seriously; but for Hippolitus a tragedy of one sort or another is inevitable. James was not a man of easy affections; he made the acquaintance of people with a feeling of hostility rather than with the more usual sensation of friendly curiosity. He was shy, and even with his best friends could not lessen his reserve. Some persons are able to form close intimacies with admirable facility, but James felt always between himself and his fellows a sort of barrier. He could not realise that deep and sudden sympathy was even possible, and was apt to look with mistrust upon the appearance thereof. He seemed frigid and perhaps supercilious to those with whom he came in contact; he was forced to go his way, hiding from all eyes the emotions he felt. And when at last he fell passionately in love, it meant to him ten times more than to most men; it was a sudden freedom from himself. He was like a prisoner who sees for the first time in his life the trees and the hurrying clouds, and all the various movement of the world. For a little while James had known a wonderful liberty, an ineffable bliss which coloured the whole universe with new, strange colours. But then he learnt that the happiness was only sin, and he returned voluntarily to his cold prison.... Till he tried to crush it, he did not know how strong was this passion; he did not realise that it had made of him a different man; it was the only thing in the world to him, beside which everything else was meaningless. He became ruthless towards himself, undergoing every torture which he fancied might cleanse him of the deadly sin.

And when Mrs. Wallace, against his will, forced herself upon his imagination, he tried to remember her vulgarity, her underbred manners, her excessive use of scent. She had merely played with him, without thinking or caring what the result to him might be. She was bent on as much enjoyment as possible without exposing herself to awkward consequences; common scandal told him that he was not the first callow youth that she had entangled with her provoking glances and her witty tongue. The epithet by which his brother officers qualified her was expressive, though impolite. James repeated these things a hundred times: he said that Mrs. Wallace was not fit to wipe Mary's boots; he paraded before himself, like a set of unread school-books, all Mary's excellent qualities. He recalled her simple piety, her good-nature, and kindly heart; she had every attribute that a man could possibly want in his wife. And yet—and yet, when he slept he dreamed he was talking to the other; all day her voice sang in his ears, her gay smile danced before his eyes. He remembered every word she had ever said; he remembered the passionate kisses he had given her. How could he forget that ecstasy? He writhed, trying to expel the importunate image; but nothing served.

Time could not weaken the impression. Since then he had never seen Mrs. Wallace, but the thought of her was still enough to send the blood racing through his veins. He had done everything to kill the mad, hopeless passion; and always, like a rank weed, it had thriven with greater strength. James knew it was his duty to marry Mary Clibborn, and yet he felt he would rather die. As the months passed on, and he knew he must shortly see her, he was never free from a sense of terrible anxiety. Doubt came to him, and he could not drive it away. The recollection of her was dim, cold, formless; his only hope was that when he saw her love might rise up again, and kill that other passion which made him so utterly despise himself. But he had welcomed the war as a respite, and the thought came to him that its chances might easily solve the difficulty. Then followed the months of hardship and of fighting; and during these the image of Mrs. Wallace had been less persistent, so that James fancied he was regaining the freedom he longed for. And when he lay wounded and ill, his absolute weariness made him ardently look forward to seeing his people again. A hotter love sprang up for them; and the hope became stronger that reunion with Mary might awaken the dead emotion. He wished for it with all his heart.

But he had seen Mary, and he felt it hopeless; she left him cold, almost hostile. And with a mocking laugh, James heard Mrs. Wallace's words:

"Subalterns always get engaged to the same type of girl. They photograph so badly."

* * *

And now he did not know what to do. The long recalling of the past had left James more uncertain than ever. Some devil within him cried, "Wait, wait! Something may happen!" It really seemed better to let things slide a little. Perhaps—who could tell?—in a day or two the old habit might render Mary as dear to him as when last he had wandered with her in that green wood, James sighed, and looked about him.... The birds still sang merrily, the squirrel leaped from tree to tree; even the blades of grass stood with a certain conscious pleasure, as the light breeze rustled through them. In the mid-day sun all things took pleasure in their life; and all Nature appeared full of joy, coloured and various and insouciant. He alone was sad.

IV

When James went home he found that the Vicar of Little Primpton and his wife had already arrived. They were both of them little, dried-up persons, with an earnest manner and no sense of humour, quite excellent in a rather unpleasant way; they resembled one another like peas, but none knew whether the likeness had grown from the propinquity of twenty years, or had been the original attraction. Deeply impressed with their sacred calling—for Mrs. Jackson would never have acknowledged that the Vicar's wife held a position inferior to the Vicar's—they argued that the whole world was God's, and they God's particular ministrants; so that it was their plain duty to concern themselves with the business of their fellows—and it must be confessed that they never shrank from this duty. They were neither well-educated, nor experienced, nor tactful; but blissfully ignorant of these defects, they shepherded their flock with little moral barks, and gave them, rather self-consciously, a good example in the difficult way to eternal life. They were eminently worthy people, who thought light-heartedness somewhat indecent. They did endless good in the most disagreeable manner possible; and in their fervour not only bore unnecessary crosses themselves, but saddled them on to everyone else, as the only certain passport to the Golden City.

The Reverend Archibald Jackson had been appointed to the living of Little Primpton while James was in India, and consequently had never seen him.

"I was telling your father," said Mrs. Jackson, on shaking hands, "that I hoped you were properly grateful for all the mercies that have been bestowed upon you."

James stared at her a little. "Were you?"

He hated the fashion these people had of discussing matters which he himself thought most private.

"Mr. Jackson was asking if you'd like a short prayer offered up next Sunday, James," said his mother.

"I shouldn't at all."

"Why not?" asked the Vicar, "I think it's your duty to thank your Maker for your safe return, and I think your parents should join in the thanksgiving."

"We're probably none of us less grateful," said James, "because we don't want to express our feelings before the united congregation."

Jamie's parents looked at him with relief, for the same thought filled their minds; but thinking it their duty to submit themselves to the spiritual direction of the Vicar and his wife, they had not thought it quite right to decline the proposal. Mrs. Jackson glanced at her husband with pained astonishment, but further argument was prevented by the arrival of Colonel and Mrs. Clibborn, and Mary.

Colonel Clibborn was a tall man, with oily black hair and fierce eyebrows, both dyed; aggressively military and reminiscent He had been in a cavalry regiment, where he had come to the philosophic conclusion that all men are dust—except cavalry-men; and he was able to look upon Jamie's prowess—the prowess of an infantryman—from superior heights. He was a great authority upon war, and could tell anyone what were the mistakes in South Africa, and how they might have been avoided; likewise he had known in the service half the peers of the realm, and talked of them by their Christian names. He spent three weeks every season in London, and dined late, at seven o'clock, so he had every qualification for considering himself a man of fashion.

"I don't know what they'd do in Little Primpton without us," he said. "It's only us who keep it alive."

But Mrs. Clibborn missed society.

"The only people I can speak to are the Parsons," she told her husband, plaintively. "They're very good people—but only infantry, Reggie."

"Of course, they're only infantry," agreed Colonel Clibborn.

Mrs. Clibborn was a regimental beauty—of fifty, who had grown stout; but not for that ceased to use the weapons which Nature had given her against the natural enemies of the sex. In her dealings with several generations of adorers, she had acquired such a habit of languishing glances that now she used them unconsciously. Whether ordering meat from the butcher or discussing parochial matters with Mr. Jackson, Mrs. Clibborn's tone and manner were such that she might have been saying the most tender things. She had been very popular in the service, because she was the type of philandering woman who required no beating about the bush; her neighbour at the dinner-table, even if he had not seen her before, need never have hesitated to tell her with the soup that she was the handsomest creature he had ever seen, and with the *entrée* that he adored her.

On coming in, Mrs. Clibborn for a moment looked at James, quite speechless, her head on one side and her eyes screwing into the corner of the room.

"Oh, how wonderful!" she said, at last "I suppose I mustn't call you Jamie now." She spoke very slowly, and every word sounded like a caress. Then she looked at James again in silent ecstasy. "Colonel Parsons, how proud you must be! And when I think that soon he will be my son! How thin you look, James!"

"And how well you look, dear lady!"

It was understood that everyone must make compliments to Mrs. Clibborn; otherwise she grew cross, and when she was cross she was horrid.

She smiled to show her really beautiful teeth.

"I should like to kiss you, James. May I, Mrs. Parsons?"

"Certainly," replied Jamie's mother, who didn't approve of Mrs. Clibborn at all.

She turned her cheek to James, and assumed a seraphic expression while he lightly touched it with his lips.

"I'm only an old woman," she murmured to the company in general.

She seldom made more than one remark at a time, and at the end of each assumed an appropriate attitude—coy, Madonna-like, resigned, as the circumstances might require. Mr. Jackson came forward to shake hands, and she turned her languishing glance on him.

"Oh, Mr. Jackson, how beautiful your sermon was!"

* * *

They sat down to dinner, and ate their ox-tail soup. It is terrible to think of the subtlety with which the Evil One can insinuate himself among the most pious; for soup at middle-day is one of his most dangerous wiles, and it is precisely with the simple-minded inhabitants of the country and of the suburbs that this vice is most prevalent.

James was sitting next to Mrs. Clibborn, and presently she looked at him with the melancholy smile which had always seemed to her so effective.

"We want you to tell us how you won your Victoria Cross, Jamie."

The others, eager to hear the story from the hero's lips, had been, notwithstanding, too tactful to ask; but they were willing to take advantage of Mrs. Clibborn's lack of that quality.

"We've all been looking forward to it," said the Vicar.

"I don't think there's anything to tell," replied James.

His father and mother were looking at him with happy eyes, and the Colonel nodded to Mary.

"Please, Jamie, tell us," she said. "We only saw the shortest account in the papers, and you said nothing about it in your letters."

"D'you think it's very good form of me to tell you about it?" asked James, smiling gravely.

"We're all friends here," said the Vicar.

And Colonel Clibborn added, making sheep's eyes at his wife:

"You can't refuse a lady!"

"I'm an old woman," sighed Mrs. Clibborn, with a doleful glance. "I can't expect him to do it for me."

The only clever thing Mrs. Clibborn had done in her life was to acknowledge to old age at thirty, and then she did not mean it. It had been one of her methods in flirtation, covering all excesses under a maternal aspect. She must have told hundreds of young officers that she was old enough to be their mother; and she always said it looking plaintively at the ceiling, when they squeezed her hand.

"It wasn't a very wonderful thing I did," said James, at last, "and it was completely useless."

"No fine deed is useless," said the Vicar, sententiously.

James looked at him a moment, but proceeded with his story.

"It was only that I tried to save the life of a sub who'd just joined—and didn't."

"Would you pass me the salt?" said Mrs. Clibborn.

"Mamma!" cried Mary, with a look as near irritation as her gentle nature permitted.

"Go on, Jamie, there's a good boy," said Mrs. Parsons.

And James, seeing his father's charming, pathetic look of pride, told the story to him alone. The others did not care how much they hurt him so long as they could gape in admiration, but in his father he saw the most touching sympathy.

"It was a chap called Larcher, a boy of eighteen, with fair hair and blue eyes, who looked quite absurdly young. His people live somewhere round here, near Ashford."

"Larcher, did you say?" asked Mrs. Clibborn, "I've never heard the name. It's not a county family."

"Go on, Jamie," said Mary, with some impatience.

"Well, he'd only been with us three or four weeks; but I knew him rather well. Oddly enough, he'd taken a sort of fancy to me. He was such a nice, bright boy, so enthusiastic and simple. I used to tell him that he ought to have been at school, rather than roughing it at the Cape."

Mrs. Clibborn sat with an idiotic smile on her lips, and a fixed expression of girlish innocence.

"Well, we knew we should be fighting in a day or so; and the evening before the battle young Larcher was talking to me. 'How d'you feel?' I said. He didn't answer quite so quickly as usual. 'D'you know,' he said, 'I'm so awfully afraid that I shall funk it.' 'You needn't mind that,' I said, and I laughed. 'The first time we most of us do funk it. For five minutes or so you just have to cling on to your eyelashes to prevent yourself from running away, and then you feel all right, and you think it's rather sport.' 'I've got a sort of presentiment that I shall be killed,' he said. 'Don't be an ass,' I answered. 'We've all got a presentiment that we shall be killed the first time we're under fire. If all the people were killed who had presentiments, half the army would have gone to kingdom come long ago.'"

"You should have told him to lay his trust in the hands of Him who has power to turn the bullet and to break the sword," said Mrs. Jackson.

"He wasn't that sort," replied James, drily, "I laughed at him, thinking it the better way.... Well, next day we did really fight. We were sent to take an unoccupied hill. Our maxim was that a hill is always unoccupied unless the enemy are actually firing from it. Of course, the place was chock full of Boers; they waited till we had come within easy range for a toy-pistol, and then fired murderously. We did all we could. We tried to storm the place, but we hadn't a chance. Men tumbled down like ninepins. I've never seen anything like it. The order was given to fire, and there was nothing to fire at but the naked rocks. We had to retire—we couldn't do anything else; and presently I found that poor Larcher had been wounded. Well, I thought he couldn't be left where he was, so I went back for him. I asked him if he could move. 'No,' he said, 'I think I'm hurt in the leg.' I knelt down and bandaged him up as well as I could. He was simply bleeding like a pig; and meanwhile brother Boer potted at us for all he was worth. 'How d'you feel?' I asked. 'Bit dicky; but comfortable. I didn't funk it, did I?' 'No, of course not, you juggins!' I said. 'Can you walk, d'you think?' 'I'll try.' I lifted him up and put my arm round him, and we got along for a bit; then he became awfully white and groaned, 'I do feel so bad, Parsons,' and then he fainted. So I had to carry him; and we went a bit farther, and then—and then I was hit in the arm. 'I say, I can't carry you now,' I said; 'for God's sake, buck up.' He opened his eyes, and I prevented him from falling. 'I think I can stand,' he said, and as he spoke a bullet got him in the neck, and his blood splashed over my face. He gave a gasp and died."

James finished, and his mother and Mary wiped the tears from their eyes. Mrs. Clibborn turned to her husband.

"Reggie, I'm sure the Larchers are not a county family."

"There was a sapper of that name whom we met at Simla once, my dear," replied the Colonel.

"I thought I'd heard it before," said Mrs. Clibborn, with an air of triumph, as though she'd found out a very difficult puzzle. "Had he a red moustache?"

"Have you heard from the young man's people, Captain Parsons?" asked Mrs. Jackson.

"I had a letter from Mrs. Larcher, the boy's mother, asking me to go over and see her."

"She must be very grateful to you, Jamie."

"Why? She has no reason to be."

"You did all you could to save him."

"It would have been better if I'd left him alone. Don't you see that if he had remained where he was he might have been alive now. He would have been taken prisoner and sent to Pretoria, but that is better than rotting on the veldt. He was killed because I tried to save him."

"There are worse things than death," said Colonel Parsons. "I have often thought that those fellows who surrendered did the braver thing. It is easy to stand and be shot down, but to hoist the white flag so as to save the lives of the men under one—that requires courage."

"It is a sort of courage which seemed not uncommon," answered James, drily. "And they had a fairly pleasant time in Pretoria. Eventually, I believe, wars will be quite bloodless; rival armies will perambulate, and whenever one side has got into a good position, the other will surrender wholesale. Campaigns will be conducted like manoeuvres, and the special correspondents will decide which lot has won."

"If they were surrounded and couldn't escape, it would have been wicked not to hoist the white flag," said Mrs. Jackson.

"I daresay you know more about it than I," replied James.

But the Vicar's lady insisted:

"If you were so placed that on one hand was certain death for yourself and all your men, and on the other hand surrender, which would you chose?"

"One can never tell; and in those matters it is wiser not to boast. Certain death is an awful thing, but our fathers preferred it to surrender."

"War is horrible!" said Mary, shuddering.

"Oh, no!" cried James, shaking himself out of his despondency. "War is the most splendid thing in the world. I shall never forget those few minutes, now and then, when we got on top of the Boers and fought with them, man to man, in the old way. Ah, life seemed worth living then! One day, I remember, they'd been giving it us awfully hot all the morning, and we'd lost frightfully. At last we rushed their position, and, by Jove, we let 'em have it! How we did hate them! You should have heard the Tommies cursing as they killed! I shall never forget the exhilaration of it, the joy of thinking that we were getting our own again. By Gad, it beat cock-fighting!"

Jamie's cheeks were flushed and his eyes shone; but he had forgotten where he was, and his father's voice came to him through a mist of blood and a roar of sound.

"I have fought, too," said Colonel Parsons, looking at his son with troubled eyes—"I have fought, too, but never with anger in my heart, nor lust of vengeance. I hope I did my duty, but I never forgot that my enemy was a fellow-creature. I never felt joy at killing, but pain and grief. War is inevitable, but it is horrible, horrible! It is only the righteous cause that can excuse it; and then it must be tempered with mercy and forgiveness."

"Cause? Every cause is righteous. I can think of no war in which right has not been fairly equal on both sides; in every question there is about as much to be said on either part, and in none more than in war. Each country is necessarily convinced of the justice of its own cause."

"They can't both be right."

"Oh, yes, they can. It's generally six to one and half a dozen of the other."

"Do you mean to say that you, a military man, think the Boers were justified?" asked Colonel Clibborn, with some indignation.

James laughed.

"You must remember that if any nation but ourselves had been engaged, our sympathies would have been entirely with the sturdy peasants fighting for their independence. The two great powers in the affairs of the world are sentiment and self-interest. The Boers are the smaller, weaker nation, and they have been beaten; it is only natural that sympathy should be with them. It was with the French for the same reason, after the Franco-Prussian War. But we, who were fighting, couldn't think of sentiment; to us it was really a matter of life and death, I was interested to see how soon the English put aside their ideas of fair play and equal terms when we had had a few reverses. They forgot that one Englishman was equal to ten foreigners, and insisted on sending out as many troops as possible. I fancy you were badly panic-stricken over here."

James saw that his listeners looked at him with surprise, even with consternation; and he hastened to explain.

"Of course, I don't blame them. They were quite right to send as many men as possible. The object of war is not to do glorious actions, but to win. Other things being equal, it is obviously better to be ten to one; it is less heroic, but more reasonable."

"You take from war all the honour and all the chivalry!" cried Mary. "The only excuse for war is that it brings out the noblest qualities of man—self-sacrifice, unselfishness, endurance."

"But war doesn't want any excuse," replied James, smiling gently. "Many people say that war is inhuman and absurd; many people are uncommonly silly. When they think war can be abolished, they show a phenomenal ignorance of the conditions of all development. War in one way and another is at the very root of life. War is not conducted only by fire and sword; it is in all nature, it is the condition of existence for all created things. Even the wild flowers in the meadow wage war, and they wage it more ruthlessly even than man, for with them defeat means extermination. The law of Nature is that the fit should kill the unfit. The Lord is the Lord of Hosts. The lame, and the halt, and the blind must remain behind, while the strong man goes his way rejoicing."

"How hard you are!" said Mary. "Have you no pity, James?"

"D'you know, I've got an idea that there's too much pity in the world. People seem to be losing their nerve; reality shocks them, and they live slothfully in the shoddy palaces of Sham Ideals. The sentimentalists, the cowards, and the cranks have broken the spirit of mankind. The general in battle now is afraid to strike because men may be killed. Sometimes it is worth while to lose men. When we become soldiers, we know that we cease to be human beings, and are merely the instruments for a certain work; we know that sometimes it may be part of a general's deliberate plan that we should be killed. I have no confidence in a leader who is tender-hearted. Compassion weakens his brain, and the result, too often, is disaster."

But as he spoke, James realised with a start how his father would take what he was saying. He could have torn out his tongue, he would have given anything that the words should remain unspoken. His father, in pity and in humanity, had committed just such a fatal mistake, and trying tender-heartedly to save life had brought about death and disaster. He would take the thoughtless words as a deliberate condemnation; the wound, barely closed, was torn open by his very son, and he must feel again the humiliation which had nearly killed him.

Colonel Parsons sat motionless, as though he were stunned, his eyes fixed on James with horror and pain; he looked like some hunted animal, terror-stricken, and yet surprised, wondering that man should be so cruel.

"What can I do?" thought James. "How can I make it good for him?"

The conversation was carried on by the Clibborns and by the Vicar, all happily unconscious that a tragedy was acting under their noses. James looked at his father. He wanted to show how bitterly he regretted the pain he had caused, but knew not what to say; he wanted to give a sign of his eager love, and tortured himself, knowing the impossibility of showing in any way his devotion.

Fortunately, the maid came in to announce that the school children were without, to welcome Captain Parsons; and they all rose from the table.

V

Colonel Parsons and his wife had wished no function to celebrate the home-coming of James; but gave in to the persuasions of Mary and of Mr. Dryland, the curate, who said that a public ceremony would be undoubtedly a stimulus to the moral welfare of Little Primpton. No man could escape from his obligations, and Captain Parsons owed it to his fellow-countrymen of Little Primpton to let them show their appreciation of his great deed.

The Vicar went so far as to assert that a hearty greeting to the hero would be as salutory to the parishioners as a sermon of his own, while it would awaken James, a young man and possibly thoughtless, to a proper sense of his responsibilities. But the sudden arrival of James had disturbed the arrangements, and Mr. Dryland, in some perplexity, went to see Mary.

"What are we to do, Miss Clibborn? The school children will be so disappointed."

The original plan had been to meet the hero as he drove towards Primpton House from the station, and the curate was unwilling to give it up.

"D'you think Captain Parsons would go into Tunbridge Wells and drive in at two o'clock, as if he were just arriving?"

"I'm afraid he wouldn't," replied Mary, doubtfully, "and I think he'd only laugh if I asked him. He seemed glad when he thought he had escaped the celebration."

"Did he, indeed? How true it is that real courage is always modest! But it would be an eternal disgrace to Little Primpton if we did not welcome our hero, especially now that everything is prepared. It must not be said that Little Primpton neglects to honour him whom the Empire has distinguished."

After turning over many plans, they decided that the procession should come to Primpton House at the appointed hour, when Captain Parsons would receive it from the triumphal arch at the gate.... When the servant announced that the function was ready to begin, an announcement emphasised by the discordant notes of the brass band, Mary hurriedly explained to James what was expected of him, and they all made for the front door.

Primpton House faced the green, and opposite the little village shops were gay with bunting; at the side, against the highroad that led to Groombridge, the church and the public-house stood together in friendly neighbourhood, decorated with Union Jacks. The whole scene, with its great chestnut-trees, and the stretch of greenery beyond, was pleasantly rural, old-fashioned and very English; and to complete it, the sun shone down comfortably like a good-natured, mild old gentleman. The curate, with a fine sense of order, had arranged on the right the school-boys, nicely scrubbed and redolent of pomatum; and on the left the girls, supported by their teachers. In the middle stood the choir, the brass band, and Mr. Dryland. The village yokels were collected round in open-mouthed admiration. The little party from the house took their places under the triumphal arch, the Clibborns assuming an expression of genteel superciliousness; and as they all wore their Sunday clothes, they made quite an imposing group.

Seeing that they were ready, Mr. Dryland stepped forward, turned his back so as to command the musicians, and coughed significantly. He raised above his head his large, white clerical hand, stretching out the index-finger, and began to beat time. He bellowed aloud, and the choir, a bar or so late, followed lustily. The band joined in with a hearty braying of trumpets.

> *"See, the conquering Hero comes*
> *Sound the trumpets; beat the drums."*

But growing excited at the music issuing from his throat, the curate raised the other hand which held his soft felt hat, and beat time energetically with that also.

At the end of the verse the performers took a rapid breath, as though afraid of being left behind, and then galloped on, a little less evenly, until one by one they reached the highly-decorated Amen.

When the last note of the last cornet had died away on the startled air, Mr. Dryland made a sign to the head boy of the school, who thereupon advanced and waved his cap, shouting:

"Three cheers for Capting Parsons, V.C.!"

Then the curate, wiping his heated brow, turned round and cleared his throat.

"Captain Parsons," he said, in a loud voice, so that none should miss his honeyed words, "we, the inhabitants of Little Primpton, welcome you to your home. I need not say that it is with great pleasure that we have gathered together this day to offer you our congratulations on your safe return to those that love you. I need not remind you that there is no place like home. ("Hear, hear!" from the Vicar.) We are proud to think that our fellow-parishioner should have gained the coveted glory of the Victoria Cross. Little Primpton need not be ashamed now to hold up its head among the proudest cities of the Empire. You have brought honour to yourself, but you have brought honour to us also. You have shown that Englishmen know how to die; you have shown the rival nations of the Continent that the purity and the godliness of Old England still bear fruit. But I will say no more; I wished only to utter a few words to welcome you on behalf of those who cannot, perhaps, express themselves so well as I can. I will say no more. Captain Parsons, we hope that you will live long to enjoy your honour and glory, side by side with her who is to shortly become your wife. I would only assure you that your example has not been lost upon us; we all feel better, nobler, and more truly Christian. And we say to you, now that you have overcome all dangers and tribulation, now that you have returned to the bosom of your beloved family, take her who has also given us an example of resignation, of courage, and of—and of resignation. Take her, we say, and be happy; confident in the respect, esteem, and affection of the people of Little Primpton. James Brown, who has the honour to bear the same Christian name as yourself, and is also the top boy of the Parish School, will now recite a short poem entitled 'Casabianca.'

Mr. Dryland had wished to compose an ode especially for the occasion. It would evidently have been effective to welcome the hero, to glorify his deed, and to point the moral in a few original verses; but, unhappily, the muse was froward, which was singular, since the *élite* of Little Primpton had unimpeachable morals, ideals of the most approved character, and principles enough to build a church with; nor was an acquaintance with literature wanting. They all read the daily papers, and Mr. and Mrs. Jackson, in addition, read the *Church Times*. Mary even knew by heart whole chunks of Sir Lewis Morris, and Mr. Dryland recited Tennyson at penny readings. But when inspiration is wanting, a rhyming dictionary, for which the curate sent to London, will not help to any great extent; and finally the unanimous decision was reached to give some well-known poem apposite to the circumstance. It shows in what charming unity of spirit these simple, God-fearing people lived, and how fine was their sense of literary excellence, that without hesitation they voted in chorus for "Casabianca."

The head boy stepped forward—he had been carefully trained by Mr. Dryland—and with appropriate gestures recited the immortal verses of Felicia Hemans:

> *"The boy stood on the burning deck,*
> *Whence all but 'e 'ad fled;*
> *The flame that lit the battle's wreck,*
> *Shone round 'im o'er the dead."*

When he finished, amid the discreet applause of the little party beneath the archway, Mr. Dryland again advanced.

"Polly Game, the top girl of the Parish School, will now present Miss Clibborn with a bouquet. Step forward, Polly Game."

This was a surprise arranged by the curate, and he watched with pleasure Mary's look of delighted astonishment.

Polly Game stepped forward, and made a little speech in the ingenuous words which Mr. Dryland had thought natural to her character and station.

"Please, Miss Clibborn, we, the girls of Little Primpton, wish to present you with this bouquet as a slight token of our esteem. We wish you a long life and a 'appy marriage with the choice of your 'eart."

She then handed a very stiff bunch of flowers, surrounded with frilled paper like the knuckle of a leg of mutton.

"We will now sing hymn number one hundred and thirty-seven," said Mr. Dryland.

The verses were given vigorously, while Mrs. Clibborn, with a tender smile, murmured to Mrs. Parsons that it was beautiful to see such a nice spirit among the lower classes. The strains of the brass band died away on the summer breeze, and there was a momentary pause. Then the Vicar, with a discreet cough to clear his throat, came forward.

"Captain Parsons, ladies and gentlemen, parishioners of Little Primpton, I wish to take the opportunity to say a few words."

The Vicar made an admirable speech. The sentiments were hackneyed, the observations self-evident, and the moral obvious. His phrases had the well-known ring which distinguishes the true orator. Mr. Jackson was recognised everywhere to be a fine platform speaker, but his varied excellence could not be appreciated in a summary, and he had a fine verbosity. It is sufficient to say that he concluded by asking for more cheers, which were heartily given.

James found the whole affair distasteful and ridiculous; and indeed scarcely noticed what was going on, for his thoughts were entirely occupied with his father. At first Colonel Parsons seemed too depressed to pay attention to the ceremony, and his eyes travelled every now and again to James, with that startled, unhappy expression which was horribly painful to see. But his age and weakness prevented him from feeling very intensely for more than a short while; time had brought its own good medicine, and the old man's mind was easily turned. Presently he began to smile, and the look of pride and happiness returned to his face.

But James was not satisfied. He felt he must make active reparation. When the Vicar finished, and he understood that some reply was expected, it occurred to him that he had an opportunity of salving the bitter wound he had caused. The very hatred he felt at making open allusion to his feelings made him think it a just punishment; none knew but himself how painful it was to talk in that strain to stupid, curious people.

"I thank you very much for the welcome you have all given me," he said.

His voice trembled in his nervousness, so that he could hardly command it, and he reddened. It seemed to James a frightful humiliation to have to say the things he had in mind, it made them all ugly and vulgar; he was troubled also by his inability to express what he felt. He noticed a reporter for the local newspaper rapidly taking notes.

"I have been very much touched by your kindness. Of course, I am extremely proud to have won the Victoria Cross, but I feel it is really more owing to my father than to any deed of mine. You all know my father, and you know what a brave and gallant soldier he was. It was owing to his fine example, and to his teaching, and to his constant, loving care, that I was able to do the little I did. And I should like to say that it is to him and to my mother that I owe everything. It is the thought of his unblemished and exquisite career, of the beautiful spirit which brightly coloured all his actions, that has supported me in times of difficulty. And my earnest desire has always been to prove myself worthy of my father and the name he has handed on to me. You have cheered me very kindly; now I should like to ask you for three cheers for my father."

Colonel Parsons looked at his son as he began to speak. When he realised Jamie's meaning, tears filled his eyes and streamed down his cheeks—tears of happiness and gratitude. All recollection of the affront quickly vanished, and he felt an ecstatic joy such as he had never known before. The idea came to him in his weakness: "Now I can die happy!" He was too overcome to be ashamed of his emotion, and taking out his handkerchief, quite unaffectedly wiped his eyes.

The band struck up "Rule, Britannia" and "God Save the Queen"; and in orderly fashion, as Mr. Dryland had arranged, they all marched off. The group under the triumphal arch broke up, and the Jacksons and Colonel and Mrs. Clibborn went their ways.

Mary came into the house. She took Jamie's hands, her eyes wet with tears.

"Oh, Jamie," she said, "you are good! It was charming of you to speak as you did of your father. You don't know how happy you've made him."

"I'm very glad you are pleased," he said gravely, and bending forward, put his arm round her waist and kissed her.

For a moment she leant her head against his shoulder; but with her emotion was a thing soon vanquished. She wished, above all things, to be manly, as befitted a soldier's wife. She shook herself, and withdrew from Jamie's arms.

"But I must be running off, or mamma will be angry with me. Good-bye for the present."

* * *

James went into the dining-room, where his father, exhausted by the varied agitations of the day, was seeking composure in the leading articles of the morning paper. Mrs. Parsons sat on her usual chair, knitting, and she greeted him with a loving smile. James saw that they were both pleased with his few awkward words, which still rang in his own ears as shoddy and sentimental, and he tasted, somewhat ruefully, the delight of making the kind creatures happy.

"Has Mary gone?" asked Mrs. Parsons.

"Yes. She said her mother would be angry if she stayed."

"I saw that Mrs. Clibborn was put out. I suppose because someone besides herself attracted attention. I do think she is the wickedest woman I've ever known."

"Frances, Frances!" expostulated the Colonel.

"She is, Richmond. She's a thoroughly bad woman. The way she treats Mary is simply scandalous."

"Poor girl!" said the Colonel.

"Oh, Jamie, it makes my blood boil when I think of it. Sometimes the poor thing used to come here quite upset, and simply cry as if her heart was breaking."

"But what does Mrs. Clibborn do?" asked James, surprised.

"Oh, I can't tell you! She's dreadfully unkind. She hates Mary because she's grown up, and because she sometimes attracts attention. She's always making little cruel remarks. You only see her when she's on her good behaviour; but when she's alone with Mary, Mrs. Clibborn is simply horrible. She abuses her; she tells her she's ugly, and that she dresses badly. How can she dress any better when Mrs. Clibborn spends all the money on herself? I've heard her myself say to Mary: 'How stupid and clumsy you are! I'm ashamed to take you anywhere.' And Mary's the very soul of goodness. She teaches in the Sunday School, and she trains the choir-boys, and she visits the poor; and yet Mrs. Clibborn complains that she's useless. I wanted Richmond to talk to Colonel Clibborn about it."

"Mary particularly asked me not to," said Colonel Parsons. "She preferred to bear anything rather than create unhappiness between her father and mother."

"She's a perfect angel of goodness!" cried Mrs. Parsons, enthusiastically. "She's simply a martyr, and all the time she's as kind and affectionate to her mother as if she were the best woman in the world. She never lets anyone say a word against her."

"Sometimes," murmured Colonel Parsons, "she used to say that her only happiness was in the thought of you, Jamie."

"The thought of me?" said James; and then hesitatingly: "Do you think she is very fond of me, mother?"

"Fond of you?" Mrs Parsons laughed. "She worships the very ground you tread on. You can't imagine all you are to her."

"You'll make the boy vain," said Colonel Parsons, laughing.

"Often the only way we could comfort her was by saying that you would come back some day and take her away from here."

"We shall have to be thinking of weddings soon, I suppose?" said Colonel Parsons, looking at James, with a bantering smile.

James turned white. "It's rather early to think of that just yet."

"We spoke of June," said his mother.

"We must see."

"You've waited so long," said Colonel Parsons; "I'm sure you don't want to wait any longer."

"She *will* make you a good wife, Jamie. You are lucky to have found such a dear, sweet girl. It's a blessing to us to think that you will be so happy."

"As I was saying to Mary the other day," added Colonel Parsons, laughing gently, "'you must begin thinking of your trousseau, my dear,' I said, 'If I know anything of Jamie, he'll want to get married in a week. These young fellows are always impatient.'"

Mrs Parsons smiled.

"Well, it's a great secret, and Mary would be dreadfully annoyed if she thought you knew; but when we heard you were coming home, she started to order things. Her father has given her a hundred pounds to begin with."

They had no mercy, thought James. They were horribly cruel in their loving-kindness, in their affectionate interest for his welfare.

VI

James had been away from England for five years; and in that time a curious change, long silently proceeding, had made itself openly felt—becoming manifest, like an insidious disease, only when every limb and every organ were infected. A new spirit had been in action, eating into the foundations of the national character; it worked through the masses of the great cities, unnerved by the three poisons of drink, the Salvation Army, and popular journalism. A mighty force of hysteria and sensationalism was created, seething, ready to burst its bonds ... The canker spread through the country-side; the boundaries of class and class are now so vague that quickly the whole population was affected; the current literature of the day flourished upon it; the people of England, neurotic from the stress of the last sixty years, became unstable as water. And with the petty reverses of the beginning of the war, the last barriers of shame were broken down; their arrogance was dissipated, and suddenly the English became timorous as a conquered nation, deprecating, apologetic; like frightened women, they ran to and fro, wringing their hands. Reserve, restraint, self-possession, were swept away ... And now we are frankly emotional; reeds tottering in the wind, our boast is that we are not even reeds that think; we cry out for idols. Who is there that will set up a golden ass that we may fall down and worship? We glory in our shame, in our swelling hearts, in our eyes heavy with tears. We want sympathy at all costs; we run about showing our bleeding vitals, asking one another whether they are not indeed a horrible sight. Englishmen now are proud of being womanish, and nothing is more manly than to weep. To be a man of feeling is better than to be a gentleman—it is certainly much easier. The halt of mind, the maim, the blind of wit, have come by their own; and the poor in spirit have inherited the earth.

James had left England when this emotional state was contemptible. Found chiefly in the dregs of the populace, it was ascribed to ignorance and to the abuse of stimulants. When he returned, it had the public conscience behind it. He could not understand the change. The persons he had known sober, equal-minded, and restrained, now seemed violently hysterical. James still shuddered, remembering the curate's allusions to his engagement; and he wondered that Mary, far from thinking them impertinent, had been vastly gratified. She seemed to take pleasure in publicly advertising her connection, in giving her private affairs to the inspection of all and sundry. The whole ceremony had been revolting; he loathed the adulation and the fulsome sentiment. His own emotions seemed vulgar now that he had been forced to display them to the gaping crowd.

But the function of the previous day had the effect also of sealing his engagement. Everyone knew of it. Jamie's name was indissolubly joined with Mary's; he could not break the tie now without exposing her to the utmost humiliation. And how could he offer her such an affront when she loved him devotedly? It was not vanity that made him think so, his mother had told him outright; and he saw it in every look of Mary's eyes, in the least inflection of her voice. James asked himself desperately why Mary should care for him. He was not good-looking; he was silent; he was not amusing; he had no particular attraction.

James was sitting in his room, and presently heard Mary's voice calling from the hall.

"Jamie! Jamie!"

He got up and came downstairs.

"Why, Jamie," said his father, "you ought to have gone to fetch Mary, instead of waiting here for her to come to you."

"You certainly ought, Jamie," said Mary, laughing; and then, looking at him, with sudden feeling: "But how seedy you look!"

James had hardly slept, troubling over his perplexity, and he looked haggard and tired.

"I'm all right," he said; "I'm not very strong yet, and I was rather exhausted yesterday."

"Mary thought you would like to go with her this morning, while she does her district visiting."

"It's a beautiful morning, Jamie; it will do you good!" cried Mary.

"I should like it very much."

They started out. Mary wore her every-day costume—a serge gown, a sailor hat, and solid, square-toed boots. She walked fast, with long steps and firm carriage. James set himself to talk, asking her insignificant questions about the people she visited. Mary answered with feeling and at length, but was interrupted by arriving at a cottage.

"You'd better not come in here," she said, blushing slightly; "although I want to take you in to some of the people. I think it will be a lesson to them."

"A lesson in what?" "Oh, I can't tell you to your face, I don't want to make you conceited; but you can guess while you're waiting for me."

Mary's patient was about to be confined, and thinking her condition rather indecent, quite rightly, Mary had left James outside. But the good lady, since it was all in the way of nature, was not so ashamed of herself as she should have been, and insisted on coming to the door to show Miss Clibborn out.

"Take care he doesn't see you!" cried Mary in alarm, pushing her back.

"Well, there's no harm in it. I'm a married woman. You'll have to go through it yourself one day, miss."

Mary rejoined her lover, suffused in blushes, hoping he had seen nothing.

"It's very difficult to teach these people propriety. Somehow the lower classes seem to have no sense of decency."

"What's the matter?"

"Oh, nothing I can tell you," replied Mary, modestly. Then, to turn the conversation: "She asked after my young man, and was very anxious to see you."

"Was she? How did she know you had a young man?" asked James, grimly.

"Oh, everyone knows that! You can't keep secrets in Primpton. And besides, I'm not ashamed of it. Are you?"

"I haven't got a young man."

Mary laughed.

They walked on. The morning was crisp and bright, sending a healthy colour through Mary's cheeks. The blue sky and the bracing air made her feel more self-reliant, better assured than ever of her upright purpose and her candid heart. The road, firm underfoot and delightful to walk upon, stretched before them in a sinuous line. A pleasant odour came from the adjoining fields, from the farm-yards, as they passed them; the larks soared singing with happy heart, while the sparrows chirruped in the hedges. The hawthorn was bursting into leaf, all bright and green, and here and there the wild flowers were showing themselves, the buttercup and the speedwell. But while the charm of Nature made James anxious to linger, to lean on a gate and look for a while at the cows lazily grazing, Mary had too sound a constitution to find in it anything but a stimulus to renewed activity.

"We mustn't dawdle, you lazy creature!" she cried merrily. "I shall never get through my round before one o'clock if we don't put our best foot foremost."

"Can't you see them some other time?"

The limpid air softened his heart; he thought for a moment that if he could wander aimlessly with Mary, gossiping without purpose, they might end by understanding one another. The sun, the wild flowers, the inconstant breeze, might help to create a new feeling.

But Mary turned to him with grave tenderness.

"You know I'd do anything to please you, Jamie. But even for you I cannot neglect my duty."

James froze.

"Of course, you're quite right," he said. "It really doesn't matter."

They came to another cottage, and this time Mary took James in.

"It's a poor old man," she said. "I'm so sorry for him; he's always so grateful for what I do."

They found him lying in bed, writhing with pain, his head supported by a pillow.

"Oh, how uncomfortable you look!" cried Mary. "You poor thing! Who on earth arranged your pillows like that?"

"My daughter, miss."

"I must talk to her; she ought to know better."

Miss Clibborn drew away the pillows very gently, smoothed them out, and replaced them.

"I can't bear 'em like that, miss. The other is the only way I'm comfortable."

"Nonsense, John!" cried Mary, brightly. "You couldn't be comfortable with your head all on one side; you're much better as you are."

James saw the look of pain in the man's face, and ventured to expostulate.

"Don't you think you'd better put them back in the old way? He seemed much easier."

"Nonsense, Jamie. You must know that the head ought to be higher than the body."

"Please, miss, I can't bear the pillow like this."

"Oh, yes, you can. You must show more forbearance and fortitude. Remember that God sends you pain in order to try you. Think of Our Lord suffering silently on the Cross."

"You're putting him to quite unnecessary torture, Mary," said James. "He must know best how he's comfortable."

"It's only because he's obstinate. Those people are always complaining. Really, you must permit me to know more about nursing than you do, Jamie."

Jamie's face grew dark and grim, but he made no answer.

"I shall send you some soup, John," said Mary, as they went out, "You know, one can never get these people to do anything in a rational way," she added to James. "It's perfectly heartrending trying to teach them even such a natural thing as making themselves comfortable."

James was silent.

They walked a few yards farther, and passed a man in a dog-cart Mary turned very red, staring in front of her with the fixed awkwardness of one not adept in the useful art of cutting.

"Oh," she said, with vexation, "he's going to John."

"Who is it?"

"It's Dr. Higgins—a horrid, vulgar man. He's been dreadfully rude to me, and I make a point of cutting him."

"Really?"

"Oh, he behaved scandalously. I can't bear doctors, they're so dreadfully interfering. And they seem to think no one can know anything about doctoring but themselves! He was attending one of my patients; it was a woman, and of course I knew what she wanted. She was ill and weak, and needed strengthening; so I sent her down a bottle of port. Well, Dr. Higgins came to the house, and asked to see me. He's not a gentleman, you know, and he was so rude! 'I've come to see you about Mrs. Gandy,' he said. 'I particularly ordered her not to take stimulants, and I find you've sent her down port.' 'I thought she wanted it,' I said. 'She told me that you had said she wasn't to touch anything, but I thought a little port would do her good.'

Then he said, 'I wish to goodness you wouldn't interfere with what you know nothing about.' 'I should like you to remember that you're speaking to a gentlewoman,' I said. 'I don't care twopence,' he answered, in the rudest way. 'I'm not going to allow you to interfere with my patients. I took the port away, and I wish you to understand that you're not to send any more.'

"Then I confess I lost my temper. 'I suppose you took it away to drink yourself?' I said. Then what d'you think he did? He burst out laughing, and said: 'A bottle of port that cost two bob at the local grocer's! The saints preserve us!'"

James repressed a smile.

"'You impertinent man!' I said. 'You ought to be ashamed to talk to a woman like that. I shall at once send Mrs. Gandy another bottle of port, and it's no business of yours how much it cost.' 'If you do,' he said, 'and anything happens, by God, I'll have you up for manslaughter.' I rang the bell. 'Leave the house,' I said, 'and never dare come here again!' Now don't you think I was right, Jamie?"

"My dear Mary, you always are!"

James looked back at the doctor entering the cottage. It was some comfort to think that he would put the old man into a comfortable position.

"When I told papa," added Mary, "he got in a most fearful rage. He insisted on going out with a horsewhip, and said he meant to thrash Dr. Higgins. He looked for him all the morning, but couldn't find him; and then your mother and I persuaded him it was better to treat such a vulgar man with silent contempt."

James had noticed that the doctor was a burly, broad-shouldered fellow, and he could not help thinking Colonel Clibborn's resolution distinctly wise. How sad it is that in this world right is so often subordinate to brute force!

"But he's not received anywhere. We all cut him; and I get everyone I can not to employ him."

"Ah!" murmured James.

Mary's next patient was feminine, and James was again left to cool his heels in the road; but not alone, for Mr. Dryland came out of the cottage. The curate was a big, stout man, with reddish hair, and a complexion like squashed strawberries and cream; his large, heavy face, hairless except for scanty red eyebrows, gave a disconcerting impression of nakedness. His eyes were blue and his mouth small, with the expression which young ladies, eighty years back, strove to acquire by repeating the words prune and prism. He had a fat, full voice, with unctuous modulations not entirely under his control, so that sometimes, unintentionally, he would utter the most commonplace remark in a tone fitted for a benediction. Mr. Dryland was possessed by the laudable ambition to be all things to all men; and he tried, without conspicuous success, always to suit his conversation to his hearers. With old ladies he was bland; with sportsmen slangy; with yokels he was broadly humorous; and with young people aggressively juvenile. But above all, he wished to be manly, and cultivated a boisterous laugh and a jovial manner.

"I don't know if you remember me," he cried, with a ripple of fat laughter, going up to James, "I had the pleasure of addressing a few words to you yesterday in my official capacity. Miss Clibborn told me you were waiting, and I thought I would introduce myself. My name is Dryland."

"I remember quite well."

"I'm the Vicar's bottle-washer, you know," added the curate, with a guffaw. "Change for you—going round to the sick and needy of the parish—after fighting the good fight. I hear you were wounded."

"I was, rather badly."

"I wish I could have gone out and had a smack at the Boers. Nothing I should have liked better. But, of course, I'm only a parson, you know. It wouldn't have been thought the correct thing." Mr. Dryland, from his superior height, beamed down on James. "I don't know whether you remember the few words which I was privileged to address to you yesterday—"

"Perfectly," put in James.

"Impromptu, you know; but they expressed my feelings. That is one of the best things the war has done for us. It has permitted us to express our emotions more openly. I thought it a beautiful sight to see the noble tears coursing down your father's furrowed cheeks. Those few words of yours have won all our hearts. I may say that our little endeavours were nothing beside that short, unstudied speech. I hope there will be a full report in the Tunbridge Wells papers."

"I hope not!" cried James.

"You're too modest, Captain Parsons. That is what I said to Miss Clibborn yesterday; true courage is always modest. But it is our duty to see that it does not hide its light under a bushel. I hope you won't think it a liberty, but I myself gave the reporter a few notes."

"Will Miss Clibborn be long?" asked James, looking at the cottage.

"Ah, what a good woman she is, Captain Parsons. My dear sir, I assure you she's an angel of mercy."

"It's very kind of you to say so."

"Not at all! It's a pleasure. The good she does is beyond praise. She's a wonderful help in the parish. She has at heart the spiritual welfare of the people, and I may say that she is a moral force of the first magnitude."

"I'm sure that's a very delightful thing to be."

"You know I can't help thinking," laughed Mr. Dryland fatly, "that she ought to be the wife of a clergyman, rather than of a military man."

Mary came out.

"I've been telling Mrs. Gray that I don't approve of the things her daughter wears in church," she said. "I don't think it's nice for people of that class to wear such bright colours."

"I don't know what we should do in the parish without you," replied the curate, unctuously. "It's so rare to find someone who knows what is right, and isn't afraid of speaking out."

Mary said that she and James were walking home, and asked Mr. Dryland whether he would not accompany them.

"I shall be delighted, if I'm not *de trop*."

He looked with laughing significance from one to the other.

"I wanted to talk to you about my girls," said Mary.

She had a class of village maidens, to whom she taught sewing, respect for their betters, and other useful things.

"I was just telling Captain Parsons that you were an angel of mercy, Miss Clibborn."

"I'm afraid I'm not that," replied Mary, gravely. "But I try to do my duty."

"Ah!" cried Mr. Dryland, raising his eyes so that he looked exactly like a codfish, "how few of us can say that!"

"I'm seriously distressed about my girls. They live in nasty little cottages, and eat filthy things; they pass their whole lives under the most disgusting conditions, and yet they're happy. I can't get them to see that they ought to be utterly miserable."

"Oh, I know," sighed the curate; "it makes me sad to think of it."

"Surely, if they're happy, you can want nothing better," said James, rather impatiently.

"But I do. They have no right to be happy under such circumstances. I want to make them feel their wretchedness."

"What a brutal thing to do!" cried James.

"It's the only way to improve them. I want them to see things as I see them."

"And how d'you know that you see them any more correctly than they do?"

"My dear Jamie!" cried Mary; and then as the humour of such a suggestion dawned upon her, she burst into a little shout of laughter.

"What d'you think is the good of making them dissatisfied?" asked James, grimly.

"I want to make them better, nobler, worthier; I want to make their lives more beautiful and holy."

"If you saw a man happily wearing a tinsel crown, would you go to him and say, 'My good friend, you're making a fool of yourself. Your crown isn't of real gold, and you must throw it away. I haven't a golden crown to give you instead, but you're wicked to take pleasure in that sham thing.' They're just as comfortable, after their fashion, in a hovel as you in your fine house; they enjoy the snack of fat pork they have on Sunday just as much as you enjoy your boiled chickens and blanc-manges. They're happy, and that's the chief thing."

"Happiness is not the chief thing in this world, James," said Mary, gravely.

"Isn't it? I thought it was."

"Captain Parsons is a cynic," said Mr. Dryland, with a slightly supercilious smile.

"Because I say it's idiotic to apply your standards to people who have nothing in common with you? I hate all this interfering. For God's sake let us go our way; and if we can get a little pleasure out of dross and tinsel, let us keep it."

"I want to give the poor high ideals," said Mary.

"I should have thought bread and cheese would be more useful."

"My dear Jamie," said Mary, good-naturedly, "I think you're talking of things you know nothing about."

"You must remember that Miss Clibborn has worked nobly among the poor for many years."

"My own conscience tells me I'm right," pursued Mary, "and you see Mr. Dryland agrees with me. I know you mean well, Jamie; but I don't think you quite understand the matter, and I fancy we had better change the conversation."

VII

Next day Mary went into Primpton House. Colonel Parsons nodded to her as she walked up the drive, and took off his spectacles. The front door was neither locked nor bolted in that confiding neighbourhood, and Mary walked straight in.

"Well, my dear?" said the Colonel, smiling with pleasure, for he was as fond of her as of his own son.

"I thought I'd come and see you alone. Jamie's still out, isn't he? I saw him pass our house. I was standing at the window, but he didn't look up."

"I daresay he was thinking. He's grown very thoughtful now."

Mrs. Parsons came in, and her quiet face lit up, too, as she greeted Mary. She kissed her tenderly.

"Jamie's out, you know."

"Mary has come to see us," said the Colonel. "She doesn't want us to feel neglected now that she has the boy."

"We shall never dream that you can do anything unkind, dear Mary," replied Mrs. Parsons, stroking the girl's hair. "It's natural that you should think more of him than of us."

Mary hesitated a moment.

"Don't you think Jamie has changed?"

Mrs. Parsons looked at her quickly.

"I think he has grown more silent. But he's been through so much. And then he's a man now; he was only a boy when we saw him last."

"D'you think he cares for me any more?" asked Mary, with a rapid tremor in her voice.

"Mary!"

"Of course he does! He talks of you continually," said Colonel Parsons, "and always as if he were devoted. Doesn't he, Frances?"

The old man's deep love for Mary had prevented him from seeing in Jamie's behaviour anything incongruous with that of a true lover.

"What makes you ask that question, Mary?" said Mrs. Parsons.

Her feminine tact had led her to notice a difference in Jamie's feeling towards his betrothed; but she had been unwilling to think that it amounted even to coldness. Such a change could be explained in a hundred natural ways, and might, indeed, exist merely in her own imagination.

"Oh, he's not the same as he was!" cried Mary, "I don't know what it is, but I feel it in his whole manner. Yesterday evening he barely said a word."

James had dined with the Clibborns in solemn state.

"I daresay he's not very well yet. His wound troubles him still."

"I try to put it down to that," said Mary, "but he seems to force himself to speak to me. He's not natural. I've got an awful fear that he has ceased to care for me."

She looked from Colonel Parsons to his wife, who stared at her in dismay.

"Don't be angry with me," she said; "I couldn't talk like this to anyone else, but I know you love me. I look upon you already as my father and mother. I don't want to be unkind to mamma, but I couldn't talk of it to her; she would only sneer at me. And I'm afraid it's making me rather unhappy."

"Of course, we want you to treat us as your real parents, Mary. We both love you as we love Jamie. We have always looked upon you as our daughter."

"You're so good to me!"

"Has your mother said anything to annoy you?"

Mary faltered.

"Last night, when he went away, she said she didn't think he was devoted to me."

"Oh, I knew it was your mother who'd put this in your head! She has always been jealous of you. I suppose she thinks he's in love with her."

"Mrs. Parsons!" cried Mary, in a tone of entreaty.

"I know you can't bear anything said against your mother, and it's wicked of me to vex you; but she has no right to suggest such things."

"It's not only that. It's what I feel."

"I'm sure Jamie is most fond of you," said Colonel Parsons, kindly. "You've not seen one another for five years, and you find yourselves altered. Even we feel a little strange with Jamie sometimes; don't we, Frances? What children they are, Frances!" Colonel Parsons laughed in that irresistibly sweet fashion of his. "Why, it was only the day before yesterday that Jamie came to us with a long face and asked if you cared for *him*."

"Did he?" asked Mary, with pleased surprise, anxious to believe what the Colonel suggested. "Oh, he must see that I love him! Perhaps he finds me unresponsive.... How could I help caring for him? I think if he ceased to love me, I should die."

"My dearest Mary," cried Mrs. Parsons, the tears rising to her eyes, "don't talk like that! I'm sure he can't help loving you, either; you're so good and sweet. You're both of you fanciful, and he's not well. Be patient. Jamie is shy and reserved; he hasn't quite got used to us yet. He doesn't know how to show his feelings. It will all come right soon."

"Of course he loves you!" said Colonel Parsons. "Who could help it? Why, if I were a young fellow I should be mad to marry you."

"And what about me, Richmond?" asked Mrs. Parsons, smiling.

"Well, I think I should have to commit bigamy, and marry you both."

They laughed at the Colonel's mild little joke, happy to break through the cloud of doubt which oppressed them.

"You're a dear thing," said Mary, kissing the old man, "and I'm a very silly girl. It's wrong of me to give way to whims and fancies."

"You must be very brave when you're the wife of a V.C.," said the Colonel, patting her hand.

"Oh, it was a beautiful action!" cried Mary. "And he's as modest about it as though he had done nothing that any man might not do. I think there can be no sight more pleasing to God than that of a brave man risking his life to save a comrade."

"And that ought to be an assurance to you, Mary, that James will never do anything unkind or dishonourable. Trust him, and forgive his little faults of manner. I'm sure he loves you, and soon you'll get married and be completely happy."

Mary's face darkened once more.

"He's been here three days, and he's not said a word about getting married. Oh, I can't help it; I'm so frightened! I wish he'd say something—just one word to show that he really cares for me. He seems to have forgotten that we're even engaged."

Colonel Parsons looked at his wife, begging her by his glance to say something that would comfort Mary. Mrs. Parsons looked down, uncertain, ill at ease.

"You don't despise me for talking like this, Mrs. Parsons?"

"Despise you, my dear! How can I, when I love you so dearly? Shall I speak to Jamie? I'm sure when he understands that he's making you unhappy, he'll be different. He has the kindest heart in the world; I've never known him do an unkind thing in his life."

"No, don't say anything to him," replied Mary. "I daresay it's all nonsense. I don't want him to be driven into making love to me."

* * *

Meanwhile James wandered thoughtfully. The country was undulating, and little hill rose after little hill, affording spacious views of the fat Kentish fields, encircled by oak trees and by chestnuts. Owned by rich landlords, each generation had done its best, and the fruitful land was tended like a garden. But it had no abandonment, no freedom; the hand of man was obvious, perpetually, in the trimness and in the careful arrangement, so that the landscape, in its formality, reminded one of those set pieces chosen by the classic painters. But the fields were fresh with the tall young grass of the new year, the buttercups flaunted themselves gaily, careless of the pitiless night, rejoicing in the sunshine, as before they had rejoiced in the enlivening rain. The pleasant rain-drops still lingered on the daisies. The feathery ball of the dandelion, carried by the breeze, floated past like a symbol of the life of man—a random thing, resistless to the merest breath, with no mission but to spread its seed upon the fertile earth, so that things like unto it should spring up in the succeeding summer, and flower uncared for, and reproduce themselves, and die.

James decided finally that he must break that very evening his engagement with Mary. He could not put it off. Every day made his difficulty greater, and it was impossible any longer to avoid the discussion of their marriage, nor could he continue to treat Mary with nothing better than friendliness. He realised all her good qualities; she was frank, and honest, and simple; anxious to do right; charitable according to her light;

kindness itself. James felt sincerely grateful for the affectionate tenderness which Mary showed to his father and mother. He was thankful for that and for much else, and was prepared to look upon her as a very good friend, even as a sister; but he did not love her. He could not look upon the prospect of marriage without repulsion. Nor did Mary, he said, really love him. He knew what love was—something different entirely from that pallid flame of affection and esteem, of which alone she was capable. Mary loved him for certain qualities of mind, because his station in life was decent, his manners passable, his morals beyond reproach.

"She might as well marry the Ten Commandments!" he cried impatiently.

Mary cared for him from habit, from a sense of decorum, and for the fitness of things; but that was not love. He shrugged his shoulders scornfully, looking for some word to express the mildly pleasant, unagitating emotion. James, who had been devoured by it, who had struggled with it as with a deadly sin, who had killed it finally while, like a serpent of evil, it clung to his throat, drinking his life's blood, James knew what love was—a fire in the veins, a divine affliction, a passion, a frenzy, a madness. The love he knew was the love of the body of flesh and blood, the love that engenders, the love that kills. At the bottom of it is sex, and sex is not ugly or immoral, for sex is the root of life. The woman is fair because man shall love her body; her lips are red and passionate that he may kiss them; her hair is beautiful that he may take it in his hands—a river of living gold.

James stopped, and the dead love rose again and tore his entrails like a beast of prey. He gasped with agony, with bitter joy. Ah, that was the true love! What did he care that the woman lacked this and that? He loved her because he loved her; he loved her for her faults. And in spite of the poignant anguish, he thanked her from the bottom of his heart, for she had taught him love. She had caused him endless pain, but she had given him the strength to bear it. She had ruined his life, perhaps, but had shown him that life was worth living. What were the agony, the torture, the despair, beside that radiant passion which made him godlike? It is only the lover who lives, and of his life every moment is intense and fervid. James felt that his most precious recollection was that ardent month, during which, at last, he had seen the world in all its dazzling movement, in its manifold colour, singing with his youth and laughing to his joy.

And he did not care that hideous names have been given to that dear passion, to that rich desire. The vulgar call it lust, and blush and hide their faces; in their folly is the shame, in their prurience the disgrace. They do not know that the appetite which shocks them is the very origin of the highest qualities of man. It is they, weaklings afraid to look life in the face, dotards and sentimentalists, who have made the body unclean. They have covered the nakedness of Aphrodite with the rags of their own impurity. They have disembowelled the great lovers of antiquity till Cleopatra serves to adorn a prudish tale and Lancelot to point a moral. Oh, Mother Nature, give us back our freedom, with its strength of sinew and its humour! For lack of it we perish in false shame, and our fig-leaves point our immodesty to all the world. Teach us that love is not a tawdry sentiment, but a fire divine in order to the procreation of children; teach us not to dishonour our bodies, for they are beautiful and pure, and all thy works are sweet. Teach us, again, in thy merciful goodness, that man is made for woman, his body for her body, and that the flesh cannot sin.

Teach us also not to rant too much, even in thy service; and though we do set up for prophets and the like, let us not forget occasionally to laugh at our very august selves.

* * *

Then, harking back, Jamie's thoughts returned to the dinner of the previous evening at the Clibborns. He was the only guest, and when he arrived, found Mary and the Colonel by themselves in the drawing-room. It was an old habit of Mrs. Clibborn's not to appear till after her visitors, thinking that so she created a greater effect. The Colonel wore a very high collar, which made his head look like some queer flower on a long white stalk; hair and eyebrows were freshly dyed, and glistened like the oiled locks of a young Jewess. He was the perfect dandy, even to his bejewelled fingers and his scented handkerchief. His manner was a happy mixture of cordiality and condescension, by the side of which Mary's unaffected simplicity contrasted oddly. She seemed less at home in an evening dress than in the walking costume she vastly preferred; her free, rather masculine movements were ungainly in the silk frock, badly made and countrified, while lace and ribbons suited her most awkwardly. She was out of place, too, in that room, decorated with all the abominations of pseudo-fashion, with draperies and tissue-paper, uncomfortable little chairs and rickety tables. In every available place stood photographs of Mrs. Clibborn—Mrs. Clibborn sitting, standing, lying; Mrs. Clibborn full face, three-quarter face, side face; Mrs. Clibborn in this costume or in that costume—grave, gay, thoughtful, or smiling; Mrs. Clibborn showing her beautiful teeth, her rounded arms, her vast shoulders; Mrs. Clibborn dressed to the nines, and Mrs. Clibborn as undressed as she dared.

Finally, the beauty swept in with a great rustle of silk, displaying to the full her very opulent charms. Her hair was lightly powdered, and honestly she looked remarkably handsome.

"Don't say I've kept you waiting," she murmured. "I could never forgive myself."

James made some polite reply, and they went down to dinner. The conversation was kept at the high level which one naturally expects from persons fashionable enough to dine late. They discussed Literature, by which they meant the last novel but one; Art, by which they meant the Royal Academy; and Society, by which they meant their friends who kept carriages.

Mrs. Clibborn said that, of course, she could not expect James to pay any attention to her, since all his thoughts must be for Mary, and then proceeded entirely to absorb him.

"You must find it very dull here," she moaned. "I'm afraid you'll be bored to death." And she looked at Mary with her most smilingly cruel expression. "Oh, Mary, why did you put on that dreadfully dowdy frock? I've asked you over and over again to give it away, but you never pay attention to your poor mother."

"It's all right," said Mary, looking down at it, laughing and blushing a little.

Mrs. Clibborn turned again to James.

"I think it's such a mistake for women not to dress well. I'm an old woman now, but I always try to look my best. Reggie has never seen me in a dowdy gown. Have you, Reggie?"

"Any dress would become you, my love."

"Oh, Reggie, don't say that before James. He looks upon his future mother as an old woman."

Then at the end of dinner:

"Don't sit too long over your wine. I shall be so dull with nobody but Mary to amuse me."

Mrs. Clibborn had been fond enough of Mary when she was a little girl, who could be petted on occasion and sent away when necessary; but as she grew up and exhibited a will of her own, she found her almost an intolerable nuisance. The girl developed a conscience, and refused indignantly to tell the little fibs which her mother occasionally suggested. She put her sense of right and wrong before Mrs. Clibborn's wishes, which that lady considered undutiful, if not entirely wicked. It seemed nothing short of an impertinence that Mary should disapprove of theatres when there was nothing to which the elder woman was more devoted. And Mrs. Clibborn felt that the girl saw through all her little tricks and artful dodges, often speaking out strongly when her mother proposed to do something particularly underhand. It was another grievance that Mary had inherited no good looks, and the faded beauty, in her vanity, was convinced that the girl spitefully observed every fresh wrinkle that appeared upon her face. But Mrs. Clibborn was also a little afraid of her daughter; such meekness and such good temper were difficult to overcome; and when she snubbed her, it was not only to chasten a proud spirit, but also to reassure herself.

When the ladies had retired, the Colonel handed James an execrable cigar.

"Now, I'm going to give you some very special port I've got," he said.

He poured out a glass with extreme care, and passed it over with evident pride. James remembered Mary's story of the doctor, and having tasted the wine, entirely sympathised with him. It was no wonder that invalids did not thrive upon it.

"Fine wine, isn't it?" said Colonel Clibborn. "Had it in my cellar for years." He shook it so as to inhale the aroma. "I got it from my old friend, the Duke of St. Olphert's. 'Reggie, my boy,' he said—'Reggie, do you want some good port?' 'Good port, Bill!' I cried—I always called him Bill, you know; his Christian name was William—'I should think I do, Billy, old boy.' 'Well,' said the Duke, 'I've got some I can let you have.'"

"He was a wine-merchant, was he?" asked James.

"Wine-merchant! My dear fellow, he was the Duke of St. Olphert's. He'd bought up the cellar of an Austrian nobleman, and he had more port than he wanted."

"And this is some of it?" asked James, gravely, holding the murky fluid to the light.

Then the Colonel stretched his legs and began to talk of the war. James, rather tired of the subject, sought to change the conversation; but Colonel Clibborn was anxious to tell one who had been through it how the thing should have been conducted; so his guest, with a mixture of astonishment and indignation, resigned himself to listen to the most pitiful inanities. He marvelled that a man should have spent his life in the service, and yet apparently be ignorant of the very elements of warfare;

but having already learnt to hold his tongue, he let the Colonel talk, and was presently rewarded by a break. Something reminded the gallant cavalryman of a hoary anecdote, and he gave James that dreary round of stories which have dragged their heavy feet for thirty years from garrison to garrison. Then, naturally, he proceeded to the account of his own youthful conquests. The Colonel had evidently been a devil with the ladies, for he knew all about the forgotten ballet-dancers of the seventies, and related with gusto a number of scabrous tales.

"Ah, my boy, in my day we went the pace! I tell you in confidence, I was a deuce of a rake before I got married."

When they returned to the drawing-room, Mrs. Clibborn was ready with her langorous smile, and made James sit beside her on the sofa. In a few minutes the Colonel, as was his habit, closed his eyes, dropped his chin, and fell comfortably asleep. Mrs. Clibborn slowly turned to Mary.

"Will you try and find me my glasses, darling," she murmured. "They're either in my work-basket or on the morning-room table. And if you can't see them there, perhaps they're in your father's study. I want to read Jamie a letter."

"I'll go and look, mother."

Mary went out, and Mrs. Clibborn put her hand on Jamie's arm.

"Do you dislike me very much, Jamie?" she murmured softly.

"On the contrary!"

"I'm afraid your mother doesn't care for me."

"I'm sure she does."

"Women have never liked me. I don't know why. I can't help it if I'm not exactly—plain, I'm as God made me."

James thought that the Almighty in that case must have an unexpected familiarity with the rouge-pot and the powder-puff.

"Do you know that I did all I could to prevent your engagement to Mary?"

"You!" cried James, thunderstruck. "I never knew that."

"I thought I had better tell you myself. You mustn't be angry with me. It was for your own good. If I had had my way you would never have become engaged. I thought you were so much too young."

"Five years ago, d'you mean—when it first happened?"

"You were only a boy—a very nice boy, Jamie. I always liked you. I don't approve of long engagements, and I thought you'd change your mind. Most young men are a little wild; it's right that they should be."

James looked at her, wondering suddenly whether she knew or divined anything. It was impossible, she was too silly.

"You're very wise."

"Oh, don't say that!" cried Mrs. Clibborn, with a positive groan. "It sounds so middle-aged.... I always thought Mary was too old for you. A woman should be ten years younger than her husband."

"Tell me all about it," insisted James.

"They wouldn't listen to me. They said you had better be engaged. They thought it would benefit your morals. I was very much against it. I think boys are so much nicer when they haven't got encumbrances—or morals."

At that moment Mary came in.

"I can't find your glasses, mamma."

"Oh, it doesn't matter," replied Mrs. Clibborn, smiling softly; "I've just remembered that I sent them into Tunbridge Wells yesterday to be mended."

VIII

James knew he would see Mary at the tea-party which Mrs. Jackson that afternoon was giving at the Vicarage. Society in Little Primpton was exclusive, with the result that the same people met each other day after day, and the only intruders were occasional visitors of irreproachable antecedents from Tunbridge Wells. Respectability is a plant which in that fashionable watering-place has been so assiduously cultivated that it flourishes now in the open air; like the yellow gorse, it is found in every corner, thriving hardily under the most unfavourable conditions; and the keener the wind, the harder the frost, the more proudly does it hold its head. But on this particular day the gathering was confined to the immediate neighbours, and when the Parsons arrived they found, beside their hosts, only the Clibborns and the inevitable curate. There was a prolonged shaking of hands, inquiries concerning the health of all present, and observations suggested by the weather; then they sat down in a circle, and set themselves to discuss the questions of the day.

"Oh, Mr. Dryland," cried Mary, "thanks so much for that book! I am enjoying it!"

"I thought you'd like it," replied the curate, smiling blandly. "I know you share my admiration for Miss Corelli."

"Mr. Dryland has just lent me 'The Master Christian,'" Mary explained, turning to Mrs. Jackson.

"Oh, I was thinking of putting it on the list for my next book."

They had formed a club in Little Primpton of twelve persons, each buying a six-shilling book at the beginning of the year, and passing it on in return for another after a certain interval, so that at the end of twelve months all had read a dozen masterpieces of contemporary fiction.

"I thought I'd like to buy it at once," said Mr. Dryland. "I always think one ought to possess Marie Corelli's books. She's the only really great novelist we have in England now."

Mr. Dryland was a man of taste and authority, so that his literary judgments could always be relied on.

"Of course, I don't pretend to know much about the matter," said Mary, modestly. "There are more important things in life than books; but I do think she's splendid. I can't help feeling I'm wasting my time when I read most novels, but I never feel that with Marie Corelli."

"No one would think she was a woman," said the Vicar.

To which the curate answered: *"Le genie n'a pas de sexe."*

The others, being no scholars, did not quite understand the remark, but they looked intelligent.

"I always think it's so disgraceful the way the newspapers sneer at her," said Mrs. Jackson. "And, I'm sure, merely because she's a woman."

"And because she has genius, my dear," put in the Vicar. "Some minds are so contemptibly small that they are simply crushed by greatness. It requires an eagle to look at the sun."

And the excellent people looked at one another with a certain self-satisfaction, for they had the fearless gaze of the king of birds in face of that brilliant orb.

"The critics are willing to do anything for money. Miss Corelli has said herself that there is a vile conspiracy to blacken her, and for my part I am quite prepared to believe it. They're all afraid of her because she dares to show them up."

"Besides, most of the critics are unsuccessful novelists," added Mr. Dryland, "and they are as envious as they can be."

"It makes one boil with indignation," cried Mary, "to think that people can be so utterly base. Those who revile her are not worthy to unloose the latchet of her shoes."

"It does one good to hear such whole-hearted admiration," replied the curate, beaming. "But you must remember that genius has always been persecuted. Look at Keats and Shelley. The critics abused them just as they abuse Marie Corelli. Even Shakespeare was slandered. But time has vindicated our immortal William; time will vindicate as brightly our gentle Marie."

"I wonder how many of us here could get through Hamlet without yawning!" meditatively said the Vicar.

"I see your point!" cried Mr. Dryland, opening his eyes. "While we could all read the 'Sorrows of Satan' without a break. I've read it three times, and each perusal leaves me more astounded. Miss Corelli has her revenge in her own hand; what can she care for the petty snarling of critics when the wreath of immortality is on her brow. I don't hesitate to say it, I'm not ashamed of my opinion; I consider Miss Corelli every bit as great as William Shakespeare. I've gone into the matter carefully, and if I may say so, I'm speaking of what I know something about. My deliberate opinion is that in wit, and humour, and language, she's every bit his equal."

"Her language is beautiful," said Mrs. Jackson. "When I read her I feel just as if I were listening to hymns."

"And where, I should like to know," continued the curate, raising his voice, "can you find in a play of Shakespeare's such a gallery of portraits as in the 'Master Christian'?"

"And there is one thing you must never forget," said the Vicar, gravely, "she has a deep, religious feeling which you will find in none of Shakespeare's plays. Every one of her books has a lofty moral purpose. That is the justification of fiction. The novelist has a high vocation, if he could only see it; he can inculcate submission to authority, hope, charity, obedience—in fact, all the higher virtues; he can become a handmaid of the Church. And now, when irreligion, and immorality, and scepticism are rampant, we must not despise the humblest instruments."

"How true that is!" said Mrs. Jackson.

"If all novelists were like Marie Corelli, I should willingly hold them out my hand. I think every Christian ought to read 'Barabbas.' It gives an entirely new view of Christ. It puts the incidents of the Gospel in a way that one had never dreamed. I was never so impressed in my life."

"But all her books are the same in that way!" cried Mary. "They all make me feel so much better and nobler, and more truly Christian."

"I think she's vulgar and blasphemous," murmured Mrs. Clibborn quietly, as though she were making the simplest observation.

"Mamma!" cried Mary, deeply shocked; and among the others there was a little movement of indignation and disgust.

Mrs. Clibborn was continually mortifying her daughter by this kind of illiterate gaucherie. But the most painful part of it was that the good lady always remained perfectly unconscious of having said anything incredibly silly, and continued with perfect self-assurance:

"I've never been able to finish a book of hers. I began one about electricity, which I couldn't understand, and then I tried another. I forget what it was, but there was something in it about a bed of roses, and I thought it very improper. I don't think it was a nice book for Mary to read, but girls seem to read everything now."

There was a pained hush, such as naturally occurs when someone has made a very horrible *faux pas*. They all looked at one another awkwardly; while Mary, ashamed at her mother's want of taste, kept her eyes glued to the carpet But Mrs. Clibborn's folly was so notorious that presently anger was succeeded by contemptuous amusement, and the curate came to the rescue with a loud guffaw.

"Of course, you know your Marie Corelli by heart, Captain Parsons?"

"I'm afraid I've never read one of them."

"Not?" they all cried in surprise.

"Oh, I'll send them to you to Primpton House," said Mr. Dryland. "I have them all. Why, no one's education is complete till he's read Marie Corelli."

This was considered a very good hit at Mrs. Clibborn, and the dear people smiled at one another significantly. Even Mary could scarcely keep a straight face.

The tea then appeared, and was taken more or less silently. With the exception of the fashionable Mrs. Clibborn, they were all more used to making a sit-down meal of it, and the care of holding a cup, with a piece of cake unsteadily balanced in the saucer, prevented them from indulging in very brilliant conversational feats; they found one gymnastic exercise quite sufficient at a time. But when the tea-cups were safely restored to the table, Mrs. Jackson suggested a little music.

"Will you open the proceedings, Mary?"

The curate went up to Miss Clibborn with a bow, gallantly offering his arm to escort her to the piano. Mary had thoughtfully brought her music, and began to play a 'Song Without Words,' by Mendelssohn. She was considered a fine pianist in Little Primpton. She attacked the notes with marked resolution, keeping the loud pedal down throughout; her eyes were fixed on the music with an intense, determined air, in which you saw an eagerness to perform a social duty, and her lips moved as conscientiously she counted time. Mary played the whole piece without making a single mistake, and at the end was much applauded.

"There's nothing like classical music, is there?" cried the curate enthusiastically, as Mary stopped, rather out of breath, for she played, as she did everything else, with energy and thoroughness.

"It's the only music I really love."

"And those 'Songs Without Words' are beautiful," said Colonel Parsons, who was standing on Mary's other side.

"Mendelssohn is my favourite composer," she replied. "He's so full of soul."

"Ah, yes," murmured Mr. Dryland. "His heart seems to throb through all his music. It's strange that he should have been a Jew."

"But then Our Lord was a Jew, wasn't He?" said Mary.

"Yes, one is so apt to forget that."

Mary turned the leaves, and finding another piece which was familiar to her, set about it. It was a satisfactory thing to listen to her performance. In Mary's decided touch one felt all the strength of her character, with its simple, unaffected candour and its eminent sense of propriety. In her execution one perceived the high purpose which animated her whole conduct; it was pure and wholesome, and thoroughly English. And her piano-playing served also as a moral lesson, for none could listen without remembering that life was not an affair to be taken lightly, but a strenuous endeavour: the world was a battlefield (this one realised more particularly when Mary forgot for a page or so to take her foot off the pedal); each one of us had a mission to perform, a duty to do, a function to fulfill.

Meanwhile, James was trying to make conversation with Mrs. Clibborn.

"How well Mary plays!"

"D'you think so? I can't bear amateurs. I wish they wouldn't play."

James looked at Mrs. Clibborn quickly. It rather surprised him that she, the very silliest woman he had ever known, should say the only sensible things he had heard that day. Nor could he forget that she had done her best to prevent his engagement.

"I think you're a very wonderful woman," he said.

"Oh, Jamie!"

Mrs. Clibborn smiled and sighed, slipping forward her hand for him to take; but James was too preoccupied to notice the movement.

"I'm beginning to think you really like me," murmured Mrs. Clibborn, cooing like an amorous dove.

Then James was invited to sing, and refused.

"Please do, Jamie!" cried Mary, smiling. "For my sake. You used to sing so nicely!"

He still tried to excuse himself, but finding everyone insistent, went at last, with very bad grace, to the piano. He not only sang badly, but knew it, and was irritated that he should be forced to make a fool of himself. Mr. Dryland sang badly, but perfectly satisfied with himself, needed no pressing when his turn came. He made a specialty of old English songs, and thundered out in his most ecclesiastical manner a jovial ditty entitled, "Down Among the Dead Men."

The afternoon was concluded by an adjournment to the dining-room to play bagatelle, the most inane of games, to which the billiard-player goes with contempt, changed quickly to wrath when he cannot put the balls into absurd little holes. Mary was an adept, and took pleasure in showing James how the thing should be done. He noticed that she and the curate managed the whole affair between them, arranging partners and advising freely. Mrs. Clibborn alone refused to play, saying frankly it was too idiotic a pastime.

At last the party broke up, and in a group bade their farewells.

"I'll walk home with you, Mary, if you don't mind," said James, "and smoke a pipe."

Mary suddenly became radiant, and Colonel Parsons gave her a happy little smile and a friendly nod.... At last James had his opportunity. He lingered while Mary gathered together her music, and waited again to light his pipe, so that when they came out of the Vicarage gates the rest of the company were no longer in sight. The day had become overcast and sombre; on the even surface of the sky floated little ragged black clouds, like the fragments cast to the wind of some widowed, ample garment. It had grown cold, and James, accustomed to a warmer air, shivered a little. The country suddenly appeared cramped and circumscribed; in the fading light a dullness of colour came over tree and hedgerow which was singularly depressing. They walked in silence, while James looked for words. All day he had been trying to find some manner to express himself, but his mind, perplexed and weary, refused to help him. The walk to Mary's house could not take more than five minutes, and he saw the distance slipping away rapidly. If he meant to say anything it must be said at once; and his mouth was dry, he felt almost a physical inability to speak. He did not know how to prepare the way, how to approach the subject; and he was doubly tormented by the absolute necessity of breaking the silence.

But it was Mary who spoke first.

"D'you know, I've been worrying a little about you, Jamie."

"Why?"

"I'm afraid I hurt your feelings yesterday. Don't you remember, when we were visiting my patients—I think I spoke rather harshly. I didn't mean to. I'm very sorry."

"I had forgotten all about it," he said, looking at her. "I have no notion what you said to offend me."

"I'm glad of that," she answered, smiling, "but it does me good to apologise. Will you think me very silly if I say something to you?"

"Of course not!"

"Well, I want to say that if I ever do anything you don't like, or don't approve of, I wish you would tell me."

After that, how could he say immediately that he no longer loved her, and wished to be released from his engagement?

"I'm afraid you think I'm a very terrifying person," answered James.

Her words had made his announcement impossible; another day had gone, and weakly he had let it pass.

"What shall I do?" he murmured under his breath. "What a coward I am!"

They came to the door of the Clibborns' house and Mary turned to say good-bye. She bent forward, smiling and blushing, and he quickly kissed her.

* * *

In the evening, James was sitting by the fire in the dining-room, thinking of that one subject which occupied all his thoughts. Colonel Parsons and his wife were at the table, engaged upon the game of backgammon which invariably filled the interval between supper and prayers. The rattle of dice came to James indistinctly, as in a dream, and he imagined fantastically that unseen powers were playing for his life. He sat with his head between his hands, staring at the flames as though to find in them a solution to his difficulty; but mockingly they spoke only of Mrs. Wallace and the caress of her limpid eyes. He turned away with a gesture of impatience. The game was just finished, and Mrs. Parsons, catching the expression on his face, asked:

"What are you thinking of, Jamie?"

"I?" he answered, looking up quickly, as though afraid that his secret had been divined. "Nothing!"

Mrs. Parsons put the backgammon board away, making up her mind to speak, for she too suffered from a shyness which made the subjects she had nearest at heart precisely those that she could least bear to talk about.

"When do you think of getting married, Jamie?"

James started.

"Why, you asked me that yesterday," He tried to make a joke of it. "Upon my word, you're very anxious to get rid of me."

"I wonder if it's occurred to you that you're making Mary a little unhappy?"

James stood up and leaned against the mantelpiece, his face upon his hand.

"I should be sorry to do that, mother."

"You've been home four days, and you've not said a word to show you love her."

"I'm afraid I'm not very demonstrative."

"That's what I said!" cried the Colonel, triumphantly.

"Can't you try to say a word or two to prove you care for her, Jamie? She *is* so fond of you," continued his mother. "I don't want to interfere with your private concerns, but I think it's only thoughtlessness on your part; and I'm sure you don't wish to make Mary miserable. Poor thing, she's so unhappy at home; she yearns for a little affection.... Won't you say something to her about your marriage?"

"Has she asked you to speak to me?" inquired James.

"No, dear. You know that she would never do anything of the kind. She would hate to think that I had said anything."

James paused a moment.

"I will speak to her to-morrow, mother."

"That's right!" said the Colonel, cheerfully. "I know she's going to be in all the morning. Colonel and Mrs. Clibborn are going into Tunbridge Wells."

"It will be a good opportunity."

IX

In the morning Mrs. Parsons was in the hall, arranging flowers, when James passed through to get his hat.

"Are you going to see Mary now?"

"Yes, mother."

"That's a good boy."

She did not notice that her son's usual gravity was intensified, or that his very lips were pallid, and his eyes careworn and lustreless.

It was raining. The young fresh leaves, in the colourless day, had lost their verdure, and the massive shapes of the elm trees were obscured in the mist. The sky had so melancholy a tone that it seemed a work of man—a lifeless hue of infinite sorrow, dreary and cheerless.

James arrived at the Clibborns' house.

"Miss Mary is in the drawing-room," he was told by a servant, who smiled on him, the accepted lover, with obtrusive friendliness.

He went in and found her seated at the piano, industriously playing scales. She wore the weather-beaten straw hat without which she never seemed comfortable.

"Oh, I'm glad you've come," she said. "I'm alone in the house, and I was taking the opportunity to have a good practice."

She turned round on the music-stool, and ran one hand chromatically up the piano, smiling the while with pleasure at Jamie's visit. "Would you like to go for a walk?" she asked. "I don't mind the rain a bit."

"I would rather stay here, if you don't mind."

James sat down and began playing with a paper-knife. Still he did not know how to express himself. He was torn asunder by rival emotions; he felt absolutely bound to speak, and yet could not bear the thought of the agony he must cause. He was very tender-hearted; he had never in his life consciously given pain to any living creature, and would far rather have inflicted hurt upon himself.

"I've been wanting to have a long talk with you alone ever since I came back."

"Have you? Why didn't you tell me?"

"Because what I want to say is very difficult, Mary; and I'm afraid it must be very—distressing to both of us."

"What do you mean?"

Mary suddenly became grave, James glanced at her, and hesitated; but there was no room for hesitation now. Somehow he must get to the end of what he had to say, attempting only to be as gentle as possible. He stood up and leant against the mantelpiece, still toying with the paper-knife; Mary also changed her seat, and took a chair by the table.

"Do you know that we've been engaged for over five years now, Mary?"

"Yes."

She looked at him steadily, and he dropped his eyes.

"I want to thank you for all you've done for my sake, Mary. I know how good you have been to my people; it was very kind of you. I cannot think how they would have got along without you."

"I love them as I love my own father and mother, Jamie. I tried to act towards them as though I was indeed their daughter."

He was silent for a while.

"We were both very young when we became engaged," he said at last.

He looked up quickly, but she did not answer. She stared with frightened eyes, as if already she understood. It was harder even than he thought. James asked himself desperately whether he could not stop there, taking back what he had said. The cup was too bitter! But what was the alternative? He could not go on pretending one thing when he felt another; he could not live a constant, horrible lie. He felt there was only one course open to him. Like a man with an ill that must be fatal unless instantly treated, he was bound to undergo everything, however great the torture.

"And it's a very bad return I'm making you for all your kindness. You have done everything for me, Mary. You've waited for me patiently and lovingly; you've sacrificed yourself in every way; and I'm afraid I must make you very unhappy—Oh, don't think I'm not grateful to you; I can never thank you sufficiently."

He wished Mary would say something to help him, but she kept silent. She merely dropped her eyes, and now her face seemed quite expressionless.

"I have asked myself day and night what I ought to do, and I can see no way clear before me. I've tried to say this to you before, but I've funked it. You think I'm brave—I'm not; I'm a pitiful coward! Sometimes I can only loathe and despise myself. I want to do my duty, but I can't tell what my duty is. If I only knew for sure which way I ought to take, I should have strength to take it; but it is all so uncertain."

James gave Mary a look of supplication, but she did not see it; her glance was still riveted to the ground.

"I think it's better to tell you the whole truth, Mary; I'm afraid I'm speaking awfully priggishly. I feel I'm acting like a cad, and yet I don't know how else to act. God help me!"

"I've known almost from the beginning that you no longer cared for me," said Mary quietly, her face showing no expression, her voice hushed till it was only a whisper.

"Forgive me, Mary; I've tried to love you. Oh, how humiliating that must sound! I hardly know what I'm saying. Try to understand me. If my words are harsh and ugly, it's because I don't know how to express myself. But I must tell you the whole truth. The chief thing is that I should be honest with you. It's the only return I can make for all you've done for me."

Mary bent her head a little lower, and heavy tears rolled down her cheeks.

"Oh, Mary, don't cry!" said James, his voice breaking; and he stepped forward, with outstretched arms, as though to comfort her.

"I'm sorry," she said; "I didn't mean to."

She took out her handkerchief and dried her eyes, trying to smile. Her courageous self-command was like a stab in Jamie's heart.

"I am an absolute cad!" he said, hoarsely.

Mary made no gesture; she sat perfectly still, rigid, not seeking to hide her emotion, but merely to master it. One could see the effort she made.

"I'm awfully sorry, Mary! Please forgive me—I don't ask you to release me. All I want to do is to explain exactly what I feel, and then leave you to decide."

"Are you—are you in love with anyone else?"

"No!"

The smile of Mrs. Wallace flashed scornfully across his mind, but he set his teeth. He hated and despised her; he would not love her.

"Is there anything in me that you don't like which I might be able to correct?"

Her humility was more than he could bear.

"No, no, no!" he cried. "I can never make you understand. You must think me simply brutal. You have all that a man could wish for. I know how kind you are, and how good you are. I think you have every quality which a good woman should have. I respect you entirely; I can never help feeling for you the most intense gratitude and affection."

In his own ears the words he spoke rang hollow, awkward, even impertinent. He could say nothing which did not seem hideously supercilious; and yet he wanted to abase himself! He knew that Mary's humiliation must be very, very bitter.

"I'm afraid that I am distressing you frightfully, and I don't see how I can make things easier."

"Oh, I knew you didn't love me! I felt it. D'you think I could talk to you for five minutes without seeing the constraint in your manner? They told me I was foolish and fanciful, but I knew better."

"I must have caused you very great unhappiness?"

Mary did not answer, and James looked at her with pity and remorse. At last he broke out passionately:

"I can't command my love! It's not a thing I have at my beck and call. If it were, do you think I should give you this pain? Love is outside all calculation. You think love can be tamed, and led about on a chain like a dog. You think it's a gentle sentiment that one can subject to considerations of propriety and decorum, and God knows what. Oh, you don't know! Love is a madness that seizes one and shakes one like a leaf in the wind. I can't counterfeit love; I can't pretend to have it. I can't command the nerves of my body."

"Do you think I don't know what love is, James? How little you know me."

James sank on a chair and hid his face.

"We none of us understand one another. We're all alike, and yet so different. I don't even know myself. Don't think I'm a prig when I say that I've tried with all my might to love you. I would have given worlds to feel as I felt five years ago. But I can't. God help me!... Oh, you must hate and despise me, Mary!"

"I, my dear?" she shook her head sadly. "I shall never do that. I want you to speak frankly. It is much better that we should try to understand one another."

"That is what I felt. I did not think it honest to marry you with a lie in my heart. I don't know whether we can ever be happy; but our only chance is to speak the whole truth."

Mary looked helplessly at him, cowed by her grief.

"I knew it was coming. Every day I dreaded it."

The pain in her eyes was more than James could bear; it was cruel to make her suffer so much. He could not do it. He felt an intense pity, and the idea came to him that there might be a middle way, which would lessen the difficulty. He hesitated a moment, and then, looking down, spoke in a low voice:

"I am anxious to do my duty, Mary. I have promised to marry you. I do not wish to break my word. I don't ask you to release me. Will you take what I can offer? I will be a good husband to you. I will do all I can to make you happy. I can give you affection and confidence—friendship; but I can't give you love. It is much better that I should tell you than that you should find out painfully by yourself—perhaps when it is too late."

"You came to ask me to release you. Why do you hesitate now? Do you think I shall refuse?"

James was silent.

"You cannot think that I will accept a compromise. Do you suppose that because I am a woman I am not made of flesh and blood? You said you wished to be frank."

"I had not thought of the other way till just now."

"Do you imagine that it softens the blow? How could I live with you as your wife, and yet not your wife? What are affection and esteem to me without love? You must think me a very poor creature, James, when you want to make me a sort of legal housekeeper."

"I'm sorry. I didn't think you would look upon it as an impertinence. I didn't mean to say anything offensive. It struck me as a possible way out of the difficulty. You would, at all events, be happier than you are here."

"It is you who despise me now!"

"Mary!"

"I can bear pain. It's not the first humiliation I have suffered. It is very simple, and there's no reason why we should make a fuss about it. You thought you loved me, and you asked me to marry you. I don't know whether you ever really loved me; you certainly don't now, and you wish me to release you. You know that I cannot and will not refuse."

"I see no way out of it, Mary," he said, hoarsely. "I wish to God I did! It's frightfully cruel to you."

"I can bear it. I don't blame you. It's not your fault. God will give me strength." Mary thought of her mother's cruel sympathy. Her parents would have to be told that James had cast her aside like a plaything he was tired of. "God will give me strength."

"I'm so sorry, Mary," cried James, kneeling by her side. "You'll have to suffer dreadfully; and I can't think how to make it any better for you."

"There is no way. We must tell them the whole truth, and let them say what they will."

"Would you like me to go away from Primpton?"

"Why?"

"It might make it easier for you."

"Nothing can make it easier. I can face it out. And I don't want you to run away and hide yourself as if you had done something to be ashamed of. And your people want you. Oh, Jamie, you will be as gentle with them as you can, won't you? I'm afraid it will—disappoint them very much."

"They had set their hearts upon our marriage."

"I'm afraid they'll feel it a good deal. But it can't be helped. Anything is better than a loveless marriage."

James was profoundly touched that at the time of her own bitter grief, Mary could think of the pain of others.

"I wish I had your courage, Mary. I've never seen such strength."

"It's well that I have some qualities. I haven't the power to make you love me, and I deserve something to make up."

"Oh, Mary, don't speak like that! I do love you! There's no one for whom I have a purer, more sincere affection. Why won't you take me with what I can offer? I promise that you will never regret it. You know exactly what I am now—weak, but anxious to do right. Why shouldn't we be married? Perhaps things may change. Who can tell what time may bring about?"

"It's impossible. You ask me to do more than I can. And I know very well that you only make the offer out of charity. Even from you I cannot accept charity."

"My earnest wish is to make you happy."

"And I know you would sacrifice yourself willingly for that; but I can sacrifice myself, too. You think that if we got married love might arise; but it wouldn't. You would feel perpetually that I was a reproach to you; you would hate me."

"I should never do that."

"How can you tell? We are the same age now, but each year I should seem older. At forty I should be an old woman, and you would still be a young man. Only the deepest love can make that difference endurable; but the love would be all on my side—if *I* had any then. I should probably have grown bitter and ill-humoured. Ah, no, Jamie, you know it is utterly impracticable. You know it as well as I do. Let us part altogether. I give you back your word. It is not your fault that you do not love me. I don't blame you. One gets over everything in this world eventually. All I ask you is not to trouble too much about me; I shan't die of it."

She stretched out her hand, and he took it, his eyes all blurred, unable to speak.

"And I thank you," she continued, "for having come to me frankly and openly, and told me everything. It is still something that you have confidence in me. You need never fear that I shall feel bitter towards you. I can see that you have suffered—perhaps more than you have made me suffer. Good-bye!"

"Is there nothing I can do, Mary?"

"Nothing," she said, trying to smile, "except not to worry."

"Good-bye," he said. "And don't think too ill of me."

She could not trust herself to answer. She stood perfectly quiet till he had gone out of the room; then with a moan sank to the floor and hid her face, bursting into tears. She had restrained herself too long; the composure became intolerable. She could have screamed, as though suffering some physical pain that destroyed all self-control. The heavy sobs rent her chest, and she did not attempt to stop them. She was heart-broken.

"Oh, how could he!" she groaned. "How could he!"

Her vision of happiness was utterly gone. In James she had placed the joy of her life; in him had found strength to bear every displeasure. Mary had no thought in which he did not take part; her whole future was inextricably mingled with his. But now the years to come, which had seemed so bright and sunny, turned suddenly grey as the melancholy sky without. She saw her life at Little Primpton, continuing as in the past years, monotonous and dull—a dreary round of little duties, of little vexations, of little pleasures.

"Oh, God help me!" she cried.

And lifting herself painfully to her knees, she prayed for strength to bear the woeful burden, for courage to endure it steadfastly, for resignation to believe that it was God's will.

X

James felt no relief. He had looked forward to a sensation of freedom such as a man might feel when he had escaped from some tyrannous servitude, and was at liberty again to breathe the buoyant air of heaven. He imagined that his depression would vanish like an evil spirit exorcised so soon as ever he got from Mary his release; but instead it sat more heavily upon him. Unconvinced even yet that he had acted rightly, he went over the conversation word for word. It seemed singularly ineffectual. Wishing to show Mary that he did not break with her from caprice or frivolous reason, but with sorrowful reluctance, and full knowledge of her suffering, he had succeeded only in being futile and commonplace.

He walked slowly towards Primpton House. He had before him the announcement to his mother and father; and he tried to order his thoughts.

Mrs. Parsons, her household work finished, was knitting the inevitable socks; while the Colonel sat at the table, putting new stamps into his album. He chattered delightedly over his treasures, getting up now and then gravely to ask his wife some question or to point out a surcharge; she, good woman, showed interest by appropriate rejoinders.

"There's no one in Tunbridge Wells who has such a fine collection as I have."

"General Newsmith showed me his the other day, but it's not nearly so good as yours, Richmond."

"I'm glad of that. I suppose his Mauritius are fine?" replied the Colonel, with some envy, for the general had lived several years on the island.

"They're fair," said Mrs. Parsons, reassuringly; "but not so good as one would expect."

"It takes a clever man to get together a good collection of stamps, although I shouldn't say it."

They looked up when James entered.

"I've just been putting in those Free States you brought me, Jamie. They look very well."

The Colonel leant back to view them, with the satisfied look with which he might have examined an old master.

"It was very thoughtful of Jamie to bring them," said Mrs. Parsons.

"Ah, I knew he wouldn't forget his old father. Don't you remember, Frances, I said to you, 'I'll be bound the boy will bring some stamps with him.' They'll be valuable in a year or two. That's what I always say with regard to postage stamps; you can't waste your money. Now jewellery, for instance, gets old-fashioned, and china breaks; but you run no risk with stamps. When I buy stamps, I really feel that I'm as good as investing my money in consols."

"Well, how's Mary this morning?"

"I've been having a long talk with her."

"Settled the day yet?" asked the Colonel, with a knowing little laugh.

"No!"

"Upon my word, Frances, I think we shall have to settle it for them. Things weren't like this when we were young. Why, Jamie, your mother and I got married six weeks after I was introduced to her at a croquet party."

"We were married in haste, Richmond," said Mrs. Parsons, laughing.

"Well, we've taken a long time to repent of it, my dear. It's over thirty years."

"I fancy it's too late now."

The Colonel took her hand and patted it.

"If you get such a good wife as I have, Jamie, I don't think you'll have reason to complain. Will he, my dear?"

"It's not for me to say, Richmond," replied Mrs. Parsons, smiling contentedly.

"Do you want me to get married very much, father?"

"Of course I do. I've set my heart upon it. I want to see what the new generations of Parsons are like before I die."

"Listen, Richmond, Jamie has something to tell us."

Mrs. Parsons had been looking at her son, and was struck at last by the agony of his expression.

"What is it, Jamie?" she asked.

"I'm afraid you'll be dreadfully disappointed. I'm so sorry—Mary and I are no longer engaged to be married."

For a minute there was silence in the room. The old Colonel looked helplessly from wife to son.

"What does he mean, Frances?" he said at last.

Mrs. Parsons did not answer, and he turned to James.

"You're not in earnest, Jamie? You're joking with us?"

James went over to his father, as the weaker of the two, and put his arm round his shoulders.

"I'm awfully sorry to have to grieve you, father. It's quite true—worse luck! It was impossible for me to marry Mary."

"D'you mean that you've broken your engagement with her after she's waited five years for you?" said Mrs. Parsons.

"I couldn't do anything else. I found I no longer loved her. We should both have been unhappy if we had married."

The Colonel recovered himself slowly, he turned round and looked at his son.

"Jamie, Jamie, what have you done?"

"Oh, you can say nothing that I've not said to myself. D'you think it's a step I should have taken lightly? I feel nothing towards Mary but friendship. I don't love her."

"But—" the Colonel stopped, and then a light shone in his face, and he began to laugh. "Oh, it's only a lovers' quarrel, Frances. They've had a little tiff, and they say they'll never speak to one another again. I warrant they're both heartily sorry already, and before night they'll be engaged as fast as ever."

James, by a look, implored his mother to speak. She understood, and shook her head sadly.

"No, Richmond, I'm afraid it's not that. It's serious."

"But Mary loves him, Frances."

"I know," said James. "That's the tragedy of it. If I could only persuade myself that she didn't care for me, it would be all right."

Colonel Parsons sank into his chair, suddenly collapsing. He seemed smaller than ever, wizened and frail; the wisp of white hair that concealed his baldness fell forward grotesquely. His face assumed again that expression, which was almost habitual, of anxious fear.

"Oh, father, don't look like that! I can't help it! Don't make it harder for me than possible. You talk to him, mother. Explain that it's not my fault. There was nothing else I could do."

Colonel Parsons sat silent, with his head bent down, but Mrs. Parsons asked:

"What did you say to Mary this morning?"

"I told her exactly what I felt."

"You said you didn't love her?"

"I had to."

"Poor thing!"

They all remained for a while without speaking, each one thinking his painful thoughts.

"Richmond," said Mrs. Parsons at last, "we mustn't blame the boy. It's not his fault. He can't help it if he doesn't love her."

"You wouldn't have me marry her without love, father?"

The question was answered by Mrs. Parsons.

"No; if you don't love her, you mustn't marry her. But what's to be done, I don't know. Poor thing, poor thing, how unhappy she must be!"

James sat with his face in his hands, utterly wretched, beginning already to see the great circle of confusion that he had caused. Mrs. Parsons looked at him and looked at her husband. Presently she went up to James.

"Jamie, will you leave us for a little? Your father and I would like to talk it over alone."

"Yes, mother."

James got up, and putting her hands on his shoulders, she kissed him.

When James had gone, Mrs. Parsons looked compassionately at her husband; he glanced up, and catching her eye, tried to smile. But it was a poor attempt, and it finished with a sigh.

"What's to be done, Richmond?"

Colonel Parsons shook his head without answering.

"I ought to have warned you that something might happen. I saw there was a difference in Jamie's feelings, but I fancied it would pass over. I believed it was only strangeness. Mary is so fond of him, I thought he would soon love her as much as ever."

"But it's not honourable what he's done, Frances," said the old man at last, his voice trembling with emotion. "It's not honourable."

"He can't help it if he doesn't love her."

"It's his duty to marry her. She's waited five years; she's given him the best of her youth—and he jilts her. He can't, Frances; he must behave like a gentleman."

The tears fell down Mrs. Parsons' careworn cheeks—the slow, sparse tears of the woman who has endured much sorrow.

"Don't let us judge him, Richmond. We're so ignorant of the world. You and I are old-fashioned."

"There are no fashions in honesty."

"Let us send for William. Perhaps he'll be able to advise us."

William was Major Forsyth, the brother of Mrs. Parsons. He was a bachelor, living in London, and considered by his relatives a typical man of the world.

"He'll be able to talk to the boy better than we can."

"Very well, let us send for him."

They were both overcome by the catastrophe, but as yet hardly grasped the full extent of it. All their hopes had been centred on this marriage; all their plans for the future had been in it so intricately woven that they could not realise the total overthrow. They felt as a man might feel who was crippled by a sudden accident, and yet still pictured his life as though he had free use of his limbs.... Mrs. Parsons wrote a telegram, and gave it to the maid. The servant went out of the room, but as she did so, stepped back and announced:

"Miss Clibborn, ma'am."

"Mary!"

The girl came in, and lifted the veil which she had put on to hide her pallor and her eyes, red and heavy with weeping.

"I thought I'd better come round and see you quietly," she said. "I suppose you've heard?"

"Mary, Mary!"

Mrs. Parsons took her in her arms, kissing her tenderly. Mary pretended to laugh, and hastily dried the tears which came to her eyes.

"You've been crying, Mrs. Parsons. You mustn't do that.... Let us sit down and talk sensibly."

She took the Colonel's hand, and gently pressed it.

"Is it true, Mary?" he asked. "I can't believe it."

"Yes, it's quite true. We've decided that we don't wish to marry one another. I want to ask you not to think badly of Jamie. He's very—cut up about it. He's not to blame."

"We're thinking of you, my dear."

"Oh, I shall be all right. I can bear it."

"It's not honourable what he's done, Mary," said the Colonel.

"Oh, don't say that, please! That is why I came round to you quickly. I want you to think that Jamie did what he considered right. For my sake, don't think ill of him. He can't help it if he doesn't love me. I'm not very attractive; he must have known in India girls far nicer than I. How could I hope to keep him all these years? I was a fool to expect it."

"I am so sorry, Mary!" cried Mrs. Parsons. "We've looked forward to your marriage with all our hearts. You know Jamie's been a good son to us; he's never given us any worry. We did want him to marry you. We're so fond of you, and we know how really good you are. We felt that whatever happened after that—if we died—Jamie would be safe and happy."

"It can't be helped. Things never turn out in this world as one wants them. Don't be too distressed about it, and, above all things, don't let Jamie see that you think he hasn't acted—as he might have done."

"How can you think of him now, when your heart must be almost breaking?"

"You see, I've thought of him for years," answered Mary, smiling sadly. "I can't help it now. Oh, I don't want him to suffer! His worrying can do no good, I should like him to be completely happy."

Colonel Parsons sighed.

"He's my son, and he's behaved dishonourably."

"Don't say that. It's not fair to him. He did not ask me for his release. But I couldn't marry him when I knew he no longer cared for me."

"He might have learned to love you, Mary," said Mrs. Parsons.

"No, no! I could see, as he pressed me to marry him notwithstanding, he was hoping with all his might that I would refuse. He would have hated me. No; it's the end. We have separated for ever, and I will do my best to get over it."

They fell into silence, and presently Mary got up. "I must go home now, and tell mamma."

"She'll probably have hysterics," said Mrs. Parsons, with a little sniff of contempt.

"No, she'll be delighted," returned Mary. "I know her so well."

"Oh, how much you will have to suffer, dearest!"

"It'll do me good. I was too happy."

"Don't you think you could wait a little before telling anyone else?" asked the Colonel. "Major Forsyth is coming down. He may be able to arrange it; he's a man of the world."

"Can he make Jamie love me? Ah, no, it's no good waiting. Let me get it over quickly while I have the courage. And it helps me to think I have something to do. It only means a few sneers and a little false sympathy."

"A great deal of real sympathy."

"People are always rather glad when some unhappiness befalls their friends! Oh, I didn't mean that! I don't want to be bitter. Don't think badly of me either. I shall be different to-morrow."

"We can never think of you without the sincerest, fondest love."

At that moment James, who did not know that Mary was there, came into the room. He started when he saw her and turned red; but Mary, with a woman's self-possession, braced herself together.

"Oh, Jamie, I've just been having a little chat with your people."

"I'm sorry I interrupted you," he answered, awkwardly. "I didn't know you were here."

"You need not avoid me because we've broken off our engagement. At all events, you have no reason to be afraid of me now. Good-bye! I'm just going home."

She went out, and James looked uncertainly at his parents. His father did not speak, staring at the ground, but Mrs. Parsons said:

"Mary has been asking us not to be angry with you, Jamie. She says it's not your fault."

"It's very kind of her."

"Oh, how could you? How could you?"

XI

Not till luncheon was nearly finished did Mary brace herself for the further ordeal, and in a steady, unmoved voice tell Colonel and Mrs. Clibborn what had happened. The faded beauty merely smiled, and lifted her eyes to the chandelier with the expression that had melted the hearts of a thousand and one impressionable subalterns.

"I knew it," she murmured; "I knew it! You can't deceive a woman and a mother."

But the Colonel for a moment was speechless. His face grew red, and his dyed eyebrows stood up in a fury of indignation.

"Impossible!" he spluttered at last.

"You'd better drink a little water, Reggie dear," said his wife. "You look as if you were going to have a fit."

"I won't have it," he shouted, bringing his fist down on the table so that the cheese-plates clattered and the biscuits danced a rapid jig. "I'll make him marry you. He forgets he has me to deal with! I disapproved of the match from the beginning, didn't I, Clara? I said I would never allow my daughter to marry beneath her."

"Papa!"

"Don't talk to me, Mary! Do you mean to deny that James Parsons is infantry, or that his father was infantry before him? But he shall marry you now. By George! he shall marry you if I have to lead him to the altar by the scruff of his neck!"

Neglecting his cheese, the Colonel sprang to his feet and walked to and fro, vehemently giving his opinion of James, his father, and all his ancestors; of the regiments to which they had belonged, and all else that was theirs. He traced their origin from a pork butcher's shop, and prophesied their end, ignominiously, in hell. Every now and then he assured Mary that she need have no fear; the rascal should marry her, or die a violent death.

"But there's nothing more to be said now, papa. We've agreed quite amicably to separate. All I want you to do is to treat him as if nothing had happened."

"I'll horsewhip him," said Colonel Clibborn. "He's insulted you, and I'll make him beg your pardon on his bended knees. Clara, where's my horsewhip?"

"Papa, do be reasonable!"

"I am reasonable, Mary," roared the gallant soldier, becoming a rich purple. "I know my duty, thank God! and I'm going to do it. When a man insults my daughter, it's my duty, as a gentleman and an officer, to give him a jolly good thrashing. When that twopenny sawbones of a doctor was rude to you, I licked him within an inch of his life. I kicked him till he begged for mercy; and if more men had the courage to take the law into their own hands, there'd be fewer damned blackguards in the world."

As a matter of fact, the Colonel had neither thrashed nor kicked the doctor, but it pleased him to think he had. Moralists teach us that the intention is praiseworthy, rather than the brutal act; consequently, there could be no objection if the fearless cavalryman took credit for things which he had thought of doing, but, from circumstances beyond his control, had not actually done.

Mary felt no great alarm at her father's horrid threats, for she knew him well, but still was doubtful about her mother.

"You will treat James as you did before, won't you, mamma?"

Mrs. Clibborn smiled, a portly seraph.

"My dear, I trust I am a gentlewoman."

"He shall never darken my doors again!" cried the Colonel. "I tell you, Clara, keep him out of my way. If I meet him I won't be responsible for my actions; I shall knock him down."

"Reggie dear, you'll have such dreadful indigestion if you don't calm down. You know it always upsets you to get excited immediately after meals."

"It's disgraceful! I suppose he forgets all those half-crowns I gave him when he was a boy, and the cigars, and the port wine he's had since. I opened a special bottle for him only the night before last. I'll never sit down to dinner with him again—don't ask me to, Clara.... It's the confounded impertinence of it which gets over me. But he shall marry you, my dear; or I'll know the reason why."

"You can't have him up for breach of promise, Reggie," cooed Mrs. Clibborn.

"A gentleman takes the law in his own hands in these matters. Ah, it's a pity the good old days have gone when they settled such things with cold steel!"

And the Colonel, to emphasise his words, flung himself into the appropriate attitude, throwing his left hand up behind his head, and lunging fiercely with the right.

"Go and look for my *pince-nez*, my dear," said Mrs. Clibborn, turning to Mary. "I think they're in my work-basket or in your father's study."

Mary was glad to leave the room, about which the Colonel stamped in an ever-increasing rage, pausing now and then to take a mouthful of bread and cheese. The request for the glasses was Mrs. Clibborn's usual way of getting rid of Mary, a typical subterfuge of a woman who never, except by chance, put anything straightforwardly.... When the door was closed, the buxom lady clasped her hands, and cried:

"Reginald! Reginald! I have a confession to make."

"What's the matter with you?" said the Colonel, stopping short.

"I am to blame for this, Reginald." Mrs. Clibborn threw her head on one side, and looked at the ceiling as the only substitute for heaven. "James Parsons has jilted Mary—on my account."

"What the devil have you been doing now?"

"Oh, forgive me, Reginald!" she cried, sliding off the chair and falling heavily on her knees. "It's not my fault: he loves me."

"Fiddlesticks!" said her husband angrily, walking on again.

"It isn't, Reginald. How unjust you are to me!"

The facile tears began to flow down Mrs. Clibborn's well-powdered cheeks.

"I know he loves me. You can't deceive a woman and a mother."

"You're double his age!"

"These boys always fall in love with women older than themselves; I've noticed it so often. And he's almost told me in so many words, though I'm sure I've given him no encouragement."

"Fiddlesticks, Clara!"

"You wouldn't believe me when I told you that poor Algy Turner loved me, and he killed himself."

"Nothing of the kind; he died of cholera."

"Reginald," retorted Mrs. Clibborn, with asperity, "his death was most mysterious. None of the doctors understood it. If he didn't poison himself, he died of a broken heart. And I think you're very unkind to me."

With some difficulty, being a heavy woman, she lifted herself from the floor; and by the time she was safely on her feet, Mrs. Clibborn was blowing and puffing like a grampus.

The Colonel, whose mind had wandered to other things, suddenly bethought himself that he had a duty to perform.

"Where's my horsewhip, Clara? I command you to give it me."

"Reginald, if you have the smallest remnant of affection for me, you will not hurt this unfortunate young man. Remember that Algy Turner killed himself. You can't blame him for not wanting to marry poor Mary. My dear, she has absolutely no figure. And men are so susceptible to those things."

The Colonel stalked out of the room, and Mrs. Clibborn sat down to meditate.

"I thought my day for such things was past," she murmured. "I knew it all along. The way he looked at me was enough—we women have such quick perceptions! Poor boy, how he must suffer!"

She promised herself that no harsh word of hers should drive James into the early grave where lay the love-lorn Algy Turner. And she sighed, thinking what a curse it was to possess that fatal gift of beauty!

* * *

When Little Primpton heard the news, Little Primpton was agitated. Certainly it was distressed, and even virtuously indignant, but at the same time completely unable to divest itself of that little flutter of excitement which was so rare, yet so enchanting, a variation from the monotony of its daily course. The well-informed walked with a lighter step, and held their heads more jauntily, for life had suddenly acquired a novel interest. With something new to talk about, something fresh to think over, with a legitimate object of sympathy and resentment, the torpid blood raced through their veins as might that of statesmen during some crisis in national affairs. Let us thank God, who has made our neighbours frail, and in His infinite mercy caused husband and wife to quarrel; Tom, Dick, and Harry to fall more or less discreditably in love; this dear friend of ours to lose his money, and that her reputation. In all humility, let us be grateful for the scandal which falls at our feet like ripe fruit, for the Divorce Court and for the newspapers that, with a witty semblance of horror, report for us the spicy details. If at certain intervals propriety obliges us to confess that we are miserable sinners, has not the Lord sought to comfort us in the recollection that we are not half so bad as most people?

Mr. Dryland went to the Vicarage to enter certificates in the parish books. The Vicar was in his study, and gave his curate the keys of the iron safe.

"Sophie Bunch came last night to put up her banns," he said.

"She's going to marry out of the parish, isn't she?"

"Yes, a Tunbridge Wells man."

The curate carefully blotted the entries he had made, and returned the heavy books to their place.

"Will you come into the dining-room, Dryland?" said the Vicar, with a certain solemnity. "Mrs. Jackson would like to speak to you."

"Certainly."

Mrs. Jackson was reading the *Church Times*. Her thin, sharp face wore an expression of strong disapproval; her tightly-closed mouth, her sharp nose, even the angular lines of her body, signified clearly that her moral sense was outraged. She put her hand quickly to her massive fringe to see that it was straight, and rose to shake hands with Mr. Dryland. His heavy red face assumed at once a grave look; his moral sense was outraged, too.

"Isn't this dreadful news, Mr. Dryland?"

"Oh, very sad! Very sad!"

In both their voices, hidden below an intense sobriety, there was discernible a slight ring of exultation.

"The moment I saw him I felt he would give trouble," said Mrs. Jackson, shaking her head. "I told you, Archibald, that I didn't like the look of him."

"I'm bound to say you did," admitted her lord and master.

"Mary Clibborn is much too good for him," added Mrs. Jackson, decisively. "She's a saint."

"The fact is, that he's suffering from a swollen head," remarked the curate, who used slang as a proof of manliness.

"There, Archibald!" cried the lady, triumphantly. "What did I tell you?"

"Mrs. Jackson thought he was conceited."

"I don't think it; I'm sure of it. He's odiously conceited. All the time I was talking to him I felt he considered himself superior to me. No nice-minded man would have refused our offer to say a short prayer on his behalf during morning service."

"Those army men always have a very good opinion of themselves," said Mr. Dryland, taking advantage of his seat opposite a looking-glass to arrange his hair.

He spoke in such a round, full voice that his shortest words carried a sort of polysyllabic weight.

"I can't see what he has done to be so proud of," said Mrs. Jackson. "Anyone would have done the same in his position. I'm sure it's no more heroic than what clergymen do every day of their lives, without making the least fuss about it."

"They say that true courage is always modest," answered Mr. Dryland.

The remark was not very apposite, but sounded damaging.

"I didn't like the way he had when he came to tea here—as if he were dreadfully bored. I'm sure he's not so clever as all that."

"No clever man would act in an ungentlemanly way," said the curate, and then smiled, for he thought he had unconsciously made an epigram.

"I couldn't express in words what I feel with regard to his treatment of Mary!" cried Mrs. Jackson; and then proceeded to do so—and in many, to boot.

They had all been a little oppressed by the greatness which, much against his will, they had thrust upon the unfortunate James. They had set him on a pedestal, and then were disconcerted because he towered above their heads, and the halo with which they had surrounded him dazzled their eyes. They had wished to make a lion of James, and his modest resistance wounded their self-esteem; it was a relief to learn that he was not worth making a lion of. Halo and pedestal were quickly demolished, for the golden idol had feet of clay, and his late adorers were ready to reproach him because he had not accepted with proper humility the gifts he did not want. Their little vanities were comforted by the assurance that, far from being a hero, James was, in fact, distinctly inferior to themselves. For there is no superiority like moral superiority. A man who stands akimbo on the top of the Ten Commandments need bow the knee to no earthly potentate.

Little Primpton was conscious of its virtue, and did not hesitate to condemn.

"He has lowered himself dreadfully."

"Yes, it's very sad. It only shows how necessary it is to preserve a meek and contrite spirit in prosperity. Pride always goes before a fall."

The Jacksons and Mr. Dryland discussed the various accounts which had reached them. Mary and Mrs. Parsons were determinedly silent, but Mrs. Clibborn was loquacious, and it needed little artifice to extract the whole story from Colonel Parsons.

"One thing is unfortunately certain," said Mrs. Jackson, with a sort of pious vindictiveness, "Captain Parsons has behaved abominably, and it's our duty to do something."

"Colonel Clibborn threatens to horsewhip him."

"It would do him good," cried Mrs. Jackson; "and I should like to be there to see it!"

They paused a moment to gloat over the imaginary scene of Jamie's chastisement.

"He's a wicked man. Fancy throwing the poor girl over when she's waited five years. I think he ought to be made to marry her."

"I'm bound to say that no gentleman would have acted like that," said the Vicar.

"I wanted Archibald to go and speak seriously to Captain Parsons. He ought to know what we think of him, and it's obviously our duty to tell him."

"His parents are very much distressed. One can see that, although they say so little."

"It's not enough to be distressed. They ought to have the strength of mind to insist upon his marrying Mary Clibborn. But they stick up for everything he does. They think he's perfect. I'm sure it's not respectful to God to worship a human being as they do their son."

"They certainly have a very exaggerated opinion of him," assented Mr. Dryland.

"And I should like to know why. He's not good-looking."

"Very ordinary," agreed Mr. Dryland, with a rapid glance at the convenient mirror. "I don't think his appearance is manly."

Whatever the curate's defects of person—and he flattered himself that he was modest enough to know his bad points—no one, he fancied, could deny him manliness. It is possible that he was not deceived. Put him in a bowler-hat and a bell-bottomed coat, and few could have distinguished him from a cab-driver.

"I don't see anything particular in his eyes or hair," pursued Mrs. Jackson.

"His features are fairly regular. But that always strikes me as insipid in a man."

"And he's not a good conversationalist."

"I'm bound to confess I've never heard him say anything clever," remarked the Vicar.

"No," smiled the curate; "one could hardly call him a brilliant epigrammatist."

"I don't think he's well informed."

"Oh, well, you know, one doesn't expect knowledge from army men," said the curate, with a contemptuous smile and a shrug of the shoulders. "I must say I was rather amused when he confessed he hadn't read Marie Corelli."

"I can hardly believe that. I think it was only pose."

"I'm sorry to say that my experience of young officers is that there are absolutely no bounds to their ignorance."

They had satisfactorily stripped James of every quality, mental and physical, which could have made him attractive in Mary's eyes; and the curate's next remark was quite natural.

"I'm afraid it sounds a conceited thing to say, but I can't help asking myself what Miss Clibborn saw in him."

"Love is blind," replied Mrs. Jackson. "She could have done much better for herself."

They paused to consider the vagaries of the tender passion, and the matches which Mary might have made, had she been so inclined.

"Archibald," said Mrs. Jackson at last, with the decision characteristic of her, "I've made up my mind. As vicar of the parish, *you* must go to Captain Parsons."

"I, my dear?"

"Yes, Archibald. You must insist upon him fulfilling his engagement with Mary. Say that you are shocked and grieved; and ask him if his own conscience does not tell him that he has done wrong."

"I'm not sure that he'd listen to reason," nervously remarked the Vicar.

"It's your duty to try, Archibald. We're so afraid of being called busybodies that even when we ought to step in we hesitate. No motives of delicacy should stop one when a wicked action is to be prevented. It's often the clergy's duty to interfere with other people's affairs. For my part, I will never shrink from doing my duty. People may call me a busybody if they like; hard words break no bones."

"Captain Parsons is very reserved. He might think it an impertinence if I went to him."

"How could he? Isn't it our business if he breaks his word with a parishioner of ours? If you don't talk to him, I shall. So there, Archibald!"

"Why don't you, Mrs. Jackson?"

"Nothing would please me better, I should thoroughly enjoy giving him a piece of my mind. It would do him good to be told frankly that he's not quite so great as he thinks himself. I will never shrink from doing my duty."

"My dear," remonstrated the Vicar, "if you really think I ought to speak—"

"Perhaps Mrs. Jackson would do better. A women can say many things that a man can't."

This was a grateful suggestion to the Vicar, who could not rid himself of the discomforting thought that James, incensed and hot-tempered, might use the strength of his arms—or legs— in lieu of argument. Mr. Jackson would have affronted horrid tortures for his faith, but shrank timidly before the least suspicion of ridicule. His wife was braver, or less imaginative.

"Very well, I'll go," she said. "It's true he might be rude to Archibald, and he couldn't be rude to a lady. And what's more, I shall go at once."

Mrs. Jackson kept her hat on a peg in the hall, and was quickly ready. She put on her black kid gloves; determination sat upon her mouth, and Christian virtue rested between her brows. Setting out with a brisk step, the conviction was obvious in every movement that duty called, and to that clarion note Maria Jackson would never turn a deaf ear. She went like a Hebrew prophet, conscious that the voice of the Lord was in her.

XII

James was wandering in the garden of Primpton House while Mrs. Jackson thither went her way. Since the termination of his engagement with Mary three days back, the subject had not been broached between him and his parents; but he divined their thoughts. He knew that they awaited the arrival of his uncle, Major Forsyth, to set the matter right. They did not seek to reconcile themselves with the idea that the break was final; it seemed too monstrous a thing to be true. James smiled, with bitter amusement, at their simple trust in the man of the world who was due that day.

Major Forsyth was fifty-three, a haunter of military clubs, a busy sluggard, who set his pride in appearing dissipated, and yet led the blameless life of a clergyman's daughter; preserving a spotless virtue, nothing pleased him more than to be thought a rake. He had been on half-pay for many years, and blamed the War Office on that account rather than his own incompetence. Ever since retiring he had told people that advancement, in these degenerate days, was impossible without influence: he was, indeed, one of those men to whom powerful friends offer the only chance of success; and possessing none, inveighed constantly against the corrupt officialism of those in authority. But to his Jeremiads upon the decay of the public services he added a keen interest in the world of fashion; it is always well that a man should have varied activities; it widens his horizon, and gives him a greater usefulness. If his attention had been limited to red-tape, Major Forsyth, even in his own circle, might have been thought a little one-sided; but his knowledge of etiquette and tailors effectually prevented the reproach. He was pleased to consider himself in society; he read assiduously those papers which give detailed accounts of the goings-on in the "hupper succles," and could give you with considerable accuracy the whereabouts of titled people. If he had a weakness, it was by his manner of speaking to insinuate that he knew certain noble persons whom, as a matter of fact, he had never set eyes on; he would not have told a direct lie on the subject, but his conscience permitted him a slight equivocation. Major Forsyth was well up in all the gossip of the clubs, and if he could not call himself a man of the world, he had not the least notion who could. But for all that, he had the strictest principles; he was true brother to Mrs. Parsons, and though he concealed the fact like something disreputable, regularly went to church on Sunday mornings. There was also a certain straitness in his income which confined him to the paths shared by the needy and the pure at heart.

Major Forsyth had found no difficulty in imposing upon his sister and her husband.

"Of course, William is rather rackety," they said. "It's a pity he hasn't a wife to steady him; but he has a good heart."

For them Major Forsyth had the double advantage of a wiliness gained in the turmoil of the world and an upright character. They scarcely knew how in the present juncture he could help, but had no doubt that from the boundless store of his worldly wisdom he would invent a solution to their difficulty.

James had found his uncle out when he was quite a boy, and seeing his absurdity, had treated him ever since with good-natured ridicule.

"I wonder what they think he can say?" he asked himself.

James was profoundly grieved at the unhappiness which bowed his father down. His parents had looked forward with such ecstatic pleasure to his arrival, and what sorrow had he not brought them!

"I wish I'd never come back," he muttered.

He thought of the flowing, undulating plains of the Orange Country, and the blue sky, with its sense of infinite freedom. In that trim Kentish landscape he felt hemmed in; when the clouds were low it seemed scarcely possible to breathe; and he suffered from the constraint of his father and mother, who treated him formally, as though he had become a stranger. There was always between them and him that painful topic which for the time was carefully shunned. They did not mention Mary's name, and the care they took to avoid it was more painful than would have been an open reference. They sat silent and sad, trying to appear natural, and dismally failing; their embarrassed manner was such as they might have adopted had he committed some crime, the mention of which for his sake must never be made, but whose recollection perpetually haunted them. In every action was the belief that James must be suffering from remorse, and that it was their duty not to make his burden heavier. James knew that his father was convinced that he had acted dishonourably, and he—what did he himself think?

James asked himself a hundred times a day whether he had acted well or ill; and though he forced himself to answer that he had done the only possible thing, deep down in his heart was a terrible, a perfectly maddening uncertainty. He tried to crush it, and would not listen, for his intelligence told him clearly it was absurd; but it was stronger than intelligence, an incorporeal shape through which passed harmlessly the sword-cuts of his reason. It was a little devil curled up in his heart, muttering to all his arguments, "Are you sure?"

Sometimes he was nearly distracted, and then the demon laughed, so that the mocking shrillness rang in his ears:

"Are you sure, my friend—are you sure? And where, pray, is the honour which only a while ago you thought so much of?"

* * *

James walked to and fro restlessly, impatient, angry with himself and with all the world.

But then on the breath of the wind, on the perfume of the roses, yellow and red, came suddenly the irresistible recollection of Mrs. Wallace. Why should he not think of her now? He was free; he could do her no harm; he would never see her again. The thought of her was the only sunshine in his life; he was tired of denying himself every pleasure. Why should he continue the pretence that he no longer loved her? It was, indeed, a consolation to think that the long absence had not dulled his passion; the strength of it was its justification. It was useless to fight against it, for it was part of his very soul; he might as well have fought against the beating of his heart. And if it was torture to remember those old days in India, he delighted in it; it was a pain more exquisite than the suffocating odours of tropical flowers, a voluptuous agony such as might feel the fakir lacerating his flesh in a divine possession.... Every little occurrence was clear, as if it had taken place but a day before.

James repeated to himself the conversations they had had, of no consequence, the idle gossip of a stray half-hour; but each word was opulent in the charming smile, in the caressing glance of her eyes. He was able to imagine Mrs. Wallace quite close to him, wearing the things that he had seen her wear, and with her movements he noticed the excessive scent she used. He wondered whether she had overcome that failing, whether she still affected the artificiality which was so adorable a relief from the primness of manner which he had thought the natural way of women.

If her cheeks were not altogether innocent of rouge or her eyebrows of pencil, what did he care; he delighted in her very faults; he would not have her different in the very slightest detail; everything was part of that complex, elusive fascination. And James thought of the skin which had the even softness of fine velvet, and the little hands. He called himself a fool for his shyness. What could have been the harm if he had taken those hands and kissed them? Now, in imagination, he pressed his lips passionately on the warm palms. He liked the barbaric touch in the many rings which bedecked her fingers.

"Why do you wear so many rings?" he asked. "Your hands are too fine."

He would never have ventured the question, but now there was no danger. Her answer came with a little, good-humoured laugh; she stretched out her fingers, looking complacently at the brilliant gems.

"I like to be gaudy. I should like to be encrusted with jewels. I want to wear bracelets to my elbow and diamond spangles on my arms; and jewelled belts, and jewels in my hair, and on my neck. I should like to flash from head to foot with exotic stones."

Then she looked at him with amusement.

"Of course, you think it's vulgar. What do I care? You all of you think it's vulgar to be different from other people. I want to be unique."

"You want everybody to look at you?"

"Of course I do! Is it sinful? Oh, I get so impatient with all of you, with your good taste and your delicacy, and your insupportable dullness. When you admire a woman, you think it impertinent to tell her she's beautiful; when you have good looks, you carry yourselves as though you were ashamed."

And in a bold moment he replied:

"Yet you would give your soul to have no drop of foreign blood in your veins!"

"I?" she cried, her eyes flashing with scorn. "I'm proud of my Eastern blood. It's not blood I have in my veins, it's fire—a fire of gold. It's because of it that I have no prejudices, and know how to enjoy my life."

James smiled, and did not answer.

"You don't believe me?" she asked.

"No!"

"Well, perhaps I should like to be quite English. I should feel more comfortable in my scorn of these regimental ladies if I thought they could find no reason to look down on me."

"I don't think they look down on you."

"Oh, don't they? They despise and loathe me."

"When you were ill, they did all they could for you."

"Foolish creature! Don't you know that to do good to your enemy is the very best way of showing your contempt."

And so James could go on, questioning, replying, putting little jests into her mouth, or half-cynical repartees. Sometimes he spoke aloud, and then Mrs. Wallace's voice sounded in his ears, clear and rich and passionate, as though she were really standing in the flesh beside him. But always he finished by taking her in his arms and kissing her lips and her closed eyes, the lids transparent like the finest alabaster. He knew no pleasure greater than to place his hands on that lustrous hair. What could it matter now? He was not bound to Mary; he could do no harm to Mrs. Wallace, ten thousand miles away.

* * *

But Colonel Parsons broke into the charming dream. Bent and weary, he came across the lawn to find his son. The wan, pathetic figure brought back to James all the present bitterness. He sighed, and advanced to meet him.

"You're very reckless to come out without a hat, father. I'll fetch you one, shall I?"

"No, I'm not going to stay." The Colonel could summon up no answering smile to his boy's kind words. "I only came to tell you that Mrs. Jackson is in the drawing-room, and would like to see you."

"What does she want?"

"She'll explain herself. She has asked to see you alone."

Jamie's face darkened, as some notion of Mrs. Jackson's object dawned upon him.

"I don't know what she can have to talk to me about alone."

"Please listen to her, Jamie. She's a very clever woman, and you can't fail to benefit by her advice."

The Colonel never had an unfriendly word to say of anyone, and even for Mrs. Jackson's unwarrantable interferences could always find a good-natured justification. He was one of those deprecatory men who, in every difference of opinion, are convinced that they are certainly in the wrong. He would have borne with the most cheerful submission any rebuke of his own conduct, and been, indeed, vastly grateful to the Vicar's wife for pointing out his error.

James found Mrs. Jackson sitting bolt upright on a straight-backed chair, convinced, such was her admirable sense of propriety, that a lounging attitude was incompatible with the performance of a duty. She held her hands on her lap, gently clasped; and her tight lips expressed as plainly as possible her conviction that though the way of righteousness was hard, she, thank God! had strength to walk it.

"How d'you do, Mrs. Jackson?"

"Good morning," she replied, with a stiff bow.

James, though there was no fire, went over to the mantelpiece and leant against it, waiting for the lady to speak.

"Captain Parsons, I have a very painful duty to perform."

Those were her words, but it must have been a dense person who failed to perceive that Mrs. Jackson found her duty anything but painful. There was just that hard resonance in her voice that an inquisitor might have in condemning to the stake a Jew to whom he owed much money.

"I suppose you will call me a busybody?"

"Oh, I'm sure you would never interfere with what does not concern you," replied James, slowly.

"Certainly not!" said Mrs. Jackson. "I come here because my conscience tells me to. What I wish to talk to you about concerns us all."

"Shall I call my people? I'm sure they'd be interested."

"I asked to see you alone, Captain Parsons," answered Mrs. Jackson, frigidly. "And it was for your sake. When one has to tell a person home-truths, he generally prefers that there should be no audience."

"So you're going to tell me some home-truths, Mrs. Jackson?" said James, with a laugh. "You must think me very good-natured. How long have I had the pleasure of your acquaintance?"

Mrs. Jackson's grimness did not relax.

"One learns a good deal about people in a week."

"D'you think so? I have an idea that ten years is a short time to get to know them. You must be very quick."

"Actions often speak."

"Actions are the most lying things in the world. They are due mostly to adventitious circumstances which have nothing to do with the character of the agent. I would never judge a man by his actions."

"I didn't come here to discuss abstract things with you, Captain Parsons."

"Why not? The abstract is so much more entertaining than the concrete. It affords opportunities for generalisation, which is the salt of conversation."

"I'm a very busy woman," retorted Mrs. Jackson sharply, thinking that James was not treating her with proper seriousness. He was not so easy to tackle as she had imagined.

"It's very good of you, then, to spare time to come and have a little chat with me," said James.

"I did not come for that purpose, Captain Parsons."

"Oh, I forgot—home-truths, wasn't it? I was thinking of Shakespeare and the musical glasses!"

"Would you kindly remember that I am a clergyman's wife, Captain Parsons? I daresay you are not used to the society of such."

"Pardon me, I even know an archdeacon quite well. He has a great gift of humour; a man wants it when he wears a silk apron."

"Captain Parsons," said Mrs. Jackson, sternly, "there are some things over which it is unbecoming to jest. I wish to be as gentle as possible with you, but I may remind you that flippancy is not the best course for you to pursue."

James looked at her with a good-tempered stare.

"Upon my word," he said to himself, "I never knew I was so patient."

"I can't beat about the bush any longer," continued the Vicar's lady; "I have a very painful duty to perform."

"That quite excuses your hesitation."

"You must guess why I have asked to see you alone."

"I haven't the least idea."

"Does your conscience say nothing to you?"

"My conscience is very well-bred. It never says unpleasant things."

"Then I'm sincerely sorry for you."

James smiled.

"Oh, my good woman," he thought, "if you only knew what a troublesome spirit I carry about with me!" But Mrs. Jackson saw only hardness of heart in the grave face; she never dreamed that behind those quiet eyes was a turmoil of discordant passions, tearing, rending, burning.

"I'm sorry for you," she repeated. "I think it's very sad, very sad indeed, that you should stand there and boast of the sluggishness of your conscience. Conscience is the voice of God, Captain Parsons; if it does not speak to you, it behoves others to speak in its place."

"And supposing I knew what you wanted to say, do you think I should like to hear?"

"I'm afraid not."

"Then don't you think discretion points to silence?"

"No, Captain Parsons. There are some things which one is morally bound to say, however distasteful they may be."

"The easiest way to get through life is to say pleasant things on all possible occasions."

"That is not my way, and that is not the right way."

"I think it rash to conclude that a course is right merely because it is difficult. Likewise an uncivil speech is not necessarily a true one."

"I repeat that I did not come here to bandy words with you."

"My dear Mrs. Jackson, I have been wondering why you did not come to the point at once."

"You have been willfully interrupting me."

"I'm so sorry. I thought I had been making a series of rather entertaining observations."

"Captain Parsons, what does your conscience say to you about Mary Clibborn?"

James looked at Mrs. Jackson very coolly, and she never imagined with what difficulty he was repressing himself.

"I thought you said your subject was of national concern. Upon my word, I thought you proposed to hold a thanksgiving service in Little Primpton Church for the success of the British arms."

"Well, you know different now," retorted Mrs. Jackson, with distinct asperity. "I look upon your treatment of Mary Clibborn as a matter which concerns us all."

"Then, as politely as possible, I must beg to differ from you. I really cannot permit you to discuss my private concerns.

You have, doubtless, much evil to say of me; say it behind my back."

"I presumed that you were a gentleman, Captain Parsons."

"You certainly presumed."

"And I should be obliged if you would treat me like a lady."

James smiled. He saw that it was folly to grow angry.

"We'll do our best to be civil to one another, Mrs. Jackson. But I don't think you must talk of what really is not your business."

"D'you think you can act shamefully and then slink away as soon as you are brought to book? Do you know what you've done to Mary Clibborn?"

"Whatever I've done, you may be sure that I have not acted rashly. Really, nothing you can say will make the slightest difference. Don't you think we had better bring our conversation to an end?"

James made a movement towards the door.

"Your father and mother wish me to speak with you, Colonel Parsons," said Mrs. Jackson. "And they wish you to listen to what I have to say."

James paused. "Very well."

He sat down and waited. Mrs. Jackson felt unaccountably nervous; it had never occurred to her that a mere soldier could be so hard to deal with, and it was she who hesitated now. Jamie's stern eyes made her feel singularly like a culprit; but she cleared her throat and straightened herself.

"It's very sad," she said, "to find how much we've been mistaken in you, Captain Parsons. When we were making all sorts of preparations to welcome you, we never thought that you would repay us like this. It grieves me to have to tell you that you have done a very wicked thing. I was hoping that your conscience would have something to say to you, but unhappily I was mistaken. You induced Mary to become engaged to you;

you kept her waiting for years; you wrote constantly, pretending to love her, deceiving her odiously; you let her waste the best part of her life, and then, without excuse and without reason, you calmly say that you're sick of her, and won't marry her. I think it is horrible, and brutal, and most ungentlemanly. Even a common man wouldn't have behaved in that way. Of course, it doesn't matter to you, but it means the ruin of Mary's whole life. How can she get a husband now when she's wasted her best years? You've spoilt all her chances. You've thrown a slur upon her which people will never forget. You're a cruel, wicked man, and however you won the Victoria Cross I don't know; I'm sure you don't deserve it."

Mrs. Jackson stopped.

"Is that all?" asked James, quietly.

"It's quite enough."

"Quite! In that case, I think we may finish our little interview."

"Have you nothing to say?" asked Mrs. Jackson indignantly, realising that she had not triumphed after all.

"I? Nothing."

Mrs. Jackson was perplexed, and still those disconcerting eyes were fixed upon her; she angrily resented their polite contempt.

"Well, I think it's disgraceful!" she cried. "You must be utterly shameless!"

"My dear lady, you asked me to listen to you, and I have. If you thought I was going to argue, I'm afraid you were mistaken. But since you have been very frank with me, you can hardly mind if I am equally frank with you. I absolutely object to the way in which not only you, but all the persons who took part in that ridiculous function the other day, talk of my private concerns. I am a perfect stranger to you, and you have no business to speak to me of my engagement with Miss Clibborn or the rupture of it. Finally, I would remark that I consider your particular interference a very gross piece of impertinence. I am sorry to have to speak so directly, but apparently nothing but the very plainest language can have any effect upon you."

Then Mrs. Jackson lost her temper.

"Captain Parsons, I am considerably older than you, and you have no right to speak to me like that. You forget that I am a lady; and if I didn't know your father and mother, I should say that you were no gentleman. And you forget also that I come here on the part of God. You are certainly no Christian. You've been very rude to me, indeed."

"I didn't mean to be," replied James, smiling.

"If I'd known you would be so rude to a lady, I should have sent Archibald to speak with you."

"Perhaps it's fortunate you didn't. I might have kicked him."

"Captain Parsons, he's a minister of the gospel."

"Surely it is possible to be that without being a malicious busybody."

"You're heartless and vain! You're odiously conceited."

"I should have thought it a proof of modesty that for half an hour I have listened to you with some respect and with great attention."

"I must say in my heart I'm glad that Providence has stepped in and prevented Mary from marrying you. You are a bad man. And I leave you now to the mercies of your own conscience; I am a Christian woman, thank Heaven! and I forgive you. But I sincerely hope that God will see fit to punish you for your wickedness."

Mrs. Jackson bounced to the door, which James very politely opened.

"Oh, don't trouble!" she said, with a sarcastic shake of the head. "I can find my way out alone, and I shan't steal the umbrellas."

XIII

Major Forsyth arrived in time for tea, red-faced, dapper, and immaculate. He wore a check suit, very new and very pronounced, with a beautiful line down each trouser-leg; and his collar and his tie were of the latest mode. His scanty hair was carefully parted in the middle, and his moustache bristled with a martial ardour. He had lately bought a fine set of artificial teeth, which, with pardonable pride, he constantly exhibited to the admiration of all and sundry. Major Forsyth's consuming desire was to appear juvenile; he affected slang, and carried himself with a youthful jauntiness. He vowed he felt a mere boy, and flattered himself that on his good days, with the light behind him, he might pass for five-and-thirty.

"A woman," he repeated—"a woman is as old as she looks; but a man is as old as he feels!"

The dandiness which in a crammer's pup—most overdressed of all the human race—would merely have aroused a smile, looked oddly with the Major's wrinkled skin and his old eyes. There was something almost uncanny in the exaggerated boyishness; he reminded one of some figure in a dance of death, of a living skeleton, hollow-eyed, strutting gaily by the side of a gallant youth.

It was not difficult to impose upon the Parsons, and Major Forsyth had gained over them a complete ascendancy. They took his opinion on every possible matter, accepting whatever he said with gratified respect. He was a man of the world, and well acquainted with the goings-on of society. They had an idea that he disappointed duchesses to come down to Little Primpton, and always felt that it was a condescension on his part to put up with their simple manners. They altered their hours; luncheon was served at the middle of the day, and dinner in the evening.

Mrs. Parsons put on a Sabbath garment of black silk to receive her brother, and round her neck a lace fichu. When he arrived with Colonel Parsons from the station, she went into the hall to meet him.

"Well, William, have you had a pleasant journey?"

"Oh, yes, yes! I came down with the prettiest woman I've seen for many a long day. I made eyes at her all the way, but she wouldn't look at me."

"William, William!" expostulated Mr. Parsons, smiling.

"You see he hasn't improved since we saw him last, Frances," laughed the Colonel, leading the way into the drawing-room.

"No harm in looking at a pretty woman, you know. I'm a bachelor still, thank the Lord! That reminds me of a funny story I heard at the club."

"Oh, we're rather frightened of your stories, William," said Mrs. Parsons.

"Yes, you're very risky sometimes," assented the Colonel, good-humouredly shaking his head.

Major Forsyth was anecdotal, as is only decent in an old bachelor, and he made a specialty of stories which he thought wicked, but which, as a matter of fact, would not have brought a blush to any cheek less innocent than that of Colonel Parsons.

"There's no harm in a little spice," said Uncle William. "And you're a married woman, Frances." He told an absolutely pointless story of how a man had helped a young woman across the street, and seen her ankle in the process. He told it with immense gusto, laughing and repeating the point at least six times.

"William, William!" laughed Colonel Parsons, heartily. "You should keep those things for the smoking-room."

"What d'you think of it, Frances?" asked the gallant Major, still hugely enjoying the joke.

Mrs. Parsons blushed a little, and for decency's sake prevented herself from smiling; she felt rather wicked.

"I don't want to hear any more of your tales, William."

"Ha, ha!" laughed Uncle William, "I knew you'd like it. And that one I told you in the fly, Richmond—you know, about the petticoat."

"Sh-sh!" said the Colonel, smiling. "You can't tell that to a lady."

"P'r'aps I'd better not. But it's a good story, though."

They both laughed.

"I think it's dreadful the things you men talk about as soon as you're alone," said Mrs. Parsons.

The two God-fearing old soldiers laughed again, admitting their wickedness.

"One must talk about something," said Uncle William. "And upon my word, I don't know anything better to talk about than the fair sex."

Soon James appeared, and shook hands with his uncle.

"You're looking younger than ever, Uncle William. You make me feel quite old."

"Oh, I never age, bless you! Why, I was talking to my old friend, Lady Green, the other day—she was a Miss Lake, you know—and she said to me: 'Upon my word, Major Forsyth, you're wonderful. I believe you've found the secret of perpetual youth.' 'The fact is,' I said, 'I never let myself grow old. If you once give way to it, you're done.' 'How do you manage it?' she said. 'Madam,' I answered, 'it's the simplest thing in the world. I keep regular hours, and I wear flannel next to my skin.'"

"Come, come, Uncle William," said James, with a smile. "You didn't mention your underlinen to a lady!"

"Upon my word, I'm telling you exactly what I said."

"You're very free in your conversation."

"Well, you know, I find the women expect it from me. Of course, I never go beyond the line."

Then Major Forsyth talked of the fashions, and of his clothes, of the scandal of the day, and the ancestry of the persons concerned, of the war.

"You can say what you like," he remarked, "but my opinion is that Roberts is vastly overrated. I met at the club the other day a man whose first cousin has served under Roberts in India—his first cousin, mind you, so it's good authority—and this chap told me, in strict confidence, of course, that his first cousin had no opinion of Roberts. That's what a man says who has actually served under him."

"It is certainly conclusive," said James. "I wonder your friend's first cousin didn't go to the War Office and protest against Bobs being sent out."

"What's the good of going to the War Office? They're all corrupt and incompetent there. If I had my way, I'd make a clean sweep of them. Talking of red-tape, I'll just give you an instance. Now, this is a fact. It was told me by the brother-in-law of the uncle of the man it happened to."

Major Forsyth told his story at great length, finishing up with the assertion that if the army wasn't going to the dogs, he didn't know what going to the dogs meant.

James, meanwhile, catching the glances which passed between his mother and Colonel Parsons, understood that they were thinking of the great subject upon which Uncle William was to be consulted. Half scornfully he gave them their opportunity.

"I'm going for a stroll," he said, "through Groombridge. I shan't be back till dinner-time."

"How lucky!" remarked Colonel Parsons naively, when James had gone. "We wanted to talk with you privately, William. You're a man of the world."

"I think there's not much that I don't know," replied the Major, shooting his linen.

"Tell him, Frances."

Mrs. Parsons, accustomed to the part of spokeswoman, gave her tale, interrupted now and again by a long whistle with which the Major signified his shrewdness, or by an energetic nod which meant that the difficulty was nothing to him.

"You're quite right," he said at last; "one has to look upon these things from the point of view of the man of the world."

"We knew you'd be able to help us," said Colonel Parsons.

"Of course! I shall settle the whole thing in five minutes. You leave it to me."

"I told you he would, Frances," cried the Colonel, with a happy smile. "You think that James ought to marry the girl, don't you?"

"Certainly. Whatever his feelings are, he must act as a gentleman and an officer. Just you let me talk it over with him. He has great respect for all I say; I've noticed that already."

Mrs. Parsons looked at her brother doubtfully.

"We haven't known what to do," she murmured. "We've prayed for guidance, haven't we, Richmond? We're anxious not to be hard on the boy, but we must be just."

"Leave it to me," repeated Uncle William. "I'm a man of the world, and I'm thoroughly at home in matters of this sort."

* * *

According to the little plan which, in his subtlety, Major Forsyth had suggested, Mrs. Parsons, soon after dinner, fetched the backgammon board.

"Shall we have our usual game, Richmond?"

Colonel Parsons looked significantly at his brother-in-law.

"If William doesn't mind?"

"No, no, of course not! I'll have a little chat with Jamie."

The players sat down at the corner of the table, and rather nervously began to set out the men. James stood by the window, silent as ever, looking at the day that was a-dying, with a milk-blue sky and tenuous clouds, copper and gold. Major Forsyth took a chair opposite him, and pulled his moustache.

"Well, Jamie, my boy, what is all this nonsense I hear about you and Mary Clibborn?"

Colonel Parsons started at the expected question, and stole a hurried look at his son. His wife noisily shook the dice-box and threw the dice on the board.

"Nine!" she said.

James turned to look at his uncle, noting a little contemptuously the change of his costume, and its extravagant juvenility.

"A lot of stuff and nonsense, isn't it?"

"D'you think so?" asked James, wearily. "We've been taking it very seriously."

"You're a set of old fogies down here. You want a man of the world to set things right."

"Ah, well, you're a man of the world, Uncle William," replied James, smiling.

The dice-box rattled obtrusively as Colonel Parsons and his wife played on with elaborate unconcern of the conversation.

"A gentleman doesn't jilt a girl when he's been engaged to her for five years."

James squared himself to answer Major Forsyth. The interview with Mrs. Jackson in the morning had left him extremely irritated. He was resolved to say now all he had to say and have done with it, hoping that a complete explanation would relieve the tension between his people and himself.

"It is with the greatest sorrow that I broke off my engagement with Mary Clibborn. It seemed to me the only honest thing to do since I no longer loved her. I can imagine nothing in the world so horrible as a loveless marriage."

"Of course, it's unfortunate; but the first thing is to keep one's word."

"No," answered James, "that is prejudice. There are many more important things."

Colonel Parsons stopped the pretence of his game.

"Do you know that Mary is breaking her heart?" he asked in a low voice.

"I'm afraid she's suffering very much. I don't see how I can help it."

"Leave this to me, Richmond," interrupted the Major, impatiently. "You'll make a mess of it."

But Colonel Parsons took no notice.

"She looked forward with all her heart to marrying you. She's very unhappy at home, and her only consolation was the hope that you would soon take her away."

"Am I managing this or are you, Richmond? I'm a man of the world."

"If I married a woman I did not care for because she was rich, you would say I had dishonoured myself. The discredit would not be in her wealth, but in my lack of love."

"That's not the same thing," replied Major Forsyth. "You gave your word, and now you take it back."

"I promised to do a thing over which I had no control. When I was a boy, before I had seen anything of the world, before I had ever known a woman besides my mother, I promised to love Mary Clibborn all my life. Oh, it was cruel to let me be engaged to her! You blame me; don't you think all of you are a little to blame as well?"

"What could we have done?"

"Why didn't you tell me not to be hasty? Why didn't you say that I was too young to become engaged?"

"We thought it would steady you."

"But a young man doesn't want to be steadied. Let him see life and taste all it has to offer. It is wicked to put fetters on his wrists before ever he has seen anything worth taking. What is the virtue that exists only because temptation is impossible!"

"I can't understand you, Jamie," said Mrs. Parsons, sadly. "You talk so differently from when you were a boy."

"Did you expect me to remain all my life an ignorant child. You've never given me any freedom. You've hemmed me in with every imaginable barrier. You've put me on a leading-string, and thanked God that I did not stray."

"We tried to bring you up like a good man, and a true Christian."

"If I'm not a hopeless prig, it's only by miracle."

"James, that's not the way to talk to your mother," said Major Forsyth.

"Oh, mother, I'm sorry; I don't want to be unkind to you. But we must talk things out freely; we've lived in a hot-house too long."

"I don't know what you mean. You became engaged to Mary of your own free will; we did nothing to hinder it, nothing to bring it about. But I confess we were heartily thankful, thinking that no influence could be better for you than the love of a pure, sweet English girl."

"It would have been kinder and wiser if you had forbidden it."

"We could not have taken the responsibility of crossing your affections."

"Mrs. Clibborn did."

"Could you expect us to be guided by her?"

"She was the only one who showed the least common sense."

"How you have changed, Jamie!"

"I would have obeyed you if you had told me I was too young to become engaged. After all, you are more responsible than I am. I was a child. It was cruel to let me bind myself."

"I never thought you would speak to us like that."

"All that's ancient history," said Major Forsyth, with what he flattered himself was a very good assumption of jocularity. It was his idea to treat the matter lightly, as a man of the world naturally would. But his interruption was unnoticed.

"We acted for the best. You know that we have always had your interests at heart."

James did not speak, for his only answer would have been bitter. Throughout, they had been unwilling to let him live his own life, but desirous rather that he should live theirs. They loved him tyrannically, on the condition that he should conform to all their prejudices. Though full of affectionate kindness, they wished him always to dance to their piping—a marionette of which they pulled the strings.

"What would you have me do?"

"Keep your word, James," answered his father.

"I can't, I can't! I don't understand how you can wish me to marry Mary Clibborn when I don't love her. *That* seems to me dishonourable."

"It would be nothing worse than a *mariage de convenance*," said Uncle William. "Many people marry in that sort of way, and are perfectly happy."

"I couldn't," said James. "That seems to me nothing better than prostitution. It is no worse for a street-walker to sell her body to any that care to buy."

"James, remember your mother is present."

"For God's sake, let us speak plainly. You must know what life is. One can do no good by shutting one's eyes to everything that doesn't square with a shoddy, false ideal. On one side I must break my word, on the other I must prostitute myself. There is no middle way. You live here surrounded by all sorts of impossible ways of looking at life. How can your outlook be sane when it is founded on a sham morality? You think the body is indecent and ugly, and that the flesh is shameful. Oh, you don't understand. I'm sick of this prudery which throws its own hideousness over all it sees. The soul and the body are one, indissoluble. Soul is body, and body is soul. Love is the God-like instinct of procreation. You think sexual attraction is something to be ignored, and in its place you put a bloodless sentimentality—the vulgar rhetoric of a penny novelette. If I marry a woman, it is that she may be the mother of children. Passion is the only reason for marriage; unless it exists, marriage is ugly and beastly. It's worse than beastly; the beasts of the field are clean. Don't you understand why I can't marry Mary Clibborn?"

"What you call love, James," said Colonel Parsons, "is what I call lust."

"I well believe it," replied James, bitterly.

"Love is something higher and purer."

"I know nothing purer than the body, nothing higher than the divine instincts of nature."

"But that sort of love doesn't last, my dear," said Mrs. Parsons, gently. "In a very little while it is exhausted, and then you look for something different in your wife. You look for friendship and companionship, confidence, consolation in your sorrows, sympathy with your success. Beside all that, the sexual love sinks into nothing."

"It may be. The passion arises for the purposes of nature, and dies away when those purposes are fulfilled. It seems to me that the recollection of it must be the surest and tenderest tie between husband and wife; and there remains for them, then, the fruit of their love, the children whom it is their blessed duty to rear till they are of fit age to go into the world and continue the endless cycle."

There was a pause, while Major Forsyth racked his brain for some apposite remark; but the conversation had run out of his depth.

Colonel Parsons at last got up and put his hands on Jamie's shoulders.

"And can't you bring yourself to marry that poor girl, when you think of the terrible unhappiness she suffers?"

James shook his head.

"You were willing to sacrifice your life for a mere stranger, and cannot you sacrifice yourself for Mary, who has loved you long and tenderly, and unselfishly?"

"I would willingly risk my life if she were in danger. But you ask more."

Colonel Parsons was silent for a little, looking into his son's eyes. Then he spoke with trembling voice.

"I think you love me, James. I've always tried to be a good father to you; and God knows I've done all I could to make you happy. If I did wrong in letting you become engaged, I beg your pardon. No; let me go on." This he said in answer to Jamie's movement of affectionate protest. "I don't say it to reproach you, but your mother and I have denied ourselves in all we could so that you should be happy and comfortable. It's been a pleasure to us, for we love you with all our hearts. You know what happened to me when I left the army. I told you years ago of the awful disgrace I suffered. I could never have lived except for my trust in God and my trust in you. I looked to you to regain the honour which I had lost. Ah! you don't know how anxiously I watched you, and the joy with which I said to myself, 'There is a good and honourable man.' And now you want to stain that honour. Oh, James, James! I'm old, and I can't live long. If you love me, if you think you have cause for gratitude to me, do this one little thing I ask you! For my sake, my dear, keep your word to Mary Clibborn."

"You're asking me to do something immoral, father."

Then Colonel Parsons helplessly dropped his hands from Jamie's shoulders, and turned to the others, his eyes full of tears.

"I don't understand what he means!" he groaned.

He sank on a chair and hid his face.

XIV

Major Forsyth was not at all discouraged by the issue of his intervention.

"Now I see how the land lies," he said, "it's all plain sailing. Reconnoitre first, and then wire in."

He bravely attacked James next day, when they were smoking in the garden after breakfast. Uncle William smoked nothing but gold-tipped cigarettes, which excited his nephew's open scorn.

"I've been thinking about what you said yesterday, James," he began.

"For Heaven's sake, Uncle William, don't talk about it any more. I'm heartily sick of the whole thing. I've made up my mind, and I really shall not alter it for anything you may say."

Major Forsyth changed the conversation with what might have been described as a strategic movement to the rear. He said that Jamie's answer told him all he wished to know, and he was content now to leave the seeds which he had sown to spring up of their own accord.

"I'm perfectly satisfied," he told his sister, complacently. "You'll see that if it'll all come right now."

Meanwhile, Mary conducted herself admirably. She neither avoided James nor sought him, but when chance brought them together, was perfectly natural. Her affection had never been demonstrative, and now there was in her manner but little change. She talked frankly, as though nothing had passed between them, with no suspicion of reproach in her tone. She was, indeed, far more at ease than James. He could not hide the effort it was to make conversation, nor the nervous discomfort which in her presence he felt. He watched her furtively, asking himself whether she still suffered. But Mary's face betrayed few of her emotions; tanned by exposure to all weathers, her robust colour remained unaltered; and it was only in her eyes that James fancied he saw a difference. They had just that perplexed, sorrowful expression which a dog has, unjustly beaten. James, imaginative and conscience-stricken, tortured himself by reading in their brown softness all manner of dreadful anguish. He watched them, unlit by the smile which played upon the lips, looking at him against their will, with a pitiful longing. He exaggerated the pain he saw till it became an obsession, intolerable and ruthless; if Mary desired revenge, she need not have been dissatisfied. But that apparently was the last thing she thought of. He was grateful to hear of her anger with Mrs. Jackson, whose sympathy had expressed itself in round abuse of him. His mother repeated the words.

"I will never listen to a word against Captain Parsons, Mrs. Jackson. Whatever he did, he had a perfect right to do. He's incapable of acting otherwise than as an honourable gentleman."

But if Mary's conduct aroused the admiration of all that knew her, it rendered James still more blameworthy.

The hero-worship was conveniently forgotten, and none strove to conceal the dislike, even the contempt, which he felt for the fallen idol. James had outraged the moral sense of the community; his name could not be mentioned without indignation; everything he did was wrong, even his very real modesty was explained as overweening conceit.

And curiously enough, James was profoundly distressed by the general disapproval. A silent, shy man, he was unreasonably sensitive to the opinion of his fellows; and though he told himself that they were stupid, ignorant, and narrow, their hostility nevertheless made him miserable. Even though he contemned them, he was anxious that they should like him. He refused to pander to their prejudices, and was too proud to be conciliatory; yet felt bitterly wounded when he had excited their aversion. Now he set to tormenting himself because he had despised the adulation of Little Primpton, and could not equally despise its censure.

* * *

Sunday came, and the good people of Little Primpton trooped to church. Mrs Clibborn turned round and smiled at James when he took his seat, but the Colonel sat rigid, showing by the stiffness of his backbone that his indignation was supreme.

The service proceeded, and in due course Mr. Jackson mounted the pulpit steps. He delivered his text: *"The fear of the Lord is to hate evil: pride, and arrogancy, and the evil way, and the forward mouth, do I hate."*

The Vicar of Little Primpton was an earnest man, and he devoted much care to the composition of his sermons. He was used to expound twice a Sunday the more obvious parts of Holy Scripture, making in twenty minutes or half an hour, for the benefit of the vulgar, a number of trite reflections; and it must be confessed that he had great facility for explaining at decorous length texts which were plain to the meanest intelligence.

But having a fair acquaintance with the thought of others, Mr. Jackson flattered himself that he was a thinker; and on suitable occasions attacked from his village pulpit the scarlet weed of heresy, expounding to an intelligent congregation of yokels and small boys the manifold difficulties of the Athanasian Creed. He was at his best in pouring vials of contempt upon the false creed of atheists, Romanists, Dissenters, and men of science. The theory of Evolution excited his bitterest scorn, and he would set up, like a row of nine-pins, the hypotheses of the greatest philosophers of the century, triumphantly to knock them down by the force of his own fearless intellect. His congregation were inattentive, and convinced beyond the need of argument, so they remained pious members of the Church of England.

But this particular sermon, after mature consideration, the Vicar had made up his mind to devote to a matter of more pressing interest. He repeated the text. Mrs. Jackson, who knew what was coming, caught the curate's eye, and looked significantly at James. The homily, in fact, was directed against him; his were the pride, the arrogance, and the evil way. He was blissfully unconscious of these faults, and for a minute or two the application missed him; but the Vicar of Little Primpton, intent upon what he honestly thought his duty, meant that there should be no mistake. He crossed his t's and dotted his i's, with the scrupulous accuracy of the scandal-monger telling a malicious story about some person whom charitably he does not name, yet wishes everyone to identify.

Colonel Parsons started when suddenly the drift of the sermon dawned upon him, and then bowed his head with shame. His wife looked straight in front of her, two flaming spots upon her pale cheeks. Mary, in the next pew, dared not move, hardly dared breathe; her heart sank with dismay, and she feared she would faint.

"How he must be suffering!" she muttered.

They all felt for James intensely; the form of Mr. Jackson, hooded and surpliced, had acquired a new authority, and his solemn invective was sulphurous with the fires of Hell. They wondered how James could bear it.

"He hasn't deserved this," thought Mrs. Parsons.

But the Colonel bent his head still lower, accepting for his son the reproof, taking part of it himself. The humiliation seemed merited, and the only thing to do was to bear it meekly. James alone appeared unconcerned; the rapid glances at him saw no change in his calm, indifferent face. His eyes were closed, and one might have thought him asleep. Mr. Jackson noted the attitude, and attributed it to a wicked obstinacy. For the repentant sinner, acknowledging his fault, he would have had entire forgiveness; but James showed no contrition. Stiff-necked and sin-hardened, he required a further chastisement.

"Courage, what is courage?" asked the preacher. "There is nothing more easy than to do a brave deed when the blood is hot. But to conduct one's life simply, modestly, with a meek spirit and a Christ-like submission, that is ten times more difficult Courage, unaccompanied by moral worth, is the quality of a brute-beast."

He showed how much more creditable were the artless virtues of honesty and truthfulness; how better it was to keep one's word, to be kind-hearted and dutiful. Becoming more pointed, he mentioned the case which had caused them so much sorrow, warning the delinquent against conceit and self-assurance.

"Pride goeth before a fall," he said. "And he that is mighty shall be abased."

* * *

They walked home silently, Colonel Parsons and his wife with downcast eyes, feeling that everyone was looking at them. Their hearts were too full for them to speak to one another, and they dared say nothing to James. But Major Forsyth had no scruples of delicacy; he attacked his nephew the moment they sat down to dinner.

"Well, James, what did you think of the sermon? Feel a bit sore?"

"Why should I?"

"I fancy it was addressed pretty directly to you."

"So I imagine," replied James, good-humouredly smiling. "I thought it singularly impertinent, but otherwise uninteresting."

"Mr. Jackson doesn't think much of you," said Uncle William, with a laugh, ignoring his sister's look, which implored him to be silent.

"I can bear that with equanimity. I never set up for a very wonderful person."

"He was wrong to make little of your attempt to save young Larcher," said Mrs. Parsons, gently.

"Why?" asked James. "He was partly right. Physical courage is more or less accidental. In battle one takes one's chance. One soon gets used to shells flying about; they're not so dangerous as they look, and after a while one forgets all about them. Now and then one gets hit, and then it's too late to be nervous."

"But you went back—into the very jaws of death—to save that boy."

"I've never been able to understand why. It didn't occur to me that I might get killed; it seemed the natural thing to do. It wasn't really brave, because I never realised that there was danger."

* * *

In the afternoon James received a note from Mrs. Clibborn, asking him to call upon her. Mary and her father were out walking, she said, so there would be no one to disturb them, and they could have a pleasant little chat. The invitation was a climax to Jamie's many vexations, and he laughed grimly at the prospect of that very foolish lady's indignation. Still, he felt bound to go. It was, after a fashion, a point of honour with him to avoid none of the annoyances which his act had brought upon him. It was partly in order to face every infliction that he insisted on remaining at Little Primpton.

"Why haven't you been to see me, James?" Mrs. Clibborn murmured, with a surprisingly tender smile.

"I thought you wouldn't wish me to."

"James!"

She sighed and cast up her eyes to heaven.

"I always liked you. I shall never feel differently towards you."

"It's very kind of you to say so," replied James, somewhat relieved.

"You must come and see me often. It'll comfort you."

"I'm afraid you and Colonel Clibborn must be very angry with me?"

"I could never be angry with you, James.... Poor Reginald, he doesn't understand! But you can't deceive a woman." Mrs. Clibborn put her hand on Jamie's arm and gazed into his eyes. "I want you to tell me something. Do you love anyone else?"

James looked at her quickly and hesitated.

"If you had asked me the other day, I should have denied it with all my might. But now—I don't know."

Mrs. Clibborn smiled.

"I thought so," she said. "You can tell me, you know."

She was convinced that James adored her, but wanted to hear him say so. It is notorious that to a handsome woman even the admiration of a crossing-sweeper is welcome.

"Oh, it's no good any longer trying to conceal it from myself!" cried James, forgetting almost to whom he was speaking. "I'm sorry about Mary; no one knows how much. But I do love someone else, and I love her with all my heart and soul; and I shall never get over it now."

"I knew it," sighed Mrs. Clibborn, complacently, "I knew it!" Then looking coyly at him: "Tell me about her."

"I can't. I know my love is idiotic and impossible; but I can't help it. It's fate."

"You're in love with a married woman, James."

"How d'you know?"

"My poor boy, d'you think you can deceive me! And is it not the wife of an officer?"

"Yes."

"A very old friend of yours?"

"It's just that which makes it so terrible."

"I knew it."

"Oh, Mrs. Clibborn, I swear you're the only woman here who's got two ounces of gumption. If they'd only listened to you five years ago, we might all have been saved this awful wretchedness."

He could not understand that Mrs. Clibborn, whose affectations were manifest, whose folly was notorious, should alone have guessed his secret. He was tired of perpetually concealing his thoughts.

"I wish I could tell you everything!" he cried.

"Don't! You'd only regret it. And I know all you can tell me."

"You can't think how hard I've struggled. When I found I loved her, I nearly killed myself trying to kill my love. But it's no good. It's stronger than I am."

"And nothing can ever come of it, you know," said Mrs. Clibborn.

"Oh, I know! Of course, I know! I'm not a cad. The only thing is to live on and suffer."

"I'm so sorry for you."

Mrs. Clibborn thought that even poor Algy Turner, who had killed himself for love of her, had not been so desperately hit.

"It's very kind of you to listen to me," said James. "I have nobody to speak to, and sometimes I feel I shall go mad."

"You're such a nice boy, James. What a pity it is you didn't go into the cavalry!"

James scarcely heard; he stared at the floor, brooding sorrowfully.

"Fate is against me," he muttered.

"If things had only happened a little differently. Poor Reggie!"

Mrs. Clibborn was thinking that if she were a widow, she could never have resisted the unhappy young man's pleading.

James got up to go.

"It's no good," he said; "talking makes it no better. I must go on trying to crush it. And the worst of it is, I don't want to crush it; I love my love. Though it embitters my whole life, I would rather die than lose it. Good-bye, Mrs. Clibborn. Thank you for being so kind. You can't imagine what good it does me to receive a little sympathy."

"I know. You're not the first who has told me that he is miserable. I think it's fate, too."

James looked at her, perplexed, not understanding what she meant. With her sharp, feminine intuition, Mrs. Clibborn read in his eyes the hopeless yearning of his heart, and for a moment her rigid virtue faltered.

"I can't be hard on you, Jamie," she said, with that effective, sad smile of hers. "I don't want you to go away from here quite wretched."

"What can you do to ease the bitter aching of my heart?"

Mrs. Clibborn, quickly looking at the window, noticed that she could not possibly be seen by anyone outside. She stretched out her hand.

"Jamie, if you like you may kiss me."

She offered her powdered cheek, and James, rather astonished, pressed it with his lips.

"I will always be a mother to you. You can depend on me whatever happens.... Now go away, there's a good boy."

She watched him as he walked down the garden, and then sighed deeply, wiping away a tear from the corner of her eyes.

"Poor boy!" she murmured.

Mary was surprised, when she came home, to find her mother quite affectionate and tender. Mrs. Clibborn, indeed, intoxicated with her triumph, could afford to be gracious to a fallen rival.

XV

A few days later Mary was surprised to receive a little note from Mr. Dryland:

"My Dear Miss Clibborn,—

With some trepidation I take up my pen to address you on a matter which, to me at least, is of the very greatest importance. We have so many sympathies in common that my meaning will hardly escape you. I daresay you will find my diffidence ridiculous, but, under the circumstances, I think it is not unpardonable. It will be no news to you when I confess that I am an exceptionally shy man, and that must be my excuse in sending you this letter. In short, I wish to ask you to grant me a brief interview; we have so few opportunities of seeing one another in private that I can find no occasion of saying to you what I wish. Indeed, for a long period my duty has made it necessary for me to crush my inclination. Now, however, that things have taken a different turn, I venture, as I said, to ask you to give me a few minutes' conversation.—

I am, my dear Miss Clibborn, your very sincere,

"Thomas Dryland.

"P.S.—I open this letter to say that I have just met your father on the Green, who tells me that he and Mrs. Clibborn are going into Tunbridge Wells this afternoon. Unless, therefore, I hear from you to the contrary, I shall (D.V.) present myself at your house at 3 P.M."

"What can he want to see me about?" exclaimed Mary, the truth occurring to her only to be chased away as a piece of egregious vanity. It was more reasonable to suppose that Mr. Dryland had on hand some charitable scheme in which he desired her to take part.

"Anyhow," she thought philosophically, "I suppose I shall know when he comes."

At one and the same moment the church clock struck three, and Mr. Dryland rang the Clibborns' bell.

He came into the dining-room in his best coat, his honest red face shining with soap, and with a consciousness that he was about to perform an heroic deed.

"This is kind of you, Miss Clibborn! Do you know, I feared the servant was going to say you were 'not at home.'"

"Oh, I never let her say that when I'm in. Mamma doesn't think it wrong, but one can't deny that it's an untruth."

"What a beautiful character you have!" cried the curate, with enthusiasm.

"I'm afraid I haven't really; but I like to be truthful."

"Were you surprised to receive my letter?"

"I'm afraid I didn't understand it."

"I was under the impression that I expressed myself with considerable perspicacity," remarked the curate, with a genial smile.

"I don't pretend to be clever."

"Oh, but you are, Miss Clibborn. There's no denying it."

"I wish I thought so."

"You're so modest. I have always thought that your mental powers were very considerable indeed. I can assure you it has been a great blessing to me to find someone here who was capable of taking an intelligent interest in Art and Literature. In these little country places one misses intellectual society so much."

"I'm not ashamed to say that I've learnt a lot from you, Mr. Dryland."

"No, that is impossible. All I lay claim to is that I was fortunate enough to be able to lend you the works of Ruskin and Marie Corelli."

"That reminds me that I must return you the 'Master Christian.'"

"Please don't hurry over it. I think it's a book worth pondering over; quite unlike the average trashy novel."

"I haven't had much time for reading lately."

"Ah, Miss Clibborn, I understand! I'm afraid you've been very much upset. I wanted to tell you how sorry I was; but I felt it would be perhaps indelicate."

"It is very kind of you to think of me."

"Besides, I must confess that I cannot bring myself to be very sorry. It's an ill wind that blows nobody good."

"I'm afraid I don't understand what you mean, Mr. Dryland."

"Miss Clibborn, I have come here to-day to converse with you on a matter which I venture to think of some importance. At least, it is to me. I will not beat about the bush. In these matters it is always best, I believe, to come straight to the point." The curate cleared his throat, and assumed his best clerical manner. "Miss Clibborn, I have the honour to solemnly ask you for your hand."

"Oh!"

Mary blushed scarlet, and her heart went pit-a-pat in the most alarming fashion.

"I think I should tell you that I am thirty-three years of age. I have some private means, small, but sufficient, with my income and economy, to support a wife. My father was for over a quarter of a century vicar of Easterham."

Mary by this time had recovered herself.

"I feel very much honoured by your proposal, Mr. Dryland. And no one can be more convinced than I of my unworthiness. But I'm afraid I must refuse."

"I don't press for an immediate answer, Miss Clibborn. I know at first blush it must surprise you that I should come forward with an offer so soon after the rupture of your engagement with Captain Parsons. But if you examine the matter closely, you will see that it is less surprising than it seems. While you were engaged to Captain Parsons it was my duty to stifle my feelings; but now I cannot. Indeed, I have not the right to conceal from you that for a long time they have been of the tenderest description."

"I feel very much flattered."

"Not at all," reassuringly answered Mr. Dryland. "I can honestly say that you are deserving of the very highest—er—admiration and esteem. Miss Clibborn, I have loved you in secret almost ever since I came to the parish. The moment I saw you I felt an affinity between us. Our tastes are so similar; we both understand Art and Literature. When you played to me the divine melodies of Mendelssohn, when I read to you the melodious verses of Lord Tennyson, I felt that my happiness in life would be a union with you."

"I'm afraid I can never be unfaithful to my old love."

"Perhaps I'm a little previous?"

"No; time can make no possible difference. I'm very grateful to you."

"You have no need to be. I have always tried to do my duty, and while you were engaged to another, I allowed not even a sigh to escape my lips. But now I venture to think that the circumstances are altered. I know I am not a gallant officer, I have done no doughty deeds, and the Victoria Cross does not adorn my bosom. I am comparatively poor; but I can offer an honest heart and a very sincere and respectful love. Oh, Miss Clibborn, cannot you give me hope that as time wears on you will be able to look upon my suit with favour?"

"I'm afraid my answer must be final."

"I hope to be soon appointed to a living, and I looked forward ardently to the life of usefulness and of Christian fellowship which we might have lived together. You are an angel of mercy, Miss Clibborn. I cannot help thinking that you are eminently suitable for the position which I make so bold as to offer you."

"I won't deny that nothing could attract me more than to be the wife of a clergyman. One has such influence for good, such power of improving one's fellow-men. But I love Captain Parsons. Even if he has ceased to care for me, I could never look upon him with other feelings."

"Even though it touches me to the quick, Miss. Clibborn," said the curate, earnestly, "I respect and admire you for your sentiments. You are wonderful. I wonder if you'd allow me to make a little confession?" The curate hesitated and reddened. "The fact is, I have written a few verses comparing you to Penelope, which, if you will allow me, I should very much like to send you."

"I should like to see them very much," said Mary, blushing a little and smiling.

"Of course, I'm not a poet, I'm too busy for that; but they are the outpouring of an honest, loving heart."

"I'm sure," said Mary, encouragingly, "that it's better to be sincere and upright than to be the greatest poet in the world."

"It's very kind of you to say so. I should like to ask one question, Miss Clibborn. Have you any objection to me personally?"

"Oh, no!" cried Mary. "How can you suggest such a thing? I have the highest respect and esteem for you, Mr. Dryland. I can never forget the great compliment you have paid me. I shall always think of you as the best friend I have."

"Can you say nothing more to me than that?" asked the curate, despondently.

Mary stretched out her hand. "I will be a sister to you."

"Oh, Miss Clibborn, how sad it is to think that your affections should be unrequited. Why am I not Captain Parsons? Miss Clibborn, can you give me no hope?"

"I should not be acting rightly towards you if I did not tell you at once that so long as Captain Parsons lives, my love for him can never alter."

"I wish I were a soldier!" murmured Mr. Dryland.

"Oh, it's not that. I think there's nothing so noble as a clergyman. If it is any consolation to you, I may confess that if I had never known Captain Parsons, things might have gone differently."

"Well, I suppose I had better go away now. I must try to bear my disappointment."

Mary gave him her hand, and, bending down with the utmost gallantry, the curate kissed it; then, taking up his low, clerical hat, hurriedly left her.

* * *

Mrs. Jackson was a woman of singular penetration, so that it was not strange if she quickly discovered what had happened. Mr. Dryland was taking tea at the Vicarage, whither, with characteristic manliness, he had gone to face his disappointment. Not for him was the solitary moping, nor the privacy of a bedchamber; his robust courage sent him rather into the field of battle, or what was under the circumstances the only equivalent, Mrs. Jackson's drawing-room.

But even he could not conceal the torments of unsuccessful love. He stirred his tea moodily, and his usual appetite for plum-cake had quite deserted him.

"What's the matter with you, Mr. Dryland?" asked the Vicar's wife, with those sharp eyes which could see into the best-hidden family secret.

Mr. Dryland started at the question. "Nothing!"

"You're very funny this afternoon."

"I've had a great disappointment."

"Oh!" replied Mrs. Jackson, in a tone which half-a-dozen marks of interrogation could inadequately express.

"It's nothing. Life is not all beer and skittles. Ha! ha!"

"Did you say you'd been calling on Mary Clibborn this afternoon?"

Mr. Dryland blushed, and to cover his confusion filled his mouth with a large piece of cake.

"Yes," he said, as soon as he could. "I paid her a little call."

"Mr. Dryland, you can't deceive me. You've proposed to Mary Clibborn."

He swallowed his food with a gulp. "It's quite true."

"And she's refused you?"

"Yes!"

"Mr. Dryland, it was a noble thing to do. I must tell Archibald."

"Oh, please don't, Mrs. Jackson! I don't want it to get about."

"Oh, but I shall. We can't let you hide your light under a bushel. Fancy you proposing to that poor, dear girl! But it's just what I should have expected of you. That's what I always say. The clergy are constantly doing the most beautiful actions that no one hears anything about. You ought to receive a moral Victoria Cross. I'm sure you deserve it far more than that wicked and misguided young man."

"I don't think I ought to take any credit for what I've done," modestly remonstrated the curate.

"It was a beautiful action. You don't know how much it means to that poor, jilted girl."

"It's true my indignation was aroused at the heartless conduct of Captain Parsons; but I have long loved her, Mrs. Jackson."

"I knew it; I knew it! When I saw you together I said to Archibald: 'What a good pair they'd make!' I'm sure you deserve her far more than that worthless creature."

"I wish she thought so."

"I'll go and speak to her myself. I think she ought to accept you. You've behaved like a knight-errant, Mr. Dryland. You're a true Christian saint."

"Oh, Mrs. Jackson, you embarrass me!"

The news spread like wild-fire, and with it the opinion that the curate had vastly distinguished himself. Neither pagan hero nor Christian martyr could have acted more becomingly. The consideration which had once been Jamie's was bodily transferred to Mr. Dryland. He was the man of the hour, and the contemplation of his gallant deed made everyone feel nobler, purer. The curate accepted with quiet satisfaction the homage that was laid at his feet, modestly denying that he had done anything out of the way. With James, all unconscious of what had happened, he was mildly patronising; with Mary, tender, respectful, subdued. If he had been an archbishop, he could not have behaved with greater delicacy, manliness, and decorum.

"I don't care what anyone says," cried Mrs. Jackson, "I think he's worth ten Captain Parsons! He's so modest and gentlemanly. Why, Captain Parsons simply used to look bored when one told him he was brave."

"He's a conceited creature!"

But in Primpton House the proposal was met with consternation.

"Suppose she accepted him?" said Colonel Parsons, anxiously.

"She'd never do that."

Major Forsyth suggested that James should be told, in the belief that his jealousy would be excited.

"I'll tell him," said Mrs. Parsons.

She waited till she was alone with her son, and then, without stopping her needlework, said suddenly:

"James, have you heard that Mr. Dryland has proposed to Mary?"

He looked up nonchalantly. "Has she accepted him?"

"James!" cried his mother, indignantly, "how can you ask such a question? Have you no respect for her? You must know that for nothing in the world would she be faithless to you."

"I should like her to marry the curate. I think it would be a very suitable match."

"You need not insult her, James."

XVI

The tension between James and his parents became not less, but greater. That barrier which, almost from the beginning, they had watched with pain rise up between them now seemed indestructible, and all their efforts only made it more obvious and more stable. It was like some tropical plant which, for being cut down, grew ever with greater luxuriance. And there was a mischievous devil present at all their conversations that made them misunderstand one another as completely as though they spoke in different tongues. Notwithstanding their love, they were like strangers together; they could look at nothing from the same point of view.

The Parsons had lived their whole lives in an artificial state. Ill-educated as most of their contemporaries in that particular class, they had just enough knowledge to render them dogmatic and intolerant. It requires a good deal of information to discover one's own ignorance, but to the consciousness of this the good people had never arrived. They felt they knew as much as necessary, and naturally on the most debatable questions were most assured. Their standpoint was inconceivably narrow. They had the best intentions in the world of doing their duty, but what their duty was they accepted on trust, frivolously. They walked round and round in a narrow circle, hemmed in by false ideals and by ugly prejudices, putting for the love of God unnecessary obstacles in their path and convinced that theirs was the only possible way, while all others led to damnation. They had never worked out an idea for themselves, never done a single deed on their own account, but invariably acted and thought according to the rule of their caste. They were not living creatures, but dogmatic machines.

James, going into the world, quickly realised that he had been brought up to a state of things which did not exist. He was like a sailor who has put out to sea in an ornamental boat, and finds that his sail is useless, the ropes not made to work, and the rudder immovable. The long, buoyant wind of the world blew away like thistle-down the conventions which had seemed so secure a foundation. But he discovered in himself a wonderful curiosity, an eagerness for adventure which led him boldly to affront every peril; and the unknown lands of the intellect are every bit as dangerously fascinating as are those of sober fact. He read omnivorously, saw many and varied things; the universe was spread out before him like an enthralling play. Knowledge is like the root of a tree, attaching man by its tendrils to the life about him. James found in existence new beauties, new interests, new complexities; and he gained a lighter heart and, above all, an exquisite sense of freedom. At length he looked back with something like horror at that old life in which the fetters of ignorance had weighed so terribly upon him.

On his return to Little Primpton, he found his people as he had left them, doing the same things, repeating at every well-known juncture the same trite observations. Their ingenuousness affected him as a negro, civilised and educated, on visiting after many years his native tribe, might be affected by their nose-rings and yellow ochre. James was astounded that they should ignore matters which he fancied common knowledge, and at the same time accept beliefs that he had thought completely dead. He was willing enough to shrug his shoulders and humour their prejudices, but they had made of them a rule of life which governed every action with an iron tyranny. It was in accordance with all these outworn conventions that they conducted the daily round. And presently James found that his father and mother were striving to draw him back into the prison. Unconsciously, even with the greatest tenderness, they sought to place upon his neck again that irksome yoke which he had so difficultly thrown off.

If James had learnt anything, it was at all hazards to think for himself, accepting nothing on authority, questioning, doubting; it was to look upon life with a critical eye, trying to understand it, and to receive no ready-made explanations. Above all, he had learnt that every question has two sides. Now this was precisely what Colonel Parsons and his wife could never acknowledge; for them one view was certainly right, and the other as certainly wrong. There was no middle way. To doubt what they believed could only be ascribed to arrant folly or to wickedness. Sometimes James was thrown into a blind rage by the complacency with which from the depths of his nescience his father dogmatised. No man could have been more unassuming than he, and yet on just the points which were most uncertain his attitude was almost inconceivably arrogant.

And James was horrified at the pettiness and the prejudice which he found in his home. Reading no books, for they thought it waste of time to read, the minds of his father and mother had sunk into such a narrow sluggishness that they could interest themselves only in trivialities. Their thoughts were occupied by their neighbours and the humdrum details of the life about them. Flattering themselves on their ideals and their high principles, they vegetated in stupid sloth and in a less than animal vacuity. Every topic of conversation above the most commonplace they found dull or incomprehensible. James learned that he had to talk to them almost as if they were children, and the tedium of those endless days was intolerable.

Occasionally he was exasperated that he could not avoid the discussions which his father, with a weak man's obstinacy, forced upon him. Some unhappy, baneful power seemed to drive Colonel Parsons to widen the rift, the existence of which caused him such exquisite pain; his natural kindliness was obscured by an uncontrollable irritation. One day he was reading the paper.

"I see we've had another unfortunate reverse," he said, looking up.

"Oh!"

"I suppose you're delighted, Jamie?"

"I'm very sorry. Why should I be otherwise?"

"You always stick up for the enemies of your country." Turning to his brother-in-law, he explained: "James says that if he'd been a Cape Dutchman he'd have fought against us."

"Well, he deserves to be court-martialled for saying so! "cried Major Forsyth.

"I don't think he means to be taken seriously," said his mother.

"Oh, yes, I do." It constantly annoyed James that when he said anything that was not quite an obvious truism, they should think he was speaking merely for effect. "Why, my dear mother, if you'd been a Boer woman you'd have potted at us from behind a haystack with the best of them."

"The Boers are robbers and brigands."

"That's just what they say we are."

"But we're right."

"And they're equally convinced that they are."

"God can't be on both sides, James."

"The odd thing is the certainty with which both sides claim His exclusive protection."

"I should think it wicked to doubt that God is with us in a righteous war," said Mrs. Parsons.

"If the Boers weren't deceived by that old villain Kruger, they'd never have fought us."

"The Boers are strange people," replied James. "They actually prefer their independence to all the privileges and advantages of subjection.... The wonderful thing to me is that people should really think Mr. Kruger a hypocrite. A ruler who didn't honestly believe in himself and in his mission would never have had such influence. If a man wants power he must have self-faith; but then he may be narrow, intolerant, and vicious. His fellows will be like wax in his hands."

"If Kruger had been honest, he wouldn't have put up with bribery and corruption."

"The last thing I expect is consistency in an animal of such contrary instincts as man."

"Every true Englishman, I'm thankful to say, thinks him a scoundrel and a blackguard."

"In a hundred years he will probably think him a patriot and a hero. In that time the sentimental view will be the only one of interest; and the sentimental view will put the Transvaal in the same category as Poland."

"You're nothing better than a pro-Boer, James."

"I'm nothing of the kind; but seeing how conflicting was current opinion, I took some trouble to find for myself a justification of the war. I couldn't help wondering why I went and killed people to whom I was personally quite indifferent."

"I hope because it was your duty as an officer of Her Majesty the Queen."

"Not exactly. I came to the conclusion that I killed people because I liked it. The fighting instinct is in my blood, and I'm never so happy as when I'm shooting things. Killing tigers is very good sport, but it's not in it with killing men. That is my justification, so far as I personally am concerned. As a member of society, I wage war for a different reason. War is the natural instinct of all creatures; not only do progress and civilisation arise from it, but it is the very condition of existence. Men, beasts, and plants are all in the same position: unless they fight incessantly they're wiped out; there's no sitting on one side and looking on.... When a state wants a neighbour's land, it has a perfect right to take it—if it can. Success is its justification. We English wanted the Transvaal for our greater numbers, for our trade, for the continuance of our power; that was our right to take it. The only thing that seems to me undignified is the rather pitiful set of excuses we made up."

"If those are your ideas, I think they are utterly ignoble."

"I believe they're scientific."

"D'you think men go to war for scientific reasons?"

"No, of course not; they don't realise them. The great majority are incapable of abstract ideas, but fortunately they're emotional and sentimental; and the pill can be gilded with high falutin. It's for them that the Union Jack and the honour of Old England are dragged through every newspaper and brandished in every music hall. It's for them that all these atrocities are invented—most of them bunkum. Men are only savages with a thin veneer of civilisation, which is rather easily rubbed off, and then they act just like Red Indians; but as a general rule they're well enough behaved. The Boer isn't a bad sort, and the Englishman isn't a bad sort; but there's not room for both of them on the earth, and one of them has to go."

"My father fought for duty and honour's sake, and so fought his father before him."

"Men have always fought really for the same reasons—for self-protection and gain; but perhaps they have not seen quite so clearly as now the truth behind all their big words. The world and mankind haven't altered suddenly in the last few years."

* * *

Afterwards, when Colonel Parsons and his wife were alone together, and she saw that he was brooding over his son's words, she laid her hand on his shoulder, and said:

"Don't worry, Richmond; it'll come right in the end, if we trust and pray."

"I don't know what to make of him," he returned, sadly shaking his head. "It's not our boy, Frances; he couldn't be callous and unscrupulous, and—dishonourable. God forgive me for saying it!"

"Don't be hard on him, Richmond. I daresay he doesn't mean all he says. And remember that he's been very ill. He's not himself yet."

The Colonel sighed bitterly.

"When we looked forward so anxiously to his return, we didn't know that he would be like this."

James had gone out. He wandered along the silent roads, taking in large breaths of the fresh air, for his home affected him like a hot-house. The atmosphere was close and heavy, so that he could neither think freely nor see things in any reasonable light. He felt sometimes as though a weight were placed upon his head, that pressed him down, and pressed him down till he seemed almost forced to his knees.

He blamed himself for his lack of moderation. Why, remembering ever his father's unhappiness and his infirmities, could he not humour him? He was an old man, weak and frail; it should not have been so difficult to use restraint towards him. James knew he had left them in Primpton House distressed and angry; but the only way to please them was to surrender his whole personality, giving up to their bidding all his thoughts and all his actions. They wished to exercise over him the most intolerable of all tyrannies, the tyranny of love. It was a heavy return they demanded for their affection if he must abandon his freedom, body and soul; he earnestly wished to make them happy, but that was too hard a price to pay. And then, with sudden rage, James asked himself why they should be so self-sufficiently certain that they were right. What an outrageous assumption it was that age must be infallible! Their idea of filial duty was that he should accept their authority, not because they were wise, but because they were old. When he was a child they had insisted on the utmost submission, and now they expected the same submission—to their prejudice, intolerance, and lack of knowledge. They had almost ridiculously that calm, quiet, well-satisfied assurance which a king by right divine might have in the certainty that he could do no wrong.

And James, with bitter, painful scorn, thought of that frightful blunder which had forced Colonel Parsons to leave the service. At first his belief in his father had been such that James could not conceive the possibility even that he had acted wrongly; the mere fact that his father had chosen a certain course was proof of its being right and proper, and the shame lay with his chief, who had used him ill. But when he examined the affair and thought over it, the truth became only too clear; it came to him like a blow, and for a while he was overcome with shame. The fact was evident—alas! only too evident—his father was incapable of command. James was simply astounded; he tried not to hear the cruel words that buzzed in his ears, but he could not help it—imbecility, crass idiocy, madness. It was worse than madness, the folly of it was almost criminal; he thought now that his father had escaped very easily.

James hastened his step, trying to rid himself of the irritating thoughts. He walked along the fat and fertile Kentish fields, by the neat iron railing with which they were enclosed. All about him was visible the care of man. Nothing was left wild. The trees were lopped into proper shape, cut down where their presence seemed inelegant, planted to complete the symmetry of a group. Nature herself was under the power of the formal influence, and flourished with a certain rigidity and decorum. After a while the impression became singularly irksome; it seemed to emphasise man's lack of freedom, reminding one of the iron conventions with which he is inevitably bound. In the sun, the valley, all green and wooded, was pleasantly cool; but when the clouds rolled up from the west heavily, brushing the surrounding hills, the aspect was so circumscribed that James could have cried out as with physical pain. The primness of the scene then was insufferable; the sombre, well-ordered elms, the meadows so carefully kept, seemed the garden of some great voluptuous prison, and the air was close with servitude.

James panted for breath. He thought of the vast distances of South Africa, bush and prairie stretching illimitably, and above, the blue sky, vaster still. There, at least, one could breathe freely, and stretch one's limbs.

"Why did I ever come back?" he cried.

The blood went thrilling through his veins at the mere thought of those days in which every minute had been intensely worth living. Then, indeed, was no restraint or pettiness; then men were hard and firm and strong. By comparison, people in England appeared so pitifully weak, vain, paltry, insignificant. What were the privations and the hardships beside the sense of mastery, the happy adventure, and the carelessness of life?

But the grey clouds hung over the valley, pregnant with rain. It gave him a singular feeling of discomfort to see them laden with water, and yet painfully holding it up.

"I can't stay in this place," he muttered. "I shall go mad."

A sudden desire for flight seized him. The clouds sank lower and lower, till he imagined he must bend his head to avoid them. If he could only get away for a little, he might regain his calm. At least, absence, he thought bitterly, was the only way to restore the old affection between him and his father.

He went home, and announced that he was going to London.

XVII

After the quiet of Little Primpton, the hurry and the noise of Victoria were a singular relief to James. Waiting for his luggage, he watched the various movements of the scene—the trollies pushed along with warning cries, the porters lifting heavy packages on to the bellied roof of hansoms, the people running to and fro, the crowd of cabs; and driving out, he was exhilarated by the confusion in the station yard, and the intense life, half gay, half sordid, of the Wilton Road. He took a room in Jermyn Street, according to Major Forsyth's recommendation, and walked to his club. James had been out of London so long that he came back with the emotions of a stranger; common scenes, the glitter of shops, the turmoil of the Circus, affected him with pleased surprise, and with a child's amusement he paused to stare at the advertisements on a hoarding. He looked forward to seeing old friends, and on his way down Piccadilly even expected to meet one or two of them sauntering along.

As a matter of form, James asked at his club whether there were any letters for him.

"I don't think so, sir," said the porter, but turned to the pigeon-holes and took out a bundle. He looked them over, and then handed one to James.

"Hulloa, who's this from?"

Suddenly something gripped his heart; he felt the blood rush to his cheeks, and a cold tremor ran through all his limbs. He recognised the handwriting of Mrs. Pritchard-Wallace, and there was a penny stamp on the envelope. She was in England. The letter had been posted in London. He turned away and walked towards a table that stood near the window of the hall. A thousand recollections surged across his memory tumultuously; the paper was scented (how characteristic that was of her, and in what bad taste!); he saw at once her smile and the look of her eyes. He had a mad desire passionately to kiss the letter; a load of weariness fell from his heart; he felt insanely happy, as though angry storm-clouds had been torn asunder, and the sun in its golden majesty shone calmly upon the earth.... Then, with sudden impulse, he tore the unopened letter into a dozen pieces and threw them away. He straightened himself, and walked into the smoking-room.

James looked round and saw nobody he knew, quietly took a magazine from the table, and sat down; but the blood-vessels in his brain throbbed so violently that he thought something horrible would happen to him. He heard the regular, quick beating, like the implacable hammering of gnomes upon some hidden, distant anvil.

"She's in London," he repeated.

When had the letter been posted? At least, he might have looked at the mark on the envelope. Was it a year ago? Was it lately? The letter did not look as though it had been lying about the club for many months. Had it not still the odour of those dreadful Parma violets? She must have seen in the paper his return from Africa, wounded and ill. And what did she say? Did she merely write a few cold words of congratulation or—more?

It was terrible that after three years the mere sight of her handwriting should have power to throw him into this state of eager, passionate anguish. He was seized with the old panic, the terrified perception of his surrender, of his utter weakness, which made flight the only possible resistance. That was why he had destroyed the letter unread. When Mrs. Wallace was many thousand miles away there had been no danger in confessing that he loved her; but now it was different. What did she say in the letter? Had she in some feminine, mysterious fashion discovered his secret? Did she ask him to go and see her? James remembered one of their conversations.

"Oh, I love going to London!" she had cried, opening her arms with the charming, exotic gesticulation which distinguished her from all other women. "I enjoy myself awfully."

"What do you do?"

"Everything. And I write to poor Dick three times a week, and tell him all I haven't done."

"I can't bear the grass-widow," said James.

"Poor boy, you can't bear anything that's amusing! I never knew anyone with such an ideal of woman as you have—a gloomy mixture of frumpishness and angularity."

James did not answer.

"Don't you wish we were in London now?" she went on. "You and I together? I really believe I should have to take you about. You're as innocent as a babe."

"D'you think so?" said James, rather hurt.

"Now, if we were in town, on our own, what would you do?"

"Oh, I don't know. I suppose make a little party and dine somewhere, and go to the Savoy to see the 'Mikado.'"

Mrs. Wallace laughed.

"I know. A party of four—yourself and me, and two maiden aunts. And we should be very prim, and talk about the weather, and go in a growler for propriety's sake. I know that sort of evening. And after the maiden aunts had seen me safety home, I should simply howl from boredom. My dear boy, I'm respectable enough here. When I'm on my own, I want to go on the loose. Now, I'll tell you what I want to do if ever we are in town together. Will you promise to do it?"

"If I possibly can."

"All right! Well, you shall fetch me in the fastest hansom you can find, and remember to tell the driver to go as quick as ever he dare. We'll dine alone, please, at the most expensive restaurant in London! You'll engage a table in the middle of the room, and you must see that the people all round us are very smart and very shady. It always makes me feel so virtuous to look at disreputable women! Do I shock you?"

"Not more than usual."

"How absurd you are! Then we'll go to the Empire. And after that we'll go somewhere else, and have supper where the people are still smarter and still shadier; and then we'll go to Covent Garden Ball. Oh, you don't know how I long to go on the rampage sometimes! I get so tired of propriety."

"And what will P. W. say to all this?"

"Oh, I'll write and tell him that I spent the evening with some of his poor relations, and give eight pages of corroborative evidence."

James thought of Pritchard-Wallace, gentlest and best-humoured of men. He was a great big fellow, with a heavy moustache and kind eyes; always ready to stand by anyone in difficulties, always ready with comfort or with cheery advice; whoever wanted help went to him as though it were the most natural thing in the world. And it was touching to see the dog-like devotion to his wife; he had such confidence in her that he never noticed her numerous flirtations. Pritchard-Wallace thought himself rather a dull stick, and he wanted her to amuse herself. So brilliant a creature could not be expected to find sufficient entertainment in a quiet man of easy-going habits.

"Go your own way, my girl," he said; "I know you're all right. And so long as you keep a place for me in the bottom of your heart, you can do whatever you like."

"Of course, I don't care two straws for anyone but you, silly old thing!"

And she pulled his moustache and kissed his lips; and he went off on his business, his heart swelling with gratitude, because Providence had given him the enduring love of so beautiful and enchanting a little woman.

"P. W. is worth ten of you," James told her indignantly one day, when he had been witness to some audacious deception.

"Well, he doesn't think so. And that's the chief thing."

* * *

James dared not see her. It was obviously best to have destroyed the letter. After all, it was probably nothing more than a curt, formal congratulation, and its coldness would nearly have broken his heart. He feared also lest in his never-ceasing thought he had crystallised his beloved into something quite different from reality. His imagination was very active, and its constant play upon those few recollections might easily have added many a false delight. To meet Mrs. Wallace would only bring perhaps a painful disillusion; and of that James was terrified, for without this passion which occupied his whole soul he would be now singularly alone in the world. It was a fantastic, charming figure that he had made for himself, and he could worship it without danger and without reproach. Was it not better to preserve his dream from the sullen irruption of fact? But why would that perfume come perpetually entangling itself with his memory? It gave the image new substance; and when he closed his eyes, the woman seemed so near that he could feel against his face the fragrance of her breath.

He dined alone, and spent the hours that followed in reading. By some chance he was able to find no one he knew, and he felt rather bored. He went to bed with a headache, feeling already the dreariness of London without friends.

Next morning James wandered in the Park, fresh and delightful with the rhododendrons; but the people he saw hurt him by their almost aggressive happiness—vivacious, cheerful, and careless, they were all evidently of opinion that no reasonable creature could complain with the best of all possible worlds. The girls that hurried past on ponies, or on bicycles up and down the well-kept road, gave him an impression of light-heartedness which was fascinating, yet made his own solitude more intolerable. Their cheeks glowed with healthiness in the summer air, and their gestures, their laughter, were charmingly animated. He noticed the smile which a slender Amazon gave to a man who raised his hat, and read suddenly in their eyes a happy, successful tenderness. Once, galloping towards him, he saw a woman who resembled Mrs. Wallace, and his heart stood still. He had an intense longing to behold her just once more, unseen of her; but he was mistaken. The rider approached and passed, and it was no one he knew.

Then, tired and sore at heart, James went back to his club. The day passed monotonously, and the day after he was seized by the peculiar discomfort of the lonely sojourner in great cities. The thronging, busy crowd added to his solitariness. When he saw acquaintances address one another in the club, or walk along the streets in conversation, he could hardly bear his own friendlessness; the interests of all these people seemed so fixed and circumscribed, their lives were already so full, that they could only look upon a new-comer with hostility. He would have felt less lonely on a desert island than in the multitudinous city, surrounded by hurrying strangers. He scarcely knew how he managed to drag through the day, tired of the eternal smoking-room, tired of wandering about. The lodgings which Major Forsyth had recommended were like barracks; a tall, narrow house, in which James had a room at the top, looking on to a blank wall. They were dreadfully cheerless. And as James climbed the endless stairs he felt an irritation at the joyous laughter that came from other rooms. Behind those closed, forbidding doors people were happy and light of heart; only he was alone, and must remain perpetually imprisoned within himself. He went to the theatre, but here again, half insanely, he felt a barrier between himself and the rest of the audience. For him the piece offered no illusions; he could only see painted actors strutting affectedly in unnatural costumes; the scenery was mere painted cloth, and the dialogue senseless inanity. With all his might James wished that he were again in Africa, with work to do and danger to encounter. There the solitude was never lonely, and the nights were blue and silent, rich with the countless stars.

He had been in London a week. One day, towards evening, while he walked down Piccadilly, looking aimlessly at the people and asking himself what their inmost thoughts could be, he felt a hand on his shoulder, and a cheery voice called out his name.

"I knew it was you, Parsons! Where the devil have you sprung from?"

He turned round and saw a man he had known in India. Jamie's solitude and boredom had made him almost effusive.

"By Jove, I am glad to see you!" he said, wringing the fellow's hand. "Come and have a drink. I've seen no one for days, and I'm dying to have some one to talk to."

"I think I can manage it. I've got a train to catch at eight; I'm just off to Scotland."

Jamie's face fell.

"I was going to ask you to dine with me."

"I'm awfully sorry! I'm afraid I can't."

They talked of one thing and another, till Jamie's friend said he must go immediately; they shook hands.

"Oh, by the way," said the man, suddenly remembering, "I saw a pal of yours the other day, who's clamouring for you."

"For me?"

James reddened, knowing at once, instinctively, that it could only be one person.

"D'you remember Mrs. Pritchard-Wallace? She's in London. I saw her at a party, and she asked me if I knew anything about you. She's staying in Half Moon Street, at 201. You'd better go and see her. Good-bye! I must simply bolt."

He left James hurriedly, and did not notice the effect of his few words.... She still thought of him, she asked for him, she wished him to go to her. The gods in their mercy had sent him the address; with beating heart and joyful step, James immediately set out. The throng in his way vanished, and he felt himself walking along some roadway of ethereal fire, straight to his passionate love—a roadway miraculously fashioned for his feet, leading only to her. Every thought left him but that the woman he adored was waiting, waiting, ready to welcome him with that exquisite smile, with the hands which were like the caresses of Aphrodite, turned to visible flesh. But he stopped short.

"What's the good?" he cried, bitterly.

Before him the sun was setting like a vision of love, colouring with softness and with quiet the manifold life of the city. James looked at it, his heart swelling with sadness; for with it seemed to die his short joy, and the shadows lengthening were like the sad facts of reality which crept into his soul one by one silently.

"I won't go," he cried; "I daren't! Oh, God help me, and give me strength!"

He turned into the Green Park, where lovers sat entwined upon the benches, and in the pleasant warmth the idlers and the weary slept upon the grass. James sank heavily upon a seat, and gave himself over to his wretchedness.

The night fell, and the lamps upon Piccadilly were lit, and in the increasing silence the roar of London sounded more intensely. From the darkness, as if it were the scene of a play, James watched the cabs and 'buses pass rapidly in the light, the endless procession of people like disembodied souls drifting aimlessly before the wind. It was a comfort and a relief to sit there unseen, under cover of the night. He observed the turmoil with a new, disinterested curiosity, feeling strangely as if he were no longer among the living. He found himself surprised that they thought it worth while to hurry and to trouble. The couples on the benches remained in silent ecstasy; and sometimes a dark figure slouched past, sorrowful and mysterious.

At last James went out, surprised to find it was so late. The theatres had disgorged their crowds, and Piccadilly was thronged, gay, vivacious, and insouciant. For a moment there was a certain luxury about its vice; the harlot gained the pompousness of a Roman courtesan, and the vulgar debauchee had for a little while the rich, corrupt decadence of art and splendour.

James turned into Half Moon Street, which now was all deserted and silent, and walked slowly, with anguish tearing at his heart, towards the house in which lodged Mrs. Wallace. One window was still lit, and he wondered whether it was hers; it would have been an exquisite pleasure if he could but have seen her form pass the drawn blind. Ah, he could not have mistaken it! Presently the light was put out, and the whole house was in darkness. He waited on, for no reason—pleased to be near her. He waited half the night, till he was so tired he could scarcely drag himself home.

In the morning James was ill and tired, and disillusioned; his head ached so that he could hardly bear the pain, and in all his limbs he felt a strange and heavy lassitude. He wondered why he had troubled himself about the woman who cared nothing—nothing whatever for him. He repeated about her the bitter, scornful things he had said so often. He fancied he had suddenly grown indifferent.

"I shall go back to Primpton," he said; "London is too horrible."

XVIII

The lassitude and the headache explained themselves, for the day after Jamie's arrival at Little Primpton he fell ill, and the doctor announced that he had enteric fever. He explained that it was not uncommon for persons to develop the disease after their return from the Cape. In their distress, the first thought of Mrs. Parsons and the Colonel was to send for Mary; they knew her to be quick and resourceful.

"Dr. Radley says we must have a nurse down. Jamie is never to be left alone, and I couldn't manage by myself."

Mary hesitated and reddened:

"Oh, I wish Jamie would let me nurse him! You and I could do everything much better than a strange woman. D'you think he'd mind?"

Mrs. Parsons looked at her doubtfully.

"It's very kind of you, Mary. I'm afraid he's not treated you so as to deserve that. And it would exhaust you dreadfully."

"I'm very strong; I should like it so much. Won't you ask Jamie? He can only refuse."

"Very well."

Mrs. Parsons went up to her son, by whom sat the Colonel, looking at him wistfully. James lay on his back, breathing quickly, dull, listless, and apathetic. Every now and then his dark dry lips contracted as the unceasing pain of his head became suddenly almost insufferable.

"Jamie, dear," said Mrs. Parsons, "Dr. Radley says you must have a second nurse, and we thought of getting one from Tunbridge Wells. Would you mind if Mary came instead?"

James opened his eyes, bright and unnatural, and the dilated pupils gave them a strangely piercing expression.

"Does she want to?"

"It would make her very happy."

"Does she know that enteric is horrid to nurse?"

"For your sake she will do everything willingly."

"Then let her." He smiled faintly. "It's an ill wind that blows nobody good. That's what the curate said."

He had sufficient strength to smile to Mary when she came up, and to stretch out his hand.

"It's very good of you, Mary."

"Nonsense!" she said, cheerily. "You mustn't talk. And you must do whatever I tell you, and let yourself be treated like a little boy."

For days James remained in the same condition, with aching head, his face livid in its pallor, except for the bright, the terrifying flush of the cheeks; and the lips were dark with the sickly darkness of death. He lay on his back continually, apathetic and listless, his eyes closed. Now and again he opened them, and their vacant brilliancy was almost unearthly. He seemed to see horrible things, impossible to prevent, staring in front of him with the ghastly intensity of the blind.

Meanwhile, Mrs. Parsons and Mary nursed him devotedly. Mary was quite splendid. In her loving quickness she forestalled all Jamie's wants, so that they were satisfied almost before he had realised them. She was always bright and good-tempered and fresh; she performed with constant cheerfulness the little revolting services which the disease necessitates; nothing was too difficult, or too harassing, or too unpleasant for her to do. She sacrificed herself with delight, taking upon her shoulders the major part of the work, leaving James only when Mrs. Parsons forced her to rest. She sat up night after night uncomplainingly; having sent for her clothes, and, notwithstanding Mrs. Clibborn's protests, taken up her abode altogether at Primpton House.

Mrs. Clibborn said it was a most improper proceeding; that a trained nurse would be more capable, and the Parsons could well afford it; and also that it was indelicate for Mary to force herself upon James when he was too ill to defend himself.

"I don't know what we should do without you, Mary," said Colonel Parsons, with tears in his eyes. "If we save him it will be your doing."

"Of course we shall save him! All I ask you is to say nothing of what I've done. It's been a pleasure to me to serve him, and I don't deserve, and I don't want, gratitude."

But it became more than doubtful whether it would be possible to save James, weakened by his wound and by the privations of the campaign. The disease grew worse. He was constantly delirious, and his prostration extreme. His cheeks sank in, and he seemed to have lost all power of holding himself together; he lay low down in the bed, as if he had given up trying to save himself. His face became dusky, so that it was terrifying to look upon.

The doctor could no longer conceal his anxiety, and at last Mrs. Parsons, alone with him, insisted upon knowing the truth.

"Is there any chance?" she asked, tremulously. "I would much rather know the worst."

"I'm afraid very, very little."

Mrs. Parsons shook hands silently with Dr. Radley and returned to the sick room, where Mary and the Colonel were sitting at the bedside.

"Well?"

Mrs. Parsons bent her head, and the silent tears rolled down her cheeks. The others understood only too well.

"The Lord's will be done," whispered the father. "Blessed be the name of the Lord!"

They looked at James with aching hearts. All their bitterness had long gone, and they loved him again with the old devotion of past time.

"D'you think I was hard on him, dear?" said the Colonel.

Mary took his hand and held it affectionately.

"Don't worry about that," she said. "I'm sure he never felt any bitterness towards you."

James now was comatose. But sometimes a reflex movement would pass through him, a sort of quiver, which seemed horribly as though the soul were parting from his body; and feebly he clutched at the bed-clothes.

"Was it for this that he was saved from war and pestilence?" muttered the Colonel, hopelessly.

* * *

But the Fates love nothing better than to mock the poor little creatures whose destinies ceaselessly they weave, refusing the wretched heart's desire till long waiting has made it listless, and giving with both hands only when the gift entails destruction.... James did not die; the passionate love of those three persons who watched him day by day and night by night seemed to have exorcised the might of Death. He grew a little better; his vigorous frame battled for life with all the force of that unknown mysterious power which cements into existence the myriad wandering atoms. He was listless, indifferent to the issue; but the will to live fought for him, and he grew better. Quickly he was out of danger.

His father and Mary and Mrs. Parsons looked at one another almost with surprise, hardly daring to believe that they had saved him. They had suffered so much, all three of them, that they hesitated to trust their good fortune, superstitiously fearing that if they congratulated themselves too soon, some dreadful thing would happen to plunge back their beloved into deadly danger. But at last he was able to get up, to sit in the garden, now luxuriant with the ripe foliage of August; and they felt the load of anxiety gradually lift itself from their shoulders. They ventured again to laugh, and to talk of little trivial things, and of the future. They no longer had that panic terror when they looked at him, pale and weak and emaciated.

Then again the old couple thanked Mary for what she had done; and one day, in secret, went off to Tunbridge Wells to buy a little present as a proof of their gratitude. Colonel Parsons suggested a bracelet, but his wife was sure that Mary would prefer something useful; so they brought back with them a very elaborate and expensive writing-case, which with a few shy words they presented to her. Mary, poor thing, was overcome with pleasure.

"It's awfully good of you," she said. "I've done nothing that I wouldn't have done for any of the cottagers."

"We know it was you who saved him. You—you snatched him from the very jaws of Death."

Mary paused, and held out her hand.

"Will you promise me one thing?"

"What is it?" asked Colonel Parsons, unwilling to give his word rashly.

"Well, promise that you will never tell James that he owes anything to me. I couldn't bear him to think I had forced myself on him so as to have a sort of claim. Please promise me that."

"I should never be able to keep it!" cried the Colonel.

"I think she's right, Richmond. We'll promise, Mary. Besides, James can't help knowing."

The hopes of the dear people were reviving, and they began to look upon Jamie's illness, piously, as a blessing of Providence in disguise. While Mrs. Parsons was about her household work in the morning, the Colonel would sometimes come in, rubbing his hands gleefully.

"I've been watching them from the kitchen garden," he said.

James lay on a long chair, in a sheltered, shady place, and Mary sat beside him, reading aloud or knitting.

"Oh, you shouldn't have done that, Richmond," said his wife, with an indulgent smile, "it's very cruel."

"I couldn't help it, my dear. They're sitting there together just like a pair of turtle-doves."

"Are they talking or reading?"

"She's reading to him, and he's looking at her. He never takes his eyes off her."

Mrs. Parsons sighed with a happy sadness.

"God is very good to us, Richmond."

* * *

James was surprised to find how happily he could spend his days with Mary. He was carried into the garden as soon as he got up, and remained there most of the day. Mary, as ever, was untiring in her devotion, thoughtful, anxious to obey his smallest whim.... He saw very soon the thoughts which were springing up again in the minds of his father and mother, intercepting the little significant glances which passed between them when Mary went away on some errand and he told her not to be long, when they exchanged gentle chaff, or she arranged the cushions under his head. The neighbours had asked to visit him, but this he resolutely declined, and appealed to Mary for protection.

"I'm quite happy alone here with you, and if anyone else comes I swear I'll fall ill again."

And with a little flush of pleasure and a smile, Mary answered that she would tell them all he was very grateful for their sympathy, but didn't feel strong enough to see them.

"I don't feel a bit grateful, really," he said.

"Then you ought to."

Her manner was much gentler now that James was ill, and her rigid moral sense relaxed a little in favour of his weakness. Mary's common sense became less aggressive, and if she was practical and unimaginative as ever, she was less afraid than before of giving way to him. She became almost tolerant, allowing him little petulances and little evasions—petty weaknesses which in complete health she would have felt it her duty not to compromise with. She treated him like a child, with whom it was possible to be indulgent without a surrender of principle; he could still claim to be spoiled and petted, and made much of.

And James found that he could look forward with something like satisfaction to the condition of things which was evolving. He did not doubt that if he proposed to Mary again, she would accept him, and all their difficulties would be at an end. After all, why not? He was deeply touched by the loving, ceaseless care she had taken of him; indeed, no words from his father were needed to make him realise what she had gone through. She was kindness itself, tender, considerate, cheerful; he felt an utter prig to hesitate. And now that he had got used to her again, James was really very fond of Mary. In his physical weakness, her strength was peculiarly comforting. He could rely upon her entirely, and trust her; he admired her rectitude and her truthfulness. She reminded him of a granite cross standing alone in a desolate Scotch island, steadfast to wind and weather, unyielding even to time, erect and stern, and yet somehow pathetic in its solemn loneliness.

Was it a lot of nonsense that he had thought about the immaculacy of the flesh? The world in general found his theories ridiculous or obscene. The world might be right. After all, the majority is not necessarily wrong. Jamie's illness interfered like a blank space between his present self and the old one, with its strenuous ideals of a purity of body which vulgar persons knew nothing of. Weak and ill, dependent upon the strength of others, his former opinions seemed singularly uncertain. How much more easy and comfortable was it to fall back upon the ideas of all and sundry? One cannot help being a little conscience-stricken sometimes when one thinks differently from others. That is why society holds together; conscience is its most efficient policeman. But when one shares common opinions, the whole authority of civilisation backs one up, and the reward is an ineffable self-complacency. It is the easiest thing possible to wallow in the prejudices of all the world, and the most eminently satisfactory. For nineteen hundred years we have learnt that the body is shameful, a pitfall and a snare to the soul. It is to be hoped we have one, for our bodies, since we began worrying about our souls, leave much to be desired. The common idea is that the flesh is beastly, the spirit divine; and it sounds reasonable enough. If it means little, one need not care, for the world has turned eternally to one senseless formula after another. All one can be sure about is that in the things of this world there is no absolute certainty.

James, in his prostration, felt only indifference; and his old strenuousness, with its tragic despair, seemed not a little ridiculous. His eagerness to keep clean from what he thought prostitution was melodramatic and silly, his idea of purity mere foolishness. If the body was excrement, as from his youth he had been taught, what could it matter how one used it! Did anything matter, when a few years would see the flesh he had thought divine corrupt and worm-eaten? James was willing now to float along the stream, sociably, with his fellows, and had no doubt that he would soon find a set of high-sounding phrases to justify his degradation. What importance could his actions have, who was an obscure unit in an ephemeral race? It was much better to cease troubling, and let things come as they would. People were obviously right when they said that Mary must be an excellent helpmate. How often had he not told himself that she would be all that a wife should—kind, helpful, trustworthy. Was it not enough?

And his marriage would give such pleasure to his father and mother, such happiness to Mary. If he could make a little return for all her goodness, was he not bound to do so? He smiled with bitter scorn at his dead, lofty ideals. The workaday world was not fit for them; it was much safer and easier to conform oneself to its terrestrial standard. And the amusing part of it was that these new opinions which seemed to him a falling away, to others meant precisely the reverse. They thought it purer and more ethereal that a man should marry because a woman would be a housekeeper of good character than because the divine instincts of Nature irresistibly propelled him.

James shrugged his shoulders, and turned to look at Mary, who was coming towards him with letters in her hand.

"Three letters for you, Jamie!"

"Whom are they from?"

"Look." She handed him one.

"That's a bill, I bet," he said. "Open it and see."

She opened and read out an account for boots.

"Throw it away."

Mary opened her eyes.

"It must be paid, Jamie."

"Of course it must; but not for a long time yet. Let him send it in a few times more. Now the next one."

He looked at the envelope, and did not recognise the handwriting.

"You can open that, too."

It was from the Larchers, repeating their invitation to go and see them.

"I wonder if they're still worrying about the death of their boy?"

"Oh, well, it's six months ago, isn't it?" replied Mary.

"I suppose in that time one gets over most griefs. I must go over some day. Now the third."

He reddened slightly, recognising again the handwriting of Mrs. Wallace. But this time it affected him very little; he was too weak to care, and he felt almost indifferent.

"Shall I open it?" said Mary.

James hesitated.

"No," he said; "tear it up." And then in reply to her astonishment, he added, smiling: "It's all right, I'm not off my head. Tear it up, and don't ask questions, there's a dear!"

"Of course, I'll tear it up if you want me to," said Mary, looking rather perplexed.

"Now, go to the hedge and throw the pieces in the field."

She did so, and sat down again.

"Shall I read to you?"

"No, I'm sick of the 'Antiquary.' Why the goodness they can't talk English like rational human beings, Heaven only knows!"

"Well, we must finish it now we've begun."

"D'you think something dreadful will happen to us if we don't?"

"If one begins a book I think one should finish it, however dull it is. One is sure to get some good out of it."

"My dear, you're a perfect monster of conscientiousness."

"Well, if you don't want me to read, I shall go on with my knitting."

"I don't want you to knit either. I want you to talk to me."

Mary looked almost charming in the subdued light of the sun as it broke through the leaves, giving a softness of expression and a richness of colour that James had never seen in her before. And the summer frock she wore made her more girlish and irresponsible than usual.

"You've been very, very good to me all this time, Mary," said James, suddenly.

Mary flushed. "I?"

"I can never thank you enough."

"Nonsense! Your father has been telling you a lot of rubbish, and he promised he wouldn't."

"No, he's said nothing. Did you make him promise? That was very nice, and just like you."

"I was afraid he'd say more than he ought."

"D'you think I haven't been able to see for myself? I owe my life to you."

"You owe it to God, Jamie."

He smiled, and took her hand.

"I'm very, very grateful!"

"It's been a pleasure to nurse you, Jamie. I never knew you'd make such a good patient."

"And for all you've done, I've made you wretched and miserable. Can you ever forgive me?"

"There's nothing to forgive, dear. You know I always think of you as a brother."

"Ah, that's what you told the curate!" cried James, laughing.

Mary reddened.

"How d'you know?"

"He told Mrs. Jackson, and she told father."

"You're not angry with me?"

"I think you might have made it second cousin," said James, with a smile.

Mary did not answer, but tried to withdraw her hand. He held it fast.

"Mary, I've treated you vilely. If you don't hate me, it's only because you're a perfect angel."

Mary looked down, blushing deep red.

"I can never hate you," she whispered.

"Oh, Mary, can you forgive me? Can you forget? It sounds almost impertinent to ask you again—Will you marry me, Mary?"

She withdrew her hand.

"It's very kind of you, Jamie. You're only asking me out of gratitude, because I've helped a little to look after you. But I want no gratitude; it was all pleasure. And I'm only too glad that you're getting well."

"I'm perfectly in earnest, Mary. I wouldn't ask you merely from gratitude. I know I have humiliated you dreadfully, and I have done my best to kill the love you had for me. But I really honestly love you now—with all my heart. If you still care for me a little, I beseech you not to dismiss me."

"If I still care for you!" cried Mary, hoarsely. "Oh, my God!"

"Mary, forgive me! I want you to marry me."

She looked at him distractedly, the fire burning through her heart. He took both her hands and drew her towards him.

"Mary, say yes."

She sank helplessly to her knees beside him.

"It would make me very happy," she murmured, with touching humility.

Then he bent forward and kissed her tenderly.

"Let's go and tell them," he said. "They'll be so pleased."

Mary, smiling and joyful, helped him to his feet, and supporting him as best she could, they went towards the house.

Colonel Parsons was sitting in the dining-room, twirling his old Panama in a great state of excitement; he had interrupted his wife at her accounts, and she was looking at him good-humouredly over her spectacles.

"I'm sure something's happening," he said. "I went out to take Jamie his beef-tea, and he was holding Mary's hand. I coughed as loud as I could, but they took no notice at all. So I thought I'd better not disturb them."

"Here they come," said Mrs. Parsons.

"Mother," said James, "Mary has something to tell you."

"I haven't anything of the sort!" cried Mary, blushing and laughing. "Jamie has something to tell you."

"Well, the fact is, I've asked Mary to marry me and she's said she would."

XIX

James was vastly relieved. His people's obvious delight, Mary's quiet happiness, were very grateful to him, and if he laughed at himself a little for feeling so virtuous, he could not help thoroughly enjoying the pleasure he had given. He was willing to acknowledge now that his conscience had been uneasy after the rupture of his engagement: although he had assured himself so vehemently that reason was upon his side, the common disapproval, and the influence of all his bringing-up, had affected him in his own despite.

"When shall we get married, Mary?" he asked, when the four of them were sitting together in the garden.

"Quickly!" cried Colonel Parsons.

"Well, shall we say in a month, or six weeks?"

"D'you think you'll be strong enough?" replied Mary, looking affectionately at him. And then, blushing a little: "I can get ready very soon."

The night before, she had gone home and taken out the trousseau which with tears had been put away. She smoothed out the things, unfolded them, and carefully folded them up. Never in her life had she possessed such dainty linen. Mary cried a while with pleasure to think that she could begin again to collect her little store. No one knew what agony it had been to write to the shops at Tunbridge Wells countermanding her orders, and now she looked forward with quiet delight to buying all that remained to get.

Finally, it was decided that the wedding should take place at the beginning of October. Mrs. Parsons wrote to her brother, who answered that he had expected the event all along, being certain that his conversation with James would eventually bear fruit. He was happy to be able to congratulate himself on the issue of his diplomacy; it was wonderful how easily all difficulties were settled, if one took them from the point of view of a man of the world. Mrs. Jackson likewise flattered herself that the renewed engagement was due to her intervention.

"I saw he was paying attention to what I said," she told her husband. "I knew all he wanted was a good, straight talking to."

"I am sorry for poor Dryland," said the Vicar.

"Yes, I think we ought to do our best to console him. Don't you think he might go away for a month, Archibald?"

Mr. Dryland came to tea, and the Vicar's wife surrounded him with little attentions. She put an extra lump of sugar in his tea, and cut him even a larger piece of seed-cake than usual.

"Of course you've heard, Mr. Dryland?" she said, solemnly.

"Are you referring to Miss Clibborn's engagement to Captain Parsons?" he asked, with a gloomy face. "Bad news travels fast."

"You have all our sympathies. We did everything we could for you."

"I can't deny that it's a great blow to me. I confess I thought that time and patience on my part might induce Miss Clibborn to change her mind. But if she's happy, I cannot complain. I must bear my misfortune with resignation."

"But will she be happy?" asked Mrs. Jackson, with foreboding in her voice.

"I sincerely hope so. Anyhow, I think it my duty to go to Captain Parsons and offer him my congratulations."

"Will you do that, Mr. Dryland?" cried Mrs. Jackson. "That is noble of you!"

"If you'd like to take your holiday now, Dryland," said the Vicar, "I daresay we can manage it."

"Oh, no, thanks; I'm not the man to desert from the field of battle."

Mrs. Jackson sighed.

"Things never come right in this world. That's what I always say; the clergy are continually doing deeds of heroism which the world never hears anything about."

The curate went to Primpton House and inquired whether he might see Captain Parsons.

"I'll go and ask if he's well enough," answered the Colonel, with his admirable respect for the cloth.

"Do you think he wants to talk to me about my soul?" asked James, smiling.

"I don't know; but I think you'd better see him."

"Very well."

Mr. Dryland came forward and shook hands with James in an ecclesiastical and suave manner, trying to be dignified, as behoved a rejected lover in the presence of his rival, and at the same time cordial, as befitted a Christian who could bear no malice.

"Captain Parsons, you will not be unaware that I asked Miss Clibborn to be my wife?"

"The fact was fairly generally known in the village," replied James, trying to restrain a smile.

Mr. Dryland blushed.

"I was annoyed at the publicity which the circumstance obtained. The worst of these little places is that people will talk."

"It was a very noble deed," said James gravely, repeating the common opinion.

"Not at all," answered the curate, with characteristic modesty. "But since it was not to be, since Miss Clibborn's choice has fallen on you, I think it my duty to inform you of my hearty goodwill. I wish, in short, to offer you again my sincerest congratulations."

"I'm sure that's very kind of you."

* * *

Two days, later Mrs. Jackson called on a similar errand.

She tripped up to James and frankly held out her hand, neatly encased as ever in a shining black kid glove.

"Captain Parsons, let us shake hands, and let bygones be bygones. You have taken my advice, and if, in the heat of the moment, we both said things which we regret, after all, we're only human."

"Surely, Mrs. Jackson, I was moderation itself?—even when you told me I should infallibly go to Hell."

"You were extremely irritating," said the Vicar's lady, smiling, "but I forgive you. After all, you paid more attention to what I said than I expected you would."

"It must be very satisfactory for you to think that."

"You know I have no ill-feeling towards you at all. I gave you a piece of my mind because I thought it was my duty. If you think I stepped over the limits of—moderation, I am willing and ready to apologise."

"What a funny woman you are!" said James, looking at her with a good-humoured, but rather astonished smile.

"I'm sure I don't know what makes you think so," she answered, bridling a little.

"It never occurred to me that you honestly thought you were acting rightly when you came and gave me a piece of your mind, as you call it. I thought your motives were simply malicious and uncharitable."

"I have a very high ideal of my duties as a clergyman's wife."

"The human animal is very odd."

"I don't look upon myself as an animal, Captain Parsons."

James smiled.

"I wonder why we all torture ourselves so unnecessarily. It really seems as if the chief use we made of our reason was to inflict as much pain upon ourselves and upon one another as we possibly could."

"I'm sure I don't know what you mean, Captain Parsons."

"When you do anything, are you ever tormented by a doubt whether you are doing right or wrong?"

"Never," she answered, firmly. "There is always a right way and a wrong way, and, I'm thankful to say, God has given me sufficient intelligence to know which is which; and obviously I choose the right way."

"What a comfortable idea! I can never help thinking that every right way is partly wrong, and every wrong way partly right. There's always so much to be said on both sides; to me it's very hard to know which is which."

"Only a very weak man could think like that."

"Possibly! I have long since ceased to flatter myself on my strength of mind. I find it is chiefly a characteristic of unintelligent persons."

* * *

It was Mary's way to take herself seriously. It flattered her to think that she was not blind to Jamie's faults; she loved him none the less on their account, but determined to correct them. He had an unusual way of looking at things, and an occasional flippancy in his conversation, both of which she hoped in time to eradicate. With patience, gentleness, and dignity a woman can do a great deal with a man.

One of Mary's friends had a husband with a bad habit of swearing, which was cured in a very simple manner. Whenever he swore, his wife swore too. For instance, he would say: "That's a damned bad job;" and his wife answered, smiling: "Yes, damned bad." He was rather surprised, but quickly ceased to employ objectionable words. Story does not relate whether he also got out of the habit of loving his wife; but that, doubtless, is a minor detail. Mary always looked upon her friend as a pattern.

"James is not really cynical," she told herself. "He says things, not because he means them, but because he likes to startle people."

It was inconceivable that James should not think on all subjects as she had been brought up to do, and the least originality struck her naturally as a sort of pose. But on account of his illness Mary allowed him a certain latitude, and when he said anything she did not approve of, instead of arguing the point, merely smiled indulgently and changed the subject. There was plenty of time before her, and when James became her husband she would have abundant opportunity of raising him to that exalted level upon which she was so comfortably settled. The influence of a simple Christian woman could not fail to have effect; at bottom James was as good as gold, and she was clever enough to guide him insensibly along the right path.

James, perceiving this, scarcely knew whether to be incensed or amused. Sometimes he could see the humour in Mary's ingenuous conceit, and in the dogmatic assurance with which she uttered the most astounding opinions; but at others, when she waved aside superciliously a remark that did not square with her prejudices, or complacently denied a statement because she had never heard it before, he was irritated beyond all endurance. And it was nothing very outrageous he said, but merely some commonplace of science which all the world had accepted for twenty years. Mary, however, entrenched herself behind the impenetrable rock of her self-sufficiency.

"I'm not clever enough to argue with you," she said; "but I know I'm right; and I'm quite satisfied."

Generally she merely smiled.

"What nonsense you talk, Jamie! You don't really believe what you say."

"But, my dear Mary, it's a solemn fact. There's no possibility of doubting it. It's a truism."

Then with admirable self-command, remembering that James was still an invalid, she would pat his hand and say:

"Well, it doesn't matter. Of course, you're much cleverer than I am. It must be almost time for your beef-tea."

James sank back, baffled. Mary's ignorance was an impenetrable cuirass; she would not try to understand, she could not even realise that she might possibly be mistaken. Quite seriously she thought that what she ignored could be hardly worth knowing. People talk of the advance of education; there may be a little among the lower classes, but it is inconceivable that the English gentry can ever have been more illiterate than they are now. Throughout the country, in the comfortable villa or in the stately mansion, you will find as much prejudice and superstition in the drawing-room as in the kitchen; and you will find the masters less receptive of new ideas than their servants; and into the bargain, presumptuously satisfied with their own nescience.

James saw that the only way to deal with Mary and with his people was to give in to all their prejudices. He let them talk, and held his tongue. He shut himself off from them, recognising that there was, and could be, no bond between them. They were strangers to him; their ways of looking at every detail of life were different from his; they had not an interest, not a thought, in common.... The preparations for the marriage went on.

One day Mary decided that it was her duty to speak with James about his religion. Some of his remarks had made her a little uneasy, and he was quite strong enough now to be seriously dealt with.

"Tell me, Jamie," she said, in reply to an observation which she was pleased to consider flippant, "you do believe in God, don't you?"

But James had learnt his lesson well.

"My dear, that seems to me a private affair of my own."

"Are you ashamed to say?" she asked, gravely.

"No; but I don't see the advantage of discussing the matter."

"I think you ought to tell me as I'm going to be your wife. I shouldn't like you to be an atheist."

"Atheism is exploded, Mary. Only very ignorant persons are certain of what they cannot possibly know."

"Then I don't see why you should be afraid to tell me."

"I'm not; only I think you have no right to ask. We both think that in marriage each should leave the other perfect freedom. I used to imagine the ideal was that married folk should not have a thought, nor an idea apart; but that is all rot. The best thing is evidently for each to go his own way, and respect the privacy of the other. Complete trust entails complete liberty."

"I think that is certainly the noblest way of looking at marriage."

"You may be quite sure I shall not intrude upon *your* privacy, Mary."

"I'm sorry I asked you any question. I suppose it's no business of mine."

James returned to his book; he had fallen into the habit again of reading incessantly, finding therein his only release from the daily affairs of life; but when Mary left him, he let his novel drop and began to think. He was bitterly amused at what he had said. The parrot words which he had so often heard on Mary's lips sounded strangely on his own. He understood now why the view of matrimony had become prevalent that it was an institution in which two casual persons lived together, for the support of one and the material comfort of the other. Without love it was the most natural thing that husband and wife should seek all manner of protection from each other; with love none was needed. It harmonised well with the paradox that a marriage of passion was rather indecent, while lukewarm affection and paltry motives of convenience were elevating and noble.

Poor Mary! James knew that she loved him with all her soul, such as it was (a delicate conscience and a collection of principles are not enough to make a great lover), and again he acknowledged to himself that he could give her only friendship. It had been but an ephemeral tenderness which drew him to her for the second time, due to weakness of body and to gratitude. If he ever thought it was love, he knew by now that he had been mistaken. Still, what did it matter? He supposed they would get along very well—as well as most people; better even than if they adored one another; for passion is not conducive to an even life. Fortunately she was cold and reserved, little given to demonstrative affection; she made few demands upon him, and occupied with her work in the parish and the collection of her trousseau, was content that he should remain with his books.

The day fixed upon for the marriage came nearer.

But at last James was seized with a wild revolt. His father was sitting by him.

"Mary's wedding-dress is nearly ready," he said, suddenly.

"So soon?" cried James, his heart sinking.

"She's afraid that something may happen at the last moment, and it won't be finished in time."

"What could happen?"

"Oh, I mean something at the dressmaker's!"

"Is that all? I imagine there's little danger."

There was a pause, broken again by the Colonel.

"I'm so glad you're going to be happily married, Jamie."

His son did not answer.

"But man is never satisfied. I used to think that when I got you spliced, I should have nothing else to wish for; but now I'm beginning to want little grandsons to rock upon my knees."

Jamie's face grew dark.

"We should never be able to afford children."

"But they come if one wants them or not, and I shall be able to increase your allowance a little, you know. I don't want you to go short of anything."

James said nothing, but he thought: "If I had children by her, I should hate them." And then with sudden dismay, losing all the artificial indifference of the last week, he rebelled passionately against his fate. "Oh, I hate and loathe her!"

He felt he could no longer continue the pretence he had been making—for it was all pretence. The effort to be loving and affectionate was torture, so that all his nerves seemed to vibrate with exasperation. Sometimes he had to clench his hands in order to keep himself under restraint. He was acting all the time. James asked himself what madness blinded Mary that she did not see? He remembered how easily speech had come in the old days when they were boy and girl together; they could pass hours side by side, without a thought of time, talking of little insignificant things, silent often, and always happy. But now he racked his brain for topics of conversation, and the slightest pause seemed irksome and unnatural. He was sometimes bored to death, savagely, cruelly; so that he was obliged to leave Mary for fear that he would say bitter and horrible things. Without his books he would have gone mad. She must be blind not to see. Then he thought of their married life. How long would it last? The years stretched themselves out endlessly, passing one after another in dreary monotony. Could they possibly be happy? Sooner or later Mary would learn how little he cared for her, and what agony must she suffer then! But it was inevitable. Now, whatever happened, he could not draw back; it was too late for explanations. Would love come? He felt it impossible; he felt, rather, that the physical repulsion which vainly he tried to crush would increase till he abhorred the very sight of his wife.

Passionately he cried out against Fate because he had escaped death so often. The gods played with him as a cat plays with a mouse. He had been through dangers innumerable; twice he had lain on the very threshold of eternal night, and twice he had been snatched back. Far rather would he have died the soldier's death, gallantly, than live on to this humiliation and despair. A friendly bullet could have saved him many difficulties and much unhappiness. And why had he recovered from the fever? What an irony it was that Mary should claim gratitude for doing him the greatest possible disservice!

"I can't help it," he cried; "I loathe her!"

The strain upon him was becoming intolerable. James felt that he could not much longer conceal the anguish which was destroying him. But what was to be done? Nothing! Nothing! Nothing!

James held his head in his hands, cursing his pitiful weakness. Why did he not realise, in his convalescence, that it was but a passing emotion which endeared Mary to him? He had been so anxious to love her, so eager to give happiness to all concerned, that he had welcomed the least sign of affection; but he knew what love was, and there could be no excuse. He should have had the courage to resist his gratitude.

"Why should I sacrifice myself?" he cried. "My life is as valuable as theirs. Why should it be always I from whom sacrifice is demanded?"

But it was no use rebelling. Mary's claims were too strong, and if he lived he must satisfy them. Yet some respite he could not do without; away from Primpton he might regain his calm. James hated London, but even that would be better than the horrible oppression, the constraint he was forced to put upon himself.

He walked up and down the garden for a few minutes to calm down, and went in to his mother. He spoke as naturally as he could.

"Father tells me that Mary's wedding-dress is nearly ready."

"Yes; it's a little early. But it's well to be on the safe side."

"It's just occurred to me that I can hardly be married in rags. I think I had better go up to town for a few days to get some things."

"Must you do that?"

"I think so. And there's a lot I want to do."

"Oh, well, I daresay Mary won't mind, if you don't stay too long. But you must take care not to tire yourself."

XX

On his second visit to London, James was more fortunate, for immediately he got inside his club he found an old friend, a man named Barker, late adjutant of his regiment. Barker had a great deal to tell James of mutual acquaintance, and the pair dined together, going afterwards to a music-hall. James felt in better spirits than for some time past, and his good humour carried him well into the following day. In the afternoon, while he was reading a paper, Barker came up to him.

"I say, old chap," he said, "I quite forgot to tell you yesterday. You remember Mrs. Wallace, don't you—Pritchard, of that ilk? She's in town, and in a passion with you. She says she's written to you twice, and you've taken no notice."

"Really? I thought nobody was in town now."

"She is; I forget why. She told me a long story, but I didn't listen, as I knew it would be mostly fibs. She's probably up to some mischief. Let's go round to her place and have tea, shall we?"

"I hardly think I can," replied James, reddening. "I've got an engagement at four."

"Rot—come on! She's just as stunning as ever. By Gad, you should have seen her in her weeds!"

"In her weeds! What the devil do you mean?"

"Didn't you know? P. W. was bowled over at the beginning of the war—after Colenso, I think."

"By God!—I didn't know. I never saw!"

"Oh, well, I didn't know till I came home.... Let's stroll along, shall we? She's looking out for number two; but she wants money, so there's no danger for us!"

James rose mechanically, and putting on his hat, accompanied Barker, all unwitting of the thunder-blow that his words had been.... Mrs. Wallace was at home. James went upstairs, forgetting everything but that the woman he loved was free—free! His heart beat so that he could scarcely breathe; he was afraid of betraying his agitation, and had to make a deliberate effort to contain himself.

Mrs. Wallace gave a little cry of surprise on seeing James.... She had not changed. The black gown she wore, fashionable, but slightly fantastic, set off the dazzling olive clearness of her skin and the rich colour of her hair. James turned pale with the passion that consumed him; he could hardly speak.

"You wretch!" she cried, her eyes sparkling, "I've written to you twice—once to congratulate you, and then to ask you to come and see me—and you took not the least notice."

"Barker has just told me you wrote. I am so sorry."

"Oh, well, I thought you might not receive the letters. I'll forgive you."

She wore Indian anklets on her wrists and a barbaric chain about her neck, so that even in the London lodging-house she preserved a mysterious Oriental charm. In her movements there was a sinuous feline grace which was delightful, and yet rather terrifying. One fancied that she was not quite human, but some cruel animal turned into the likeness of a woman. Vague stories floated through the mind of Lamia, and the unhappy end of her lovers.

The three of them began to talk, chattering of the old days in India, of the war. Mrs. Wallace bemoaned her fate in having to stay in town when all smart people had left. Barker told stories. James did not know how he joined in the flippant conversation; he wondered at his self-command in saying insignificant things, in laughing heartily, when his whole soul was in a turmoil. At length the adjutant went away, and James was left alone with Mrs. Wallace.

"D'you wish me to go?" he asked. "You can turn me out if you do."

"Oh, I should—without hesitation," she retorted, laughing; "but I'm bored to death, and I want you to amuse me."

Strangely enough, James felt that the long absence had created no barrier between them. Thinking of Mrs. Wallace incessantly, sometimes against his will, sometimes with a fierce delight, holding with her imaginary conversations, he felt, on the contrary, that he knew her far more intimately than he had ever done. There seemed to be a link between them, as though something had passed which prevented them from ever again becoming strangers. James felt he had her confidence, and he was able to talk frankly as before, in his timidity, he had never ventured. He treated her with the loving friendliness with which he had been used to treat the imaginary creature of his dreams.

"You haven't changed a bit," he said, looking at her.

"Did you expect me to be haggard and wrinkled? I never let myself grow old. One only needs strength of mind to keep young indefinitely."

"I'm surprised, because you're so exactly as I've thought of you."

"Have you thought of me often?"

The fire flashed to Jamie's eyes, and it was on his lips to break out passionately, telling her how he had lived constantly with her recollection, how she had been meat and drink to him, life, and breath, and soul; but he restrained himself.

"Sometimes," he answered, smiling.

Mrs. Wallace smiled, too.

"I seem to remember that you vowed once to think of me always."

"One vows all sorts of things." He hoped she could not hear the trembling in his voice.

"You're very cool, friend Jim—and much less shy than you used to be. You were a perfect monster of bashfulness, and your conscience was a most alarming animal. It used to frighten me out of my wits; I hope you keep it now under lock and key, like the beasts in the Zoo."

James was telling himself that it was folly to remain, that he must go at once and never return. The recollection of Mary came back to him, in the straw hat and the soiled serge dress, sitting in the dining-room with his father and mother; she had brought her knitting so as not to waste a minute; and while they talked of him, her needles clicked rapidly to and fro. Mrs. Wallace was lying in a long chair, coiled up in a serpentine, characteristic attitude; every movement wafted to him the oppressive perfume she wore; the smile on her lips, the caress of her eyes, were maddening. He loved her more even than he had imagined; his love was a fury, blind and destroying. He repeated to himself that he must fly, but the heaviness in his limbs chained him to her side; he had no will, no strength; he was a reed, bending to every word she spoke and to every look. Her fascination was not human, the calm, voluptuous look of her eyes was too cruel; and she was poised like a serpent about to spring.

At last, however, James was obliged to take his leave.

"I've stayed an unconscionable time."

"Have you? I've not noticed it."

Did she care for him? He took her hand to say good-bye, and the pressure sent the blood racing through his veins. He remembered vividly the passionate embrace of their last farewell. He thought then that he should never see her again, and it was Fate which had carried him to her feet. Oh, how he longed now to take her in his arms and to cover her soft mouth with his kisses!

"What are you doing this evening?" she said.

"Nothing."

"Would you like to take me to the Carlton? You remember you promised."

"Oh, that is good of you! Of course I should like it!"

At last he could not hide the fire in his heart, and the simple words were said so vehemently that Mrs. Wallace looked up in surprise. She withdrew the hand which he was still holding.

"Very well. You may fetch me at a quarter to eight."

* * *

After taking Mrs. Wallace home, James paced the streets for an hour in a turmoil of wild excitement. They had dined at the Carlton expensively, as was her wish, and then, driving to the Empire, James had taken a box. Through the evening he had scarcely known how to maintain his calm, how to prevent himself from telling her all that was in his heart. After the misery he had gone through, he snatched at happiness with eager grasp, determined to enjoy to the full every single moment of it. He threw all scruples to the wind. He was sick and tired of holding himself in; he had checked himself too long, and now, at all hazards, must let himself go. Bridle and curb now were of no avail. He neither could nor would suppress his passion, though it devoured him like a raging fire. He thought his conscientiousness absurd. Why could he not, like other men, take the brief joy of life? Why could he not gather the roses without caring whether they would quickly fade? "Let me eat, drink, and be merry," he cried, "for to-morrow I die!"

It was Wednesday, and on the Saturday he had promised to return to Little Primpton. But he put aside all thought of that, except as an incentive to make the most of his time. He had wrestled with temptation and been overcome, and he gloried in his defeat. He would make no further effort to stifle his love. His strength had finally deserted him, and he had no will to protect himself; he would give himself over entirely to his passion, and the future might bring what it would.

"I'm a fool to torment myself!" he cried. "After all, what does anything matter but love?"

Mrs. Wallace was engaged for the afternoon of the next day, but she had invited him to dine with her.

"They feed you abominably at my place," she said, "but I'll do my best. And we shall be able to talk."

Until then he would not live; and all sorts of wild, mad thoughts ran through his head.

"Is there a greater fool on earth than the virtuous prig?" he muttered, savagely.

He could not sleep, but tossed from side to side, thinking ever of the soft hands and the red lips that he so ardently wished to kiss. In the morning he sent to Half Moon Street a huge basket of flowers.

* * *

"It was good of you," said Mrs. Wallace, when he arrived, pointing to the roses scattered through the room. She wore three in her hair, trailing behind one ear in an exotic, charming fashion.

"It's only you who could think of wearing them like that."

"Do they make me look very barbaric?" She was flattered by the admiration in his eyes. "You certainly have improved since I saw you last."

"Now, shall we stay here or go somewhere?" she asked after dinner, when they were smoking cigarettes.

"Let us stay here."

Mrs. Wallace began talking the old nonsense which, in days past, had delighted James; it enchanted him to hear her say, in the tone of voice he knew so well, just those things which he had a thousand times repeated to himself. He looked at her with a happy smile, his eyes fixed upon her, taking in every movement.

"I don't believe you're listening to a word I'm saying!" she cried at last. "Why don't you answer?"

"Go on. I like to see you talk. It's long since I've had the chance."

"You spoke yesterday as though you hadn't missed me much."

"I didn't mean it. You knew I didn't mean it."

She smiled mockingly.

"I thought it doubtful. If it had been true, you could hardly have said anything so impolite."

"I've thought of you always. That's why I feel I know you so much better now. I don't change. What I felt once, I feel always."

"I wonder what you mean by that?"

"I mean that I love you as passionately as when last I saw you. Oh, I love you ten times more!"

"And the girl with the bun and the strenuous look? You were engaged when I knew you last."

James was silent for a moment.

"I'm going to be married to her on the 10th of October," he said finally, in an expressionless voice.

"You don't say that as if you were wildly enthusiastic."

"Why did you remind me?" cried James. "I was so happy. Oh, I hate her!"

"Then why on earth are you marrying her?"

"I can't help it; I must. You've brought it all back. How could you be so cruel! When I came back from the Cape, I broke the engagement off. I made her utterly miserable, and I took all the pleasure out of my poor father's life. I knew I'd done right; I knew that unless I loved her it was madness to marry; I felt even that it was unclean. Oh, you don't know how I've argued it all out with myself time after time! I was anxious to do right, and I felt such a cad. I can't escape from my bringing-up. You can't imagine what are the chains that bind us in England. We're wrapped from our infancy in the swaddling-clothes of prejudice, ignorance, and false ideas; and when we grow up, though we know they're all absurd and horrible, we can't escape from them; they've become part of our very flesh. Then I grew ill—I nearly died; and Mary nursed me devotedly. I don't know what came over me, I felt so ill and weak. I was grateful to her. The old self seized me again, and I was ashamed of what I'd done. I wanted to make them all happy. I asked her again to marry me, and she said she would. I thought I could love her, but I can't—I can't, God help me!"

Jamie's passion was growing uncontrollable. He walked up and down the room, and then threw himself heavily on a chair.

"Oh, I know it was weakness! I used to pride myself on my strength of mind, but I'm weak. I'm weaker than a woman. I'm a poor reed—vacillating, uncertain, purposeless. I don't know my own mind. I haven't the courage to act according to my convictions. I'm afraid to give pain. They all think I'm brave, but I'm simply a pitiful coward...."

"I feel that Mary has entrapped me, and I hate her. I know she has good qualities—heaps of them—but I can't see them. I only know that the mere touch of her hand curdles my blood. She excites absolute physical repulsion in me; I can't help it. I know it's madness to marry her, but I can't do anything else. I daren't inflict a second time the humiliation and misery upon her, or the unhappiness upon my people."

Mrs. Wallace now was serious.

"And do you really care for anyone else?"

He turned savagely upon her.

"You know I do. You know I love you with all my heart and soul. You know I've loved you passionately from the first day I saw you. Didn't you feel, even when we were separated, that my love was inextinguishable? Didn't you feel it always with you? Oh, my dear, my dear, you must have known that death was too weak to touch my love! I tried to crush it, because neither you nor I was free. Your husband was my friend. I couldn't do anything blackguardly. I ran away from you. What a fool you must have thought me! And now I know that at last we were both free, I might have made you love me. I had my chance of happiness at last; what I'd longed for, cursing myself for treachery, had come to pass. But I never knew. In my weakness I surrendered my freedom. O God! what shall I do?"

He hid his face in his hands and groaned with agony. Mrs. Wallace was silent for a while.

"I don't know if it will be any consolation for you," she said at last; "you're sure to know sooner or later, and I may as well tell you now. I'm engaged to be married."

"What!" cried James, springing up. "It's not true; it's not true!"

"Why not? Of course it's true!"

"You can't—oh, my dearest, be kind to me!"

"Don't be silly, there's a good boy! You're going to be married yourself in a month, and you really can't expect me to remain single because you fancy you care for me. I shouldn't have told you, only I thought it would make things easier for you."

"You never cared two straws for me! I knew that. You needn't throw it in my face."

"After all, I was a married woman."

"I wonder how much you minded when you heard your husband was lying dead on the veldt?"

"My dear boy, he wasn't; he died of fever at Durban—quite comfortably, in a bed."

"Were you sorry?"

"Of course I was! He was extremely satisfactory—and not at all exacting."

James did not know why he asked the questions; they came to his lips unbidden. He was sick at heart, angry, contemptuous.

"I'm going to marry a Mr. Bryant—but, of course, not immediately," she went on, occupied with her own thoughts, and pleased to talk of them.

"What is he?"

"Nothing! He's a landed proprietor." She said this with a certain pride.

James looked at her scornfully; his love all through had been mingled with contrary elements; and trying to subdue it, he had often insisted upon the woman's vulgarity, and lack of taste, and snobbishness. He thought bitterly now that the daughter of the Portuguese and of the riding-master had done very well for herself.

"Really, I think you're awfully unreasonable," she said. "You might make yourself pleasant."

"I can't," he said, gravely. "Let me go away. You don't know what I've felt for you. In my madness, I fancied that you must realise my love; I thought even that you might care for me a little in return."

"You're quite the nicest boy I've ever known. I like you immensely."

"But you like the landed proprietor better. You're very wise. He can marry you. Good-bye!"

"I don't want you to think I'm horrid," she said, going up to him and taking his arm. It was an instinct with her to caress people and make them fond of her. "After all, it's not my fault."

"Have I blamed you? I'm sorry; I had no right to."

"What are you going to do?"

"I don't know—I can always shoot myself if things get unendurable. Thank God, there's always that refuge!"

"Oh, I hope you won't do anything silly!"

"It would be unlike me," James murmured, grimly. "I'm so dreadfully prosaic and matter-of-fact. Good-bye!"

Mrs. Wallace was really sorry for James, and she took his hand affectionately. She always thought it cost so little to be amiable.

"We may never meet again," she said; "but we shall still be friends, Jim."

"Are you going to say that you'll be a sister to me, as Mary told the curate?"

"Won't you kiss me before you go?"

James shook his head, not trusting himself to answer. The light in his life had all gone; the ray of sunshine was hidden; the heavy clouds had closed in, and all the rest was darkness. But he tried to smile at Mrs. Wallace as he touched her hand; he hardly dared look at her again, knowing from old experience how every incident and every detail of her person would rise tormentingly before his recollection. But at last he pulled himself together.

"I'm sorry I've made a fool of myself," he said, quietly. "I hope you'll be very happy. Please forget all I've said to you. It was only nonsense. Good-bye! I'll send you a bit of my wedding-cake."

XXI

James was again in Little Primpton, ill at ease and unhappy. The scene with Mrs. Wallace had broken his spirit, and he was listless now, indifferent to what happened; the world had lost its colour and the sun its light. In his quieter moments he had known that it was impossible for her to care anything about him; he understood her character fairly well, and realised that he had been only a toy, a pastime to a woman who needed admiration as the breath of her nostrils. But notwithstanding, some inner voice had whispered constantly that his love could not be altogether in vain; it seemed strong enough to travel the infinite distance to her heart and awaken at least a kindly feeling. He was humble, and wanted very little. Sometimes he had even felt sure that he was loved. The truth rent his heart, and filled it with bitterness; the woman who was his whole being had forgotten him, and the woman who loved him he hated.... He tried to read, striving to forget; but his trouble overpowered him, and he could think of nothing but the future, dreadful and inevitable. The days passed slowly, monotonously; and as each night came he shuddered at the thought that time was flying. He was drifting on without hope, tortured and uncertain.

"Oh, I'm so weak," he cried; "I'm so weak!"

He knew very well what he should do if he were strong of will. A firm man in his place would cut the knot brutally—a letter to Mary, a letter to his people, and flight. After all, why should he sacrifice his life for the sake of others? The catastrophe was only partly his fault; it was unreasonable that he alone should suffer.

If his Colonel came to hear of the circumstance, and disapproving, questioned him, he could send in his papers. James was bored intensely by the dull routine of regimental life in time of peace; it was a question of performing day after day the same rather unnecessary duties, seeing the same people, listening to the same chatter, the same jokes, the same chaff. And added to the incurable dullness of the mess was the irksome feeling of being merely an overgrown schoolboy at the beck and call of every incompetent and foolish senior. Life was too short to waste in such solemn trifling, masquerading in a ridiculous costume which had to be left at home when any work was to be done. But he was young, with the world before him; there were many careers free to the man who had no fear of death. Africa opened her dusky arms to the adventurer, ruthless and desperate; the world was so large and manifold, there was ample scope for all his longing. If there were difficulties, he could overcome them; perils would add salt to the attempt, freedom would be like strong wine. Ah, that was what he desired, freedom—freedom to feel that he was his own master; that he was not enchained by the love and hate of others, by the ties of convention and of habit. Every bond was tedious. He had nothing to lose, and everything to win. But just those ties which every man may divide of his own free will are the most oppressive; they are unfelt, unseen, till suddenly they burn the wrists like fetters of fire, and the poor wretch who wears them has no power to help himself.

James knew he had not strength for this fearless disregard of others; he dared not face the pain he would cause. He was acting like a fool; his kindness was only cowardly. But to be cruel required more courage than he possessed. If he went away, his anguish would never cease; his vivid imagination would keep before his mind's eye the humiliation of Mary, the unhappiness of his people. He pictured the consternation and the horror when they discovered what he had done. At first they would refuse to believe that he was capable of acting in so blackguardly a way; they would think it a joke, or that he was mad. And then the shame when they realised the truth! How could he make such a return for all the affection and the gentleness be had received? His father, whom he loved devotedly, would be utterly crushed.

"It would kill him," muttered James.

And then he thought of his poor mother, affectionate and kind, but capable of hating him if he acted contrary to her code of honour. Her immaculate virtue made her very hard; she exacted the highest from herself, and demanded no less from others. James remembered in his boyhood how she punished his petty crimes by refusing to speak to him, going about in cold and angry silence; he had never forgotten the icy indignation of her face when once she had caught him lying. Oh, these good people, how pitiless they can be!

He would never have courage to confront the unknown dangers of a new life, unloved, unknown, unfriended. He was too merciful; his heart bled at the pain of others, he was constantly afraid of soiling his hands. It required a more unscrupulous man than he to cut all ties, and push out into the world with no weapons but intelligence and a ruthless heart. Above all, he dreaded his remorse. He knew that he would brood over what he had done till it attained the proportions of a monomania; his conscience would never give him peace. So long as he lived, the claims of Mary would call to him, and in the furthermost parts of the earth he would see her silent agony. James knew himself too well.

And the only solution was that which, in a moment of passionate bitterness, had come thoughtlessly to his lips:

"I can always shoot myself."

"I hope you won't do anything silly," Mrs. Wallace had answered.

It would be silly. After all, one has only one life. But sometimes one has to do silly things.

* * *

The whim seized James to visit the Larchers, and one day he set out for Ashford, near which they lived.... He was very modest about his attempt to save their boy, and told himself that such courage as it required was purely instinctive. He had gone back without realising in the least that there was any danger. Seeing young Larcher wounded and helpless, it had seemed the obvious thing to get him to a place of safety. In the heat of action fellows were constantly doing reckless things. Everyone had a sort of idea that he, at least, would not be hit; and James, by no means oppressed with his own heroism, knew that courageous deeds without number were performed and passed unseen. It was a mere chance that the incident in which he took part was noticed.

Again, he had from the beginning an absolute conviction that his interference was nothing less than disastrous. Probably the Boer sharpshooters would have let alone the wounded man, and afterwards their doctors would have picked him up and properly attended to him.

James could not forget that it was in his very arms that Larcher had been killed, and he repeated: "If I had minded my own business, he might have been alive to this day." It occurred to him also that with his experience he was much more useful than the callow, ignorant boy, so that to risk his more valuable life to save the other's, from the point of view of the general good, was foolish rather than praiseworthy. But it appealed to his sense of irony to receive the honour which he was so little conscious of deserving.

The Larchers had been anxious to meet James, and he was curious to know what they were like. There was at the back of his mind also a desire to see how they conducted themselves, whether they were still prostrate with grief or reconciled to the inevitable. Reggie had been an only son—just as he was. James sent no message, but arrived unexpectedly, and found that they lived some way from the station, in a new, red-brick villa. As he walked to the front door, he saw people playing tennis at the side of the house.

He asked if Mrs. Larcher was at home, and, being shown into the drawing-room the lady came to him from the tennis-lawn. He explained who he was.

"Of course, I know quite well," she said. "I saw your portrait in the illustrated papers."

She shook hands cordially, but James fancied she tried to conceal a slight look of annoyance. He saw his visit was inopportune.

"We're having a little tennis-party," she said, "It seems a pity to waste the fine weather, doesn't it?"

A shout of laughter came from the lawn, and a number of voices were heard talking loudly. Mrs. Larcher glanced towards them uneasily; she felt that James would expect them to be deeply mourning for the dead son, and it was a little incongruous that on his first visit he should find the whole family so boisterously gay.

"Shall we go out to them?" said Mrs. Larcher. "We're just going to have tea, and I'm sure you must be dying for some. If you'd let us know you were coming we should have sent to meet you."

James had divined that if he came at a fixed hour they would all have tuned their minds to a certain key, and he would see nothing of their natural state.

They went to the lawn, and James was introduced to a pair of buxom, healthy-looking girls, panting a little after their violent exercise. They were dressed in white, in a rather masculine fashion, and the only sign of mourning was the black tie that each wore in a sailor's knot. They shook hands vigorously (it was a family trait), and then seemed at a loss for conversation; James, as was his way, did not help them, and they plunged at last into a discussion about the weather and the dustiness of the road from Ashford to their house.

Presently a loose-limbed young man strolled up, and was presented to James. He appeared on friendly terms with the two girls, who called him Bobbikins.

"How long have you been back?" he asked. "I was out in the Imperial Yeomanry—only I got fever and had to come home."

James stiffened himself a little, with the instinctive dislike of the regular for the volunteer.

"Oh, yes! Did you go as a trooper?"

"Yes; and pretty rough it was, I can tell you."

He began to talk of his experience in a resonant voice, apparently well-pleased with himself, while the red-faced girls looked at him admiringly. James wondered whether the youth intended to marry them both.

The conversation was broken by the appearance of Mr. Larcher, a rosy-cheeked and be-whiskered man, dapper and suave. He had been picking flowers, and handed a bouquet to one of his guests. James fancied he was a prosperous merchant, who had retired and set up as a country gentleman; but if he was the least polished of the family, he was also the most simple. He greeted the visitor very heartily, and offered to take him over his new conservatory.

"My husband takes everyone to the new conservatory," said Mrs. Larcher, laughing apologetically.

"It's the biggest round Ashford," explained the worthy man.

James, thinking he wished to talk of his son, consented, and as they walked away, Mr. Larcher pointed out his fruit trees, his pigeons. He was a fancier, said he, and attended to the birds entirely himself; then in the conservatory, made James admire his orchids and the luxuriance of his maidenhair.

"I suppose these sort of things grow in the open air at the Cape?" he asked.

"I believe everything grows there."

Of his son he said absolutely nothing, and presently they rejoined the others. The Larchers were evidently estimable persons, healthy-minded and normal, but a little common. James asked himself why they had invited him if they wished to hear nothing of their boy's tragic death. Could they be so anxious to forget him that every reference was distasteful? He wondered how Reggie had managed to grow up so simple, frank, and charming amid these surroundings. There was a certain pretentiousness about his people which caused them to escape complete vulgarity only by a hair's-breadth. But they appeared anxious to make much of James, and in his absence had explained who he was to the remaining visitors, and these beheld him now with an awe which the hero found rather comic.

Mrs. Larcher invited him to play tennis, and when he declined seemed hardly to know what to do with him. Once when her younger daughter laughed more loudly than usual at the very pointed chaff of the Imperial Yeoman, she slightly frowned at her, with a scarcely perceptible but significant glance in Jamie's direction. To her relief, however, the conversation became general, and James found himself talking with Miss Larcher of the cricket week at Canterbury.

After all, he could not be surprised at the family's general happiness. Six months had passed since Reggie's death, and they could not remain in perpetual mourning. It was very natural that the living should forget the dead, otherwise life would be too horrible; and it was possibly only the Larchers' nature to laugh and to talk more loudly than most people. James saw that it was a united, affectionate household, homely and kind, cursed with no particular depth of feeling; and if they had not resigned themselves to the boy's death, they were doing their best to forget that he had ever lived. It was obviously the best thing, and it would be cruel—too cruel—to expect people never to regain their cheerfulness.

"I think I must be off," said James, after a while; "the trains run so awkwardly to Tunbridge Wells."

They made polite efforts to detain him, but James fancied they were not sorry for him to go.

"You must come and see us another day when we're alone," said Mrs. Larcher. "We want to have a long talk with you."

"It's very kind of you to ask me," he replied, not committing himself.

Mrs. Larcher accompanied him back to the drawing-room, followed by her husband.

"I thought you might like a photograph of Reggie," she said.

This was her first mention of the dead son, and her voice neither shook nor had in it any unwonted expression.

"I should like it very much."

It was on Jamie's tongue to say how fond he had been of the boy, and how he regretted his sad end; but he restrained himself, thinking if the wounds of grief were closed, it was cruel and unnecessary to reopen them.

Mrs. Larcher found the photograph and gave it to James. Her husband stood by, saying nothing.

"I think that's the best we have of him."

She shook hands, and then evidently nerved herself to say something further.

"We're very grateful to you, Captain Parsons, for what you did. And we're glad they gave you the Victoria Cross."

"I suppose you didn't bring it to-day?" inquired Mr. Larcher.

"I'm afraid not."

They showed him out of the front door.

"Mind you come and see us again. But let us know beforehand, if you possibly can."

* * *

Shortly afterwards James received from the Larchers a golden cigarette-case, with a Victoria Cross in diamonds on one side and an inscription on the other. It was much too magnificent for use, evidently expensive, and not in very good taste.

"I wonder whether they take that as equal in value to their son?" said James.

Mary was rather dazzled.

"Isn't it beautiful!" she cried, "Of course, it's too valuable to use; but it'll do to put in our drawing-room."

"Don't you think it should be kept under a glass case?" asked James, with his grave smile.

"It'll get so dirty if we leave it out, won't it?" replied Mary, seriously.

"I wish there were no inscription. It won't fetch so much if we get hard-up and have to pop our jewels."

"Oh, James," cried Mary, shocked, "you surely wouldn't do a thing like that!"

James was pleased to have seen the Larchers. It satisfied and relieved him to know that human sorrow was not beyond human endurance: as the greatest of their gifts, the gods have vouchsafed to man a happy forgetfulness.

In six months the boy's family were able to give parties, to laugh and jest as if they had suffered no loss at all; and the thought of this cleared his way a little. If the worst came to the worst—and that desperate step of which he had spoken seemed his only refuge—he could take it with less apprehension. Pain to those he loved was inevitable, but it would not last very long; and his death would trouble them far less than his dishonour.

Time was pressing, and James still hesitated, hoping distractedly for some unforeseen occurrence that would at least delay the marriage. The House of Death was dark and terrible, and he could not walk rashly to its dreadful gates: something would surely happen! He wanted time to think—time to see whether there was really no escape. How horrible it was that one could know nothing for certain! He was torn and rent by his indecision.

Major Forsyth had been put off by several duchesses, and was driven to spend a few economical weeks at Little Primpton; he announced that since Jamie's wedding was so near he would stay till it was over. Finding also that his nephew had not thought of a best man, he offered himself; he had acted as such many times—at the most genteel functions; and with a pleasant confusion of metaphor, assured James that he knew the ropes right down to the ground.

"Three weeks to-day, my boy!" he said heartily to James one morning, on coming down to breakfast.

"Is it?" replied James.

"Getting excited?"

"Wildly!"

"Upon my word, Jamie, you're the coolest lover I've ever seen. Why, I've hardly known how to keep in some of the fellows I've been best man to."

"I'm feeling a bit seedy to-day, Uncle William."

James thanked his stars that ill-health was deemed sufficient excuse for all his moodiness. Mary spared him the rounds among her sick and needy, whom, notwithstanding the approaching event, she would on no account neglect. She told Uncle William he was not to worry her lover, but leave him quietly with his books; and no one interfered when he took long, solitary walks in the country. Jamie's reading now was a pretence; his brain was too confused, he was too harassed and uncertain to understand a word; and he spent his time face to face with the eternal problem, trying to see a way out, when before him was an impassable wall, still hoping blindly that something would happen, some catastrophe which should finish at once all his perplexities, and everything else besides.

XXII

In solitary walks James had found his only consolation. He knew even in that populous district unfrequented parts where he could wander without fear of interruption. Among the trees and the flowers, in the broad meadows, he forgot himself; and, his senses sharpened by long absence, he learnt for the first time the exquisite charm of English country. He loved the spring, with its yellow, countless buttercups, spread over the green fields like a cloth of gold, whereon might fitly walk the angels of Messer Perugino. The colours were so delicate that one could not believe it possible for paints and paint-brush to reproduce them; the atmosphere visibly surrounded things, softening their outlines. Sometimes from a hill higher than the rest James looked down at the plain, bathed in golden sunlight. The fields of corn, the fields of clover, the roads and the rivulets, formed themselves in that flood of light into an harmonious pattern, luminous and ethereal. A pleasant reverie filled his mind, unanalysable, a waking dream of half-voluptuous sensation.

On the other side of the common, James knew a wood of tall fir trees, dark and ragged, their sombre green veiled in a silvery mist, as though, like a chill vapour, the hoar-frost of a hundred winters still lingered among their branches. At the edge of the hill, up which they climbed in serried hundreds, stood here and there an oak tree, just bursting into leaf, clothed with its new-born verdure, like the bride of the young god, Spring. And the ever-lasting youth of the oak trees contrasted wonderfully with the undying age of the firs. Then later, in the height of the summer, James found the pine wood cool and silent, fitting his humour. It was like the forest of life, the grey and sombre labyrinth where wandered the poet of Hell and Death. The tall trees rose straight and slender, like the barren masts of sailing ships; the gentle aromatic odour, the light subdued; the purple mist, so faint as to be scarcely discernible, a mere tinge of warmth in the day—all gave him an exquisite sense of rest. Here he could forget his trouble, and give himself over to the love which seemed his real life; here the recollection of Mrs. Wallace gained flesh and blood, seeming so real that he almost stretched out his arms to seize her.... His footfall on the brown needles was noiseless, and the tread was soft and easy; the odours filled him like an Eastern drug with drowsy intoxication.

But all that now was gone. When, unbidden, the well-known laugh rang again in his ears, or he felt on his hands the touch of the slender fingers, James turned away with a gesture of distaste. Now Mrs. Wallace brought him only bitterness, and he tortured himself insanely trying to forget her.... With tenfold force the sensation returned which had so terribly oppressed him before his illness; he felt that Nature had become intolerably monotonous; the circumscribed, prim country was horrible. On every inch of it the hand of man was apparent. It was a prison, and his hands and feet were chained with heavy iron.... The dark, immovable clouds were piled upon one another in giant masses—so distinct and sharply cut, so rounded, that one almost saw the impressure of the fingers of some Titanic sculptor; and they hung low down, overwhelming, so that James could scarcely breathe. The sombre elms were too well-ordered, the meadows too carefully tended. All round, the hills were dark and drear; and that very fertility, that fat Kentish luxuriance, added to the oppression. It was a task impossible to escape from that iron circle. All power of flight abandoned him. Oh! he loathed it!

The past centuries of people, living in a certain way, with certain standards, influenced by certain emotions, were too strong for him. James was like a foolish bird—a bird born in a cage, without power to attain its freedom. His lust for a free life was futile; he acknowledged with cruel self-contempt that he was weaker than a woman—ineffectual. He could not lead the life of his little circle, purposeless and untrue; and yet he had not power to lead a life of his own. Uncertain, vacillating, torn between the old and the new, his reason led him; his conscience drew him back. But the ties of his birth and ancestry were too strong; he had not the energy even of the poor tramp, who carries with him his whole fortune, and leaves in the lap of the gods the uncertain future. James envied with all his heart the beggar boy, wandering homeless and penniless, but free. He, at least, had not these inhuman fetters which it was death to suffer and death to cast off; he, indeed, could make the world his servant. Freedom, freedom! If one were only unconscious of captivity, what would it matter? It is the knowledge that kills. And James walked again by the neat, iron railing which enclosed the fields, his head aching with the rigidity and decorum, wishing vainly for just one piece of barren, unkept land to remind him that all the world was not a prison.

Already the autumn had come. The rich, mouldering colours were like an air melancholy with the approach of inevitable death; but in those passionate tints, in the red and gold of the apples, in the many tones of the first-fallen leaves, there was still something which forbade one to forget that in the death and decay of Nature there was always the beginning of other life. Yet to James the autumn heralded death, with no consoling afterthought. He had nothing to live for since he knew that Mrs. Wallace could never love him. His love for her had borne him up and sustained him; but now it was hateful and despicable. After all, his life was his own to do what he liked with; the love of others had no right to claim his self-respect. If he had duties to them, he had duties to himself also; and more vehemently than ever James felt that such a union as was before him could only be a degradation. He repeated with new emotion that marriage without love was prostitution. If death was the only way in which he could keep clean that body ignorantly despised, why, he was not afraid of death! He had seen it too often for the thought to excite alarm. It was but a common, mechanical process, quickly finished, and not more painful than could be borne. The flesh is all which is certainly immortal; the dissolution of consciousness is the signal of new birth. Out of corruption springs fresh life, like the roses from a Roman tomb; and the body, one with the earth, pursues the eternal round.

But one day James told himself impatiently that all these thoughts were mad and foolish; he could only have them because he was still out of health. Life, after all, was the most precious thing in the world. It was absurd to throw it away like a broken toy. He rebelled against the fate which seemed forcing itself upon him. He determined to make the effort and, come what might, break the hateful bonds. It only required a little courage, a little strength of mind. If others suffered, he had suffered too. The sacrifice they demanded was too great.... But when he returned to Primpton House, the inevitability of it all forced itself once again upon him. He shrugged his shoulders despairingly; it was no good.

The whole atmosphere oppressed him so that he felt powerless; some hidden influence surrounded James, sucking from his blood, as it were, all manliness, dulling his brain. He became a mere puppet, acting in accordance to principles that were not his own, automatic, will-less. His father sat, as ever, in the dining-room by the fire, for only in the warmest weather could he do without artificial heat, and he read the paper, sometimes aloud, making little comments. His mother, at the table, on a stiff-backed chair, was knitting—everlastingly knitting. Outwardly there was in them a placid content, and a gentleness which made them seem pliant as wax; but really they were iron. James knew at last how pitiless was their love, how inhumanly cruel their intolerance; and of the two his father seemed more implacable, more horribly relentless. His mother's anger was bearable, but the Colonel's very weakness was a deadly weapon. His despair, his dumb sorrow, his entire dependence on the forbearance of others, were more tyrannical than the most despotic power. James was indeed a bird beating himself against the imprisoning cage; and its bars were loving-kindness and trust, tears, silent distress, bitter disillusion, and old age.

"Where's Mary?" asked James.

"She's in the garden, walking with Uncle William."

"How well they get on together," said the Colonel, smiling.

James looked at his father, and thought he had never seen him so old and feeble. His hands were almost transparent; his thin white hair, his bowed shoulders, gave an impression of utter weakness.

"Are you very glad the wedding is so near, father?" asked James, placing his hand gently on the old man's shoulder.

"I should think I was."

"You want to get rid of me so badly?"

"'A man shall leave his father and his mother, and shall cleave unto his wife; and they shall be one flesh.' We shall have to do without you."

"I wonder whether you are fonder of Mary than of me?"

The Colonel did not answer, but Mrs. Parsons laughed.

"My impression is that your father has grown so devoted to Mary that he hardly thinks you worthy of her."

"Really? And yet you want me to marry her, don't you, daddy?"

"It's the wish of my heart."

"Were you very wretched when our engagement was broken off?"

"Don't talk of it! Now it's all settled, Jamie, I can tell you that I'd sooner see you dead at my feet than that you should break your word to Mary."

James laughed.

"And you, mother?" he asked, lightly.

She did not answer, but looked at him earnestly.

"What, you too? Would you rather see me dead than not married to Mary? What a bloodthirsty pair you are!"

James, laughing, spoke so gaily, it never dawned on them that his words meant more than was obvious; and yet he felt that they, loving but implacable, had signed his death-warrant. With smiling faces they had thrown open the portals of that House, and he, smiling, was ready to enter.

Mary at that moment came in, followed by Uncle William.

"Well, Jamie, there you are!" she cried, in that hard, metallic voice which to James betrayed so obviously the meanness of her spirit and her self-complacency. "Where on earth have you been?"

She stood by the table, straight, uncompromising, self-reliant; by her immaculate virtue, by the strength of her narrow will, she completely domineered the others. She felt herself capable of managing them all, and, in fact, had been giving Uncle William a friendly little lecture upon some action of which she disapproved. Mary had left off her summer things and wore again the plain serge skirt, and because it was rainy, the battered straw hat of the preceding winter. She was using up her old things, and having got all possible wear out of them, intended on the day before her marriage generously to distribute them among the poor.

"Is my face very red?" she asked. "There's a lot of wind to-day."

To James she had never seemed more unfeminine; that physical repulsion which at first had terrified him now was grown into an ungovernable hate. Everything Mary did irritated and exasperated him; he wondered she did not see the hatred in his eyes as he looked at her, answering her question.

"Oh, no," he said to himself, "I would rather shoot myself than marry you!"

His dislike was unreasonable, but he could not help it; and the devotion of his parents made him detest her all the more; he could not imagine what they saw in her. With hostile glance he watched her movements as she took off her hat and arranged her hair, grimly drawn back and excessively neat; she fetched her knitting from Mrs. Parsons's work-basket and sat down. All her actions had in them an insufferable air of patronage, and she seemed more than usually pleased with herself. James had an insane desire to hurt her, to ruffle that self-satisfaction; and he wanted to say something that should wound her to the quick. And all the time he laughed and jested as though he were in the highest spirits.

"And what were you doing this morning, Mary?" asked Colonel Parsons.

"Oh, I biked in to Tunbridge Wells with Mr. Dryland to play golf. He plays a rattling good game."

"Did he beat you?"

"Well, no," she answered, modestly. "It so happened that I beat him. But he took his thrashing remarkably well—some men get so angry when they're beaten by a girl."

"The curate has many virtues," said James.

"He was talking about you, Jamie. He said he thought you disliked him; but I told him I was certain you didn't. He's really such a good man, one can't help liking him. He said he'd like to teach you golf."

"And is he going to?"

"Certainly not. I mean to do that myself."

"There are many things you want to teach me, Mary. You'll have your hands full."

"Oh, by the way, father told me to remind you and Uncle William that you were shooting with him the day after to-morrow. You're to fetch him at ten."

"I hadn't forgotten," replied James. "Uncle William, we shall have to clean our guns to-morrow."

James had come to a decision at last, and meant to waste no time; indeed, there was none to waste. And to remind him how near was the date fixed for the wedding were the preparations almost complete. One or two presents had already arrived. With all his heart he thanked his father and mother for having made the way easier for him. He thought what he was about to do the kindest thing both to them and to Mary. Under no circumstances could he marry her; that would be adding a greater lie to those which he had already been forced into, and the misery was more than he could bear. But his death was the only other way of satisfying her undoubted claims. He had little doubt that in six months he would be as well forgotten as poor Reggie Larcher, and he did not care; he was sick of the whole business, and wanted the quiet of death. His love for Mrs. Wallace would never give him peace upon earth; it was utterly futile, and yet unconquerable.

James saw his opportunity in Colonel Clibborn's invitation to shoot; he was most anxious to make the affair seem accidental, and that, in cleaning his gun, was easy. He had been wounded before and knew that the pain was not very great. He had, therefore, nothing to fear.

Now at last he regained his spirits. He did not read or walk, but spent the day talking with his father; he wished the last impression he would leave to be as charming as possible, and took great pains to appear at his best.

He slept well that night, and in the morning dressed himself with unusual care. At Primpton House they breakfasted at eight, and afterwards James smoked his pipe, reading the newspaper. He was a little astonished at his calm, for doubt no longer assailed him, and the indecision which paralysed all his faculties had disappeared.

"It is the beginning of my freedom," he thought. All human interests had abandoned him, except a vague sensation of amusement. He saw the humour of the comedy he was acting, and dispassionately approved himself, because he did not give way to histrionics.

"Well, Uncle William," he said, at last, "what d'you say to setting to work on our guns?"

"I'm always ready for everything," said Major Forsyth.

"Come on, then."

They went into what they called the harness-room, and James began carefully to clean his gun.

"I think I'll take my coat off," he said; "I can work better without."

The gun had not been used for several months, and James had a good deal to do. He leant over and rubbed a little rust off the lock.

"Upon my word," said Uncle William, "I've never seen anyone handle a gun so carelessly as you. D'you call yourself a soldier?"

"I am a bit slack," replied James, laughing. "People are always telling me that."

"Well, take care, for goodness' sake! It may be loaded."

"Oh, no, there's no danger. It's not loaded, and besides, it's locked."

"Still, you oughtn't to hold it like that."

"It would be rather comic if I killed myself accidentally. I wonder what Mary would say?"

"Well, you've escaped death so often by the skin of your teeth, I think you're pretty safe from everything but old age."

Presently James turned to his uncle.

"I say, this is rotten oil. I wish we could get some fresh."

"I was just thinking that."

"Well, you're a pal of the cook. Go and ask her for some, there's a good chap."

"She'll do anything for me," said Major Forsyth, with a self-satisfied smile. It was his opinion that no woman, countess or scullery-maid, could resist his fascinations; and taking the cup, he trotted off.

James immediately went to the cupboard and took out a cartridge. He slipped it in, rested the butt on the ground, pointed the barrel to his heart, and—fired!

Epilogue

A letter from Mrs. Clibborn to General Sir Charles Clow, K.C.B., 8 Gladhorn Terrace, Bath:

"DEAR CHARLES,—

I am so glad to hear you are settled in your new house in Bath, and it is *most* kind to ask us down. I am devoted to Bath; one meets such *nice* people there, and all one's friends whom one knew centuries ago. It is such a comfort to see how fearfully old they're looking! I don't know whether we can manage to accept your kind invitation, but I must say I should be glad of a change after the truly *awful* things that have happened here. I have been dreadfully upset all the winter, and have had several touches of rheumatism, which is a thing I never suffered from before.

"I wrote and told you of the sudden and *mysterious* death of poor James Parsons, a fortnight before he was going to marry my dear Mary. He shot himself accidentally while cleaning a gun—that is to say, every one *thinks* it was an accident. But I am certain it was nothing of the kind. Ever since the dreadful thing happened—six months ago—it has been on my conscience, and I assure you that the whole time I have not slept a wink. My sufferings have been *horrible!* You will be surprised at the change in me; I am beginning to look like an *old* woman. I tell you this in strict confidence. *I believe he committed suicide.* He confessed that he loved me, Charles. Of course, I told him I was old enough to be his mother; but love is blind. When I think of the tragic end of poor Algy Turner, who poisoned himself in India for my sake, I don't know how I shall ever forgive myself. I never gave James the least encouragement, and when he said that he loved me, I was so taken aback that I *nearly fainted*. I am convinced that he shot himself rather than marry a woman he did not love, and what is more, *my* daughter. You can imagine my feelings! I have taken care not to breathe a word of this to Reginald, whose gout is making him more irritable every day, or to anyone else. So no one suspects the truth.

"But I shall never get over it. I could not bear to think of poor Algy Turner, and now I have on my head as well the blood of James Parsons. They were dear boys, both of them. I think I am the only one who is really sorry for him. If it had been my son who was killed I should either have gone *raving mad* or had hysterics for a week; but Mrs. Parsons merely said: 'The Lord has given, and the Lord has taken away. Blessed be the name of the Lord.' I cannot help thinking it was rather profane, and *most* unfeeling. *I* was dreadfully upset, and Mary had to sit up with me for several nights. I don't believe Mary really loved him. I hate to say anything against my own daughter, but I feel bound to tell the truth, and my private opinion is that she loved *herself* better. She loved her constancy and the good opinion of Little Primpton; the fuss the Parsons have made of her I'm sure is very bad for anyone. It can't be good for a girl to be given way to so much; and I never really liked the Parsons. They're very good people, of course; but only infantry!

"I am happy to say that poor Jamie's death was almost instantaneous. When they found him he said: 'It was an accident; I didn't know the gun was loaded.' (*Most improbable,* I think. It's wonderful how they've all been taken in; but then they didn't know his secret!) A few minutes later, just before he died, he said: 'Tell Mary she's to marry the curate.'

"If my betrothed had died, *nothing* would have induced me to marry anybody else. I would have remained an *old maid*. But so few people have any really *nice* feeling! Mr. Dryland, the curate, had already proposed to Mary, and she had refused him. He is a pleasant-spoken young man, with a rather fine presence—not *my* ideal at all; but that, of course, doesn't matter! Well, a month after the funeral, Mary told me that he had asked her again, and she had declined. I think it was very bad taste on his part, but Mary said she thought it *most noble*.

"It appears that Colonel and Mrs. Parsons both pressed her very much to accept the curate. They said it was Jamie's dying wish, and that his last thought had been for her happiness. There is no doubt that Mr. Dryland is an excellent young man, but if the Parsons had *really* loved their son, they would never have advised Mary to get married. I think it was most *heartless*.

"Well, a few days ago, Mr. Dryland came and told us that he had been appointed vicar of Stone Fairley, in Kent. I went to see Mrs. Jackson, the wife of our Vicar, and she looked it out in the clergy list. The stipend is £300 a year, and I am told that there is a good house. Of course, it's not very much, but better than nothing. This morning Mr. Dryland called and asked for a private interview with Mary. He said he must, of course, leave Little Primpton, and his vicarage would sadly want a mistress; and finally, for the third time, *begged* her on his *bended knees* to marry her. He had previously been to the Parsons, and the Colonel sent for Mary, and told her that he hoped she would not refuse Mr. Dryland for their sake, and that they thought it was her duty to marry. The result is that Mary accepted him, and is to be married very quietly by special license in a month. The widow of the late incumbent of Stone Fairley moves out in six weeks, so this will give them time for a fortnight's honeymoon before settling down. They think of spending it in Paris.

"I think, on the whole, it is as good a match as poor Mary could *expect to make*. The stipend is paid by the Ecclesiastical Commissioners, which, of course, is much safer than glebe. She is no longer a young girl, and I think it was her last chance. Although she is my own daughter, I cannot help confessing that she is not the sort of girl that wears well; she has always been *plain*—(no one would think she was my daughter)—and as time goes on, she will grow *plainer*. When I was eighteen my mother's maid used to say: 'Why, miss, there's many a married woman of thirty who would be proud to have your bust.' But our poor, *dear* Mary has *no figure*. She will do excellently for the wife of a country vicar. She's so fond of giving people advice, and of looking after the poor, and it won't matter that she's dowdy. She has no idea of dressing herself, although I've always done my best for her.

"Mr. Dryland is, of course, in the seventh heaven of delight. He has gone into Tunbridge Wells to get a ring, and as an engagement present has just sent round a complete edition of the works of Mr. Hall Caine. He is evidently *generous*. I think they will suit one another very well, and I am glad to get my only daughter married. She was always rather a tie on Reginald and me. We are so devoted to one another that a third person has often seemed a little in the way. Although you would not believe it, and we have been married for nearly thirty years, nothing gives us more happiness than to sit holding one another's hands. I have always been sentimental, and I am not ashamed to own it. Reggie is sometimes afraid that I shall get an attack of my rheumatism when we sit out together at night; but I always take care to wrap myself up well, and I invariably make him put a muffler on.

"Give my kindest regards to your wife, and tell her I hope to see her soon.—

Yours very sincerely,

"CLARA DE TULLEVILLE CLIBBORN."

THE END

Books in beautiful packages...

Norilana Books
Classics

www.norilana.com

Publishing some of the best, rare, and precious classics of world literature in trade hardcover and paperback editions.

Lightning Source UK Ltd.
Milton Keynes UK
21 November 2009

146541UK00001B/96/P

999
YOUNG LIFESAVERS
Emergency Action for Everyone

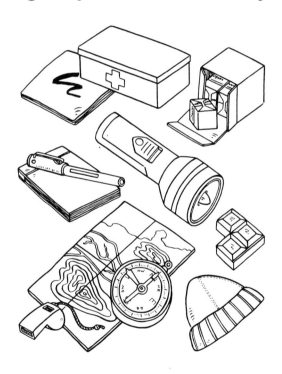

BBC CHiLDREN'S BOOKS

The Executive Producer of *999 Lifesavers* is Andy Batten-Foster.

BBC Children's Books would also like to thank Yvonne Holmes, Assistant Producer, for her help with this project.

Published by BBC Children's Books
a division of BBC Worldwide Publishing Ltd
Woodlands, 80 Wood Lane, London W12 0TT

First published in 1995

Text and illustrations © BBC Children's Books 1995
Illustrations by Jo Moore

ISBN 0 563 40431 0

Typeset by BBC Children's Books
Printed by Ebenezer Baylis, Worcester
Bound by Hunter & Foulis, Edinburgh
Cover printed by Clays Ltd, St Ives plc

Contents

Emergency!	4
Getting Help	6
Dial 999	8
Bleeding	10
First Aid	12
The Recovery Position	14
! SAFETY ALERT ! **Safety in the Street**	16
Road Accidents	18
Dangerous Loads	20
Escape from a Sinking Car	22
! SAFETY ALERT ! **Cycling Safety**	24
Broken Bones	26
Asthma Attacks	28
Epilepsy	30
Diabetes	32
! SAFETY ALERT ! **Safety at Home**	34
Be Prepared	36
Fire	38
Escape Routes	40
Stop, Drop, Roll	42
Burns and Scalds	44
Electrical Dangers	46
Electric Shocks	48
! SAFETY ALERT ! **Safety in the Country**	50
Survival Out of Doors	52
Lightning	54
Safety in the Sun	56
Safety near Water	58
Bites and Stings	60
Acknowledgements	62
Index	64

Emergency!

Imagine that you're walking across open fields on a sunny day, when the sky suddenly turns black. You find yourself in the middle of a violent thunderstorm, with streaks of lightning close by. What should you do?

Or you're out cycling with a friend, when they skid and fall, knocking themselves out as they hit the ground. How can you help them?

This book is all about emergencies – how to react if you're faced with a dangerous situation, and what to do if you're involved in an accident. Remember: by being prepared, you could help save someone's life.

EMERGENCY ACTION

In any emergency, you can follow this basic four-point plan.

- Stay calm. It will help you to think clearly and reassure other people.

- Are you in danger? Take any immediate action you can to avoid the danger or protect yourself.

- If you know what to do, give emergency aid to any casualties.

- Send for help.

Getting Help

Getting help quickly is often the most important thing you can do. If someone is ill or injured, every minute counts – a heart-attack victim, for example, has a much higher chance of survival if an ambulance arrives within 10 minutes of their attack. Don't be frightened about disturbing people or asking for help. Remember – this is an emergency.

Go to the nearest telephone. Don't waste time looking for a public phone if you can't see one straight away. Ask to use the phone in a shop or a pub, explaining that you need urgent help.

ATTRACTING ATTENTION

If you're in a quiet place or out in the countryside, it might not be so easy to attract someone's attention without leaving a casualty alone. These are some ways you might call for help.

- Shout for help at the top of your voice.

- Sound a car horn, or blow on a whistle.

- If you're near a road, lay out a coat or backpack weighed down with stones – that way, any passing cars will stop to see what's the matter.

Emergencies call for special ways of behaving. This is the one time when you might need to talk to an adult you don't know. But in normal circumstances, you should never speak to strangers.

Dial 999

All emergency calls are free – just dial 999. But before you go to the phone, check that you have all the information you need. If you send a bystander to call for help, make sure that they have all the details of the emergency too.

- **Where** is the casualty? Give a street name if you can. If you don't have the exact address, look for any other landmarks.

- **Who** is injured? For each casualty, say roughly how old they are and what sex they are.

- **What** has happened? Describe the accident and how the casualties seem to be injured.

- **Warn** the emergency services of any hazards, such as fog, fire or dangerous chemicals.

WHEN YOU PICK UP THE PHONE

* When the emergency operator answers the phone, they will ask you which service you need. Answer, "Ambulance". If you need any other services (like the police or fire brigade), the officer will call them automatically.

* The operator will ask for your phone number. If you're in a call box, this will be on the phone, or on a notice on the wall.

* The operator will put you through to the ambulance control officer. Give them all the details clearly and calmly.

* The ambulance officer may give you first aid instructions. Listen carefully.

* Do not put the phone down until the ambulance officer has rung off.

Bleeding

Every fully-grown adult has about 6 litres of blood flowing around inside them. This blood is vitally important because it carries oxygen from our lungs to all the other parts of our bodies. Without oxygen-carrying blood pumping around our bodies, we would soon die.

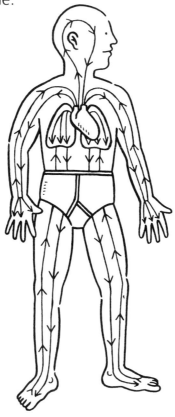

Everyone has small cuts and grazes, and they are not serious if they are treated properly and kept clean. However, large wounds that are losing a lot of blood can be very dangerous, and it's important to stop bleeding in any casualty as quickly as possible.

CUTS AND GRAZES

If you cut yourself . . .

* Wash your hands and then rinse the cut under clean, running water.

* Pat the cut dry with a clean cloth.

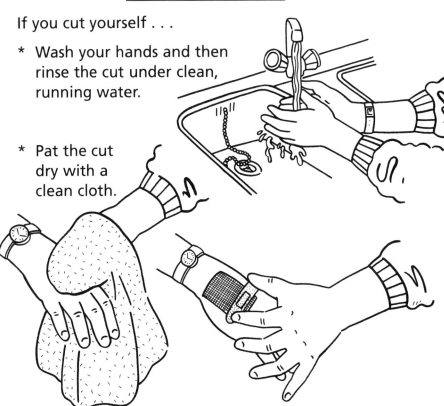

* Cover the cut with a sterile pad and hold it in place with a bandage or sticking plaster.

Small cuts should stop bleeding on their own, because the blood clots, or gets thicker, and bungs up the wound. The most important thing is to keep the cut **clean**, so that no germs can get into the blood through the broken skin.

Large wounds will not stop bleeding straight away. When you have covered the wound with a dressing pad, raise the cut part as high as possible and get medical help immediately.

First Aid

Seeing someone who is bleeding can be very frightening, but if you keep calm and cut down the amount of blood they are losing, you might help to save their life.

- Remove any clothing that covers the wound.
- Press directly on the wound. Use a clean pad or cloth.
- If you don't have any clean material, you can press down with your hand, though try to wear a glove or cover it in clingfilm first.
- If possible, raise the injured area above the casualty's head. (This cuts down the amount of blood being pumped into the injured area.)
- If something like a piece of glass is lodged inside the wound, do **not** take it out. It might be helping to plug the wound. Try to press around the wound to keep the plug as tight as possible.

MAKING A BANDAGE

You can make a bandage from any clean material. Put a pad of material on top of the wound, and then tie it firmly in place with another strip of material.

If blood starts to seep through the bandage, do not take it off. Instead, put another bandage on top.

As in all other emergencies, it's important to call an ambulance as quickly as possible if someone is losing a lot of blood.

The Recovery Position

If you find a casualty who is breathing but unconscious, the best thing you can do is to put them into the recovery position until help arrives. This position will help the casualty to breathe and stop them from choking.

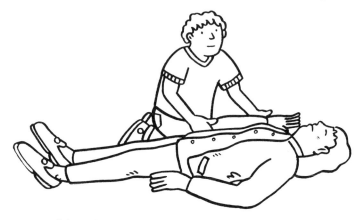

- Kneel by the casualty. Tilt the head back and straighten the legs.

- Place the arm nearest to you at right-angles to the body. Bend the arm at the elbow and lay the hand with the palm facing up.

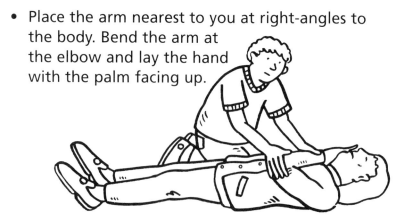

- Put the other arm across the casualty's chest and place the hand by the casualty's cheek, with the palm facing out.

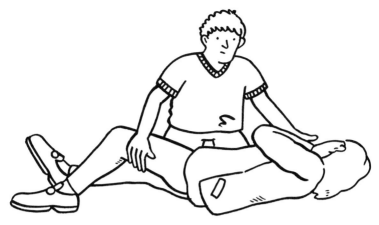

- Keep the casualty's hand by their cheek to support the head and grasp the thigh of the leg which is furthest away from you.

- Bend the leg and roll the casualty over towards you until they are on their side, with the hip and knee of the upper leg bent.

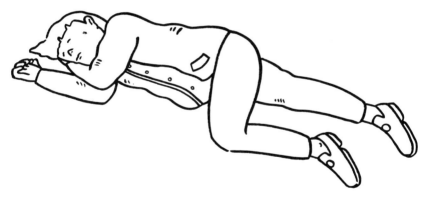

- Make sure that the casualty's head is still tilted up so that they can breathe easily.

If the casualty has injured limbs, you might need to adjust the recovery position. If you think the casualty has a back injury, you should not move them at all. (See page 27.)

!SAFETY ALERT!
Safety in the Street

Every year, hundreds of children are killed or injured in road accidents. Most of these accidents do not happen on main roads or motorways, but in quiet streets near the victims' own homes. The road outside your house might not seem very busy, but in fact it's one of the most dangerous places you'll ever go.

People are knocked down on quiet streets because they forget to watch out for traffic. **Never** play on the street, and **always** use the Green Cross Code.

Before you ever cross any road on your own, first practise the Green Cross Code with an adult until they are happy that you will be safe.

THE GREEN CROSS CODE

- Find a safe place to cross, then stop.
  – A safe place is where you can see any traffic that is coming. It is not between parked cars or near a corner. The best place to cross the road is a zebra crossing or pedestrian crossing.
- Stand on the pavement near the kerb.
  – Always stop before you cross the road. Never run straight out into the street from the pavement.
- Look all round for traffic and listen.
- If traffic is coming, let it pass. Look all round again.
- When there is no traffic near, walk straight across the road.
- Keep looking and listening for traffic while you cross.

Road Accidents

Sadly, road accidents are all too common, and they are one of the most likely emergencies that you will see on the road. If you are involved in a crash or are the first person on the scene of an accident this is what should happen.

- An adult should make sure that all approaching traffic is warned of the crash. Anyone working near the crash must wear bright, reflective or fluorescent clothing.

- All vehicles near the scene of the accident should have their hazard warning lights turned on. In the dark, headlamps should be left on too.

- An adult should also put warning triangles or flashing lamps on each side of the crash. However, on a busy motorway or road with fast traffic, this may be a dangerous thing to do.

- An adult must check to see how many people are injured. They should work out who needs help most urgently. It isn't always obvious. Someone who is shouting may not be as badly hurt as someone who is moaning or silent.

- * **No one** should run across a motorway or fast dual carriageway, even to seek help.
- * **No one** should lift a bonnet of a vehicle if it is on fire. Take all passengers as far away from a burning vehicle as possible.
- * Do **not** let anyone smoke.
- * Do **not** move anyone unless they are in immediate danger (e.g., from fire).

- An adult should go for help. On a motorway there are marker posts every 100 metres. An arrow points towards the nearest telephone. Each marker also has a number. That number should be given to the operator, so that the emergency services know exactly where you are.
- Anyone who is not helping should stay away from the crashed vehicle at all times.

Dangerous Loads

Take great care if you see an accident involving tankers, lorries or goods vans. It's possible that they are carrying dangerous loads. Look out for the special hazard signs that are painted on the side or back of a lorry.

The hazardous substances – or "hazchem" signs give you valuable information about the contents of the vehicle. This is how to understand them:

* International code number for the substance which is being carried.

* These letters and numbers are a code about the load. You must give this code to the emergency services when you report the accident so that they can bring any special equipment they need.

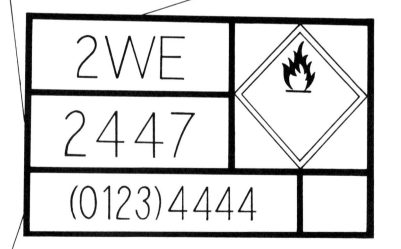

* Telephone number which the emergency services can ring for more information about the load. This is usually the number of the company that makes the substance.

Substance catches fire easily

Gas stored under pressure

Poisonous substances

Radioactive substances

When this chemical comes in contact with other substances, it might catch fire easily

Substance such as acid which eats away solid materials

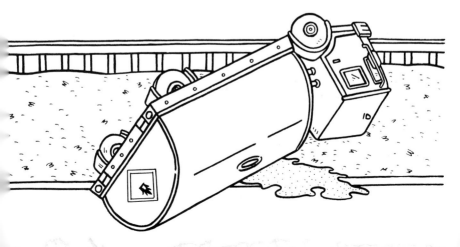

Escape from a Sinking Car

Being trapped in a sinking car might seem like a freak accident, but it does happen, especially during floods. Over the past five years, more people have been drowned inside their cars than in boating accidents.

Being caught in a sinking car is a terrifying experience. The water pressing on the outside of the car makes it difficult to open the doors. But some air will be trapped inside the car, giving you enough time to get free. Don't panic and follow these guides:

1 Undo your seatbelt. Help other passengers to undo theirs.

2 Once everyone is free to move, wind down the windows. Water will flow inside the car, making the water pressure the same inside the car as it is outside.

3 You should now be able to open the doors gently. Push them wide open and get out. If possible, get out on the downflow side.

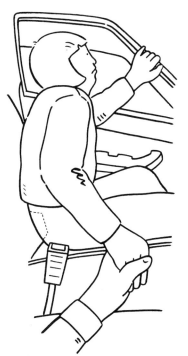

4 To make sure that everyone reaches safety, hold hands to form a human chain, staying together as you swim to the surface.

Do **not** try to escape through the sunroof. You might get stuck because it is too small for everyone to get through.

!SAFETY ALERT!
Cycling Safety

Cycling is great fun, and a good kind of exercise. But it can also be dangerous. Before you ride a bike on *any* road – even if it's just a quiet side street near your house – you should be confident that you can control it properly, and have some proper training about how to use the road. Never play around on your bicycle in the street.

CYCLE TRAINING

You should learn about road safety for cyclists *before* you go out on your bike. After all, no one would let an adult drive a car without proper lessons! Ask a teacher or the road safety officer at your local town hall about cycle training.

- **Always** wear a cycle helmet. It might save your life. Make sure that it fits properly – it shouldn't be loose. Also check that it has the official safety standard mark, to show that it has been tested.

- Wear bright clothes and plastic reflective strips at night so that motorists can always see you.

CYCLIST'S CHECKLIST

Make a checklist for your bike. Run through it every few weeks to make sure that everything is working properly.

- Good brakes are vital. Before every ride, check that the brake blocks haven't worn down.

- Do the lights still work? Have the batteries run out?

- Check the bell.

- Have the tyres worn thin? Old tyres will skid in the rain.

- Does the bike fit you properly? Do you need to adjust the saddle? When you sit on the saddle, you should be able to touch the ground with your toes and grip the brake levers firmly.

Broken Bones

Our bones are normally very strong, but a serious knock or fall can make them break. Old people are most likely to suffer broken bones, because our bones become more brittle as we get older.

Because our bones are covered in skin and muscle, it's not always obvious if one is broken, but send for help if you think there's any chance of a breakage. Bruises, swelling and limbs twisted into awkward positions are all tell-tale signs.

If you think someone might have broken a bone . . .

* Keep the injured part of the body still until help arrives.

* Support the injury with blankets or towels to make the casualty more comfortable.

* Do not let the casualty have anything to eat or drink. They might need to have an operation as soon as they reach hospital.

BACK INJURIES

The most serious breakage of all is a spine injury. A broken back can make someone completely paralysed. If you suspect someone has broken their spine, **keep them completely still**. Do not try to move them at all. Movement can cause damage that cannot be put right.

Signs that someone has broken their back are:

- Severe pain in the back and neck.
- Weak control over limbs, or no movement at all in the legs.
- Tingling feeling or no feeling at all in the limbs.

Asthma Attacks

Asthma is a common illness which affects millions of people. One in seven children is affected by it, and boys are twice as likely to suffer from it as girls.

Asthma is caused because the tiny air tubes in the lungs of asthma sufferers easily become sore and swollen. When someone has an asthma attack, the tubes get narrower and the sufferer's chest feels tight. They have difficulty breathing and begin to cough. All sorts of things can set off an attack, but some of the most common are colds and viruses, cigarette smoke, pollen or cold, dry air.

CONTROLLING ASTHMA

People who suffer from asthma usually carry blue inhalers which contain medicines they can breathe in if they have an attack. Smaller children use a simpler version of an inhaler. If a friend has an attack, this is what you should do:

- Help them to get out their inhaler and take their medicine.

- Make your friend sit down – but they should not lie down.

- Reassure your friend, and help them to stay calm and breathe slowly.

- Loosen any tight clothing.

- Make sure that no one is smoking nearby.

- Tell an adult about the attack immediately.

- If your friend is still struggling for breath after five minutes, call an ambulance. Don't be afraid to cause a fuss. A serious attack is very dangerous and needs expert help as quickly as possible.

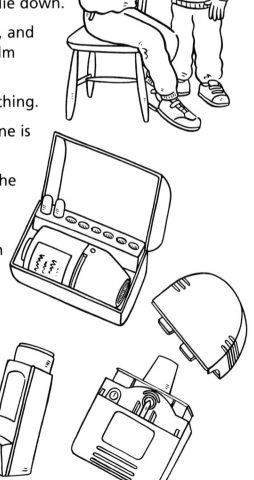

Epilepsy

Epilepsy affects at least one in every two hundred people. It's caused by a short and sudden change in the chemicals in the brain, which causes a fit or seizure. There are many different types of seizure. Some people drift into a kind of trance, but others have convulsions when the body stiffens and shakes.

Watching someone having a seizure can be frightening, but most seizures are not dangerous in themselves. The best emergency aid you can give is to make sure that the casualty doesn't injure themselves.

If someone has a seizure . . .

- Cushion their head. Use your hands or forearms, or a rolled-up jacket or cardigan if you don't have pillows or blankets.

- Move any furniture or other nearby objects that might injure the casualty.

- Once the seizure has finished, put the casualty in the recovery position (see page 14) and stay with them until they are completely recovered. Make sure they can breathe freely, but let them come round in their own way, and don't make them move until they are ready.

Don't move the casualty during the seizure unless they are in danger, and do not put anything in their mouth.

CALLING AN AMBULANCE

Usually, you won't need to call an ambulance. However, do dial 999 if the casualty has injured themselves or if the seizure lasts more than five minutes. You also need medical help if a child has a seizure for the first time.

Diabetes

Diabetes is an illness which affects about one person in every hundred. Sufferers do not have enough insulin in their bodies. Insulin is a chemical which moves sugar from the food we eat into our blood. Without enough sugar in our blood, we don't have any energy.

Most people know that they have diabetes and take injections of insulin to control the illness. However, some people do not realize that they have diabetes, or, even if they do, their insulin level may suddenly change. When this happens, the sufferer's blood sugar level drops, and they may need emergency help.

All sorts of things can cause blood sugar levels to change dramatically, but the commonest are:
* a sudden burst of unexpected activity;
* missing a meal;
* too much alcohol.

When someone's blood sugar level drops, they may:
- tremble, sweat and look pale;
- become confused, unsteady, or even aggressive (rather like someone who is drunk);
- lose consciousness.

WHAT SHOULD YOU DO?

If you know that the casualty is diabetic, make them sit down and rest. Give them something sweet to raise their blood sugar levels as soon as possible – sugary tea, chocolate or sugar lumps. When they have recovered, advise them to see their doctor.

If the casualty is unconscious, call an ambulance immediately. Smear some honey or jam between their cheeks and gums, but make sure that they can breathe properly.

If you think an unconscious casualty might be diabetic, look for tell-tale signs. Are they carrying: a warning card or bracelet; an insulin syringe; insulin tablets?

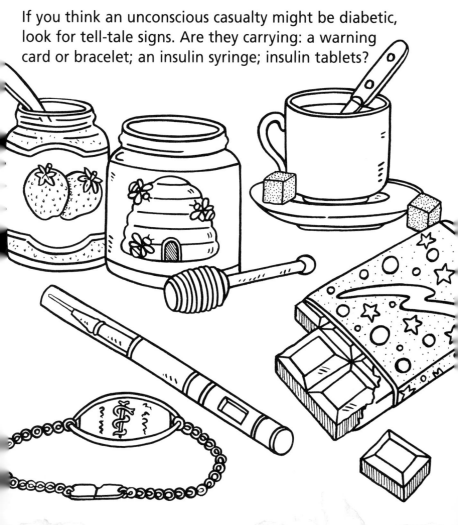

!SAFETY ALERT!
Safety at Home

You might be surprised to know that one of the most dangerous places you'll ever go is your own home! For every casualty who goes to hospital after a road accident, eight other people need hospital treatment because they have injured themselves at home.

But don't despair! The good news about accidents at home is that they're easy to avoid.

HOME ALERT!

Go through your home room by room.
Are there any dangers you can see in this house?

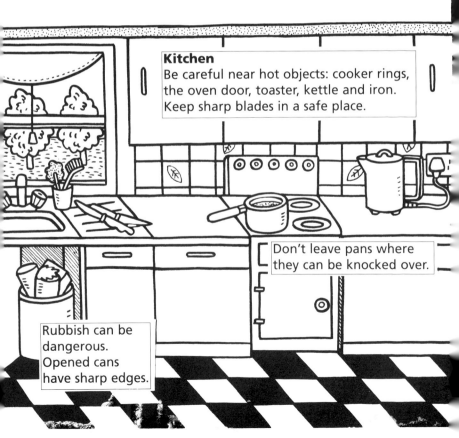

Kitchen
Be careful near hot objects: cooker rings, the oven door, toaster, kettle and iron. Keep sharp blades in a safe place.

Don't leave pans where they can be knocked over.

Rubbish can be dangerous. Opened cans have sharp edges.

Be Prepared

You need to know what to do in an emergency if you're out and about – but you should always be prepared for accidents at home. Emergencies can happen there too.

USEFUL NUMBERS

Make a list of useful phone numbers and keep it next to the telephone. You could include:

- Doctor
- Dentist
- Emergency contacts for gas and electricity
- Nearest chemist

You can add other useful pieces of information – do you know where in the house to find the mains switches for water, gas and electricity?

FIRST-AID SUPPLIES

Make up a basic first-aid kit for your home. You don't need expensive equipment. You could use an old shoe-box, and just label it clearly. You should include:

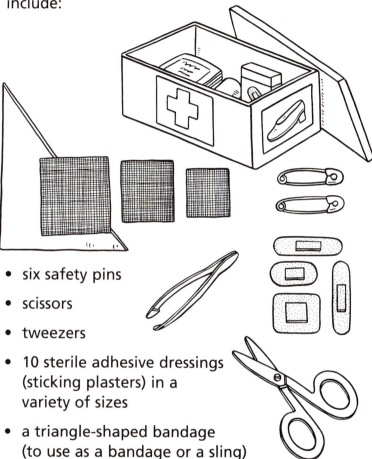

- six safety pins
- scissors
- tweezers
- 10 sterile adhesive dressings (sticking plasters) in a variety of sizes
- a triangle-shaped bandage (to use as a bandage or a sling)
- one large and one extra-large sterile dressing (these are easy to use in an emergency)
- 3 medium sterile dressings
- one sterile eye pad (any eye injuries must be protected with a sterile cover)

Fire

A fire is one of the most dangerous emergencies that can happen at home. Fires spread quickly, so you must react quickly too. Do you know what to do if fire breaks out in your home?

If fire does strike, you can be ready for it by knowing the best and quickest escape routes out of your home.

Draw a plan of your home or school, and work out the best escape routes from each room.
   Try to find an alternative route from each room in case the quickest route is blocked.
   Once your plan is finished, use it to have a fire practice with the rest of your family.

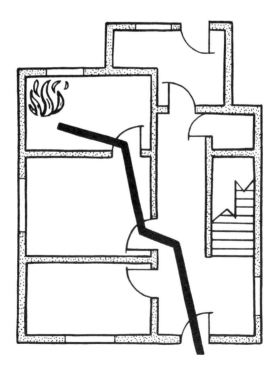

SMOKE

In many house fires, smoke is a worse danger than the fire itself. Smoke spreads very quickly and if you inhale it, just five large breaths can kill.

If you smell smoke, follow the instructions on the following page about how to leave the building.

During a fire alert, leave the building as quickly and calmly as possible.

Escape Routes

If you are caught in a fire, follow these guides as quickly as you can to escape from the building:

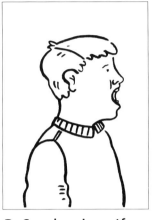

1 Shout as loudly as you can to tell everyone where the fire is. If you can, shut the door of the room where the fire started.

2 Get out of the building as quickly as you can. Never stop to pick up belongings or even pets.

3 Smoke rises. If you have to move through smoke, crawl along the floor where the air will be clearer.

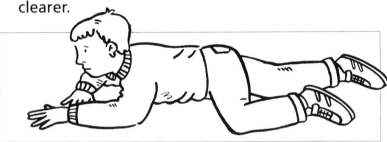

4 Don't open any doors unless they're part of your escape route. Before you open a door, feel it with the back of your hand. If it is hot, the fire is behind it, so keep it shut.

5 If all the escape routes are blocked and you are trapped inside the building, get everyone into the safest room and close the door. Block any gaps with blankets or clothing to keep the smoke out.

6 If you are trapped upstairs, open a window and shout to attract attention. Don't jump out of a window unless you have absolutely no choice. First drop cushions and bedding onto the ground below to break your fall. Then lower yourself over at arm's length before dropping to the ground. Never jump straight out of a window.

7 If you need to break a window to escape, use a heavy object. Before climbing out, cover the jagged edges with a towel or blanket.

8 Once you're out, stay out. Never return to a burning building. Dial 999 and wait for the fire brigade.

Stop, Drop, Roll

It's a terrifying experience if a person's clothes ever catch fire, but it is possible to avoid serious burns if you know what to do.

If you're alone and your clothes catch fire, you should **stop**, **drop** and **roll**.

1 **STOP**. Running about will make the fire spread more quickly.
2 **DROP** to the ground.
3 **ROLL** around on the floor to put out the flames.

If you see that another person's clothes are on fire, try to put out the flames by wrapping them tightly in a coat or a cloth blanket – but never use anything made of nylon, which might make the burns worse.

FIREWORKS

Stay safe when you use fireworks. **Remember:**

- Keep fireworks in a closed box.
- Follow the instructions on each firework.
- Light fireworks at arm's length, using a taper.
- Stand well back.
- Wear gloves and take care with sparklers.
They stay hot even when they've gone out.

Never:
- Throw fireworks.
- Put a firework in your pocket.
- Let pets outside on fireworks night.
- Go back to a firework once it's lit. You can never be sure it's gone out, and it might go off in your face.

Burns and Scalds

All burns and scalds need some attention straight away. The longer a burn is left untreated, the worse it becomes. Severe burns can cause shock and unconsciousness, and if you're at all worried about a casualty, you should get medical help as quickly as you can. Any burn or scald is a serious injury if it affects an area bigger than two square centimetres.

FIRST AID FOR BURNS

It's important to know some simple first-aid steps even for small burns.

- With all burns, you should cool the injury as soon as possible, using lots of cold water. If the burn is large, cover it in a towel soaked in cold water. Cooling a burn properly can take up to ten minutes.

- If you don't have any cold water, you can use another cool liquid such as milk or beer. However, **never** use a liquid which burns easily, such as oil.

- Once the burn is completely cooled, cover it with clean, non-fluffy material, to protect it from germs. You can use a sheet of clingfilm.

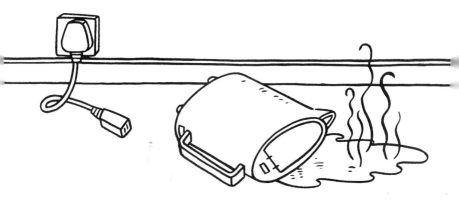

DOS AND DON'TS

* Do not put a sticking plaster or cotton wool on the injury. You won't be able to get it off later without damaging the skin beneath.

* Do not break any blisters, as they protect the skin beneath.

* Do not put butter, ointment or toothpaste on a burn.

Always get medical help if:

- The burn was caused by an electric shock or by chemicals.

- The burn affects the mouth or throat, which might make it difficult to breathe.

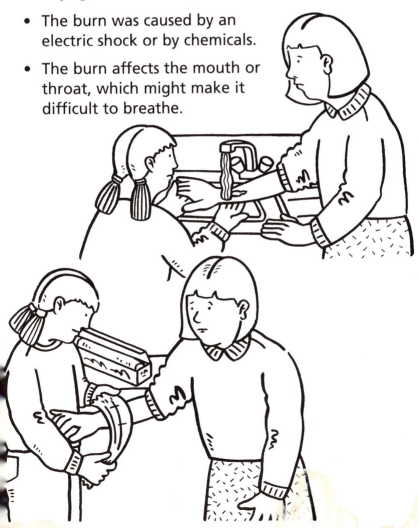

Electrical Dangers

Electricity is a type of energy. It's the power that works all kinds of machines in our home – from computers and washing machines to lights and television sets. But electricity is dangerous! If you touch bare wires or live parts that have electricity flowing through them, you could be badly injured or even killed. Always treat electricity with respect.

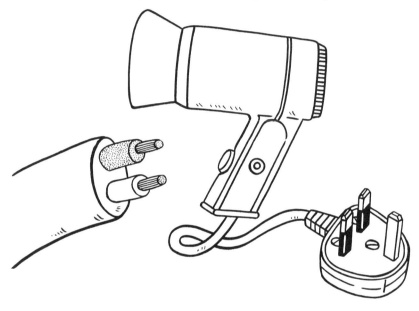

Even something as small as a hairdryer uses enough electricity to kill you.

Electricity passes through some materials (called conductors) but not through others (called insulators). It moves through metal, but not through rubber or plastic. That's why electric wires should always be covered by a rubber or plastic tube. If you see bare or frayed wires, never touch them.

Watch out for this warning sign. It means that there is danger from electricity. You'll always see it on pylons, which carry huge amounts of electricity, and are especially dangerous.

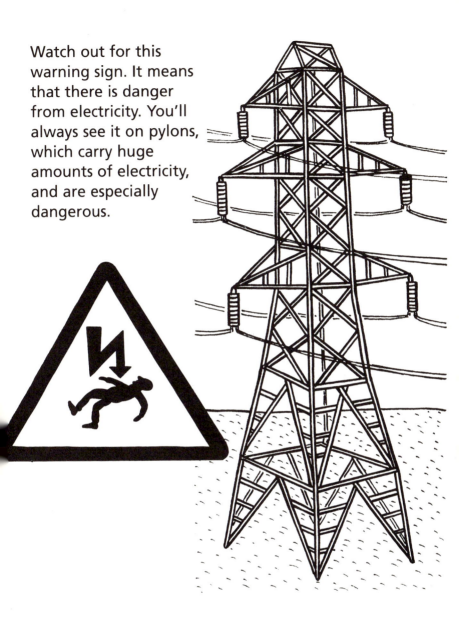

Electricity can pass through water, so water and electricity should never be allowed to mix. Never pour water onto machines powered by electricity, even if they are on fire.

Electric Shocks

Finding someone who has had an electric shock is dangerous. Electricity can pass through our bodies from one person to another. If the casualty is still connected to a live electricity supply, they can pass on the shock and injure you too.

If someone has an electric shock at home:

- Don't touch them. The electricity will pass from them to you.

- If you can, switch off the electricity supply. The safest place is the mains switch.

- If you can't switch off the electricity supply, as a last resort try to move the person away from the electricity. Stand on a wooden box, plastic or rubber mat, a phone book or pile of newspapers. Use something **wooden** (such as a chair or brush handle) to push the casualty away. Never push them with anything metal.

If someone has received an electric shock from a high-voltage cable (usually out of doors), dial 999 immediately and do not go near them. Strong electricity can 'jump' as far as 20 metres, so no one should approach the casualty until you are sure the electricity supply has been switched off.

Anyone who has received a serious electric shock should have expert medical treatment immediately.

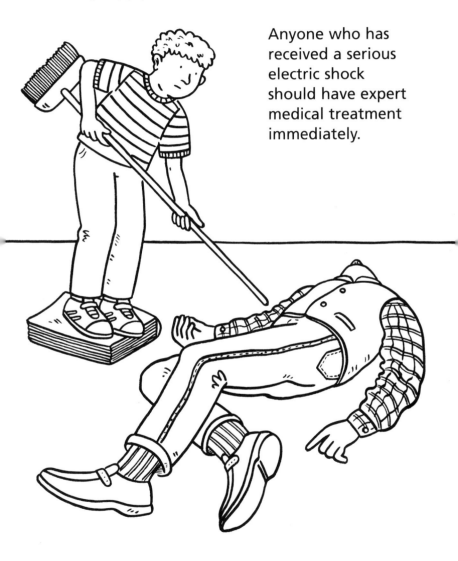

!SAFETY ALERT!
Safety in the Country

Even if you live in a town, you'll probably go walking or sightseeing out in the country now and again. We usually think of the countryside as a peaceful place, but you need to watch out for dangers in the country as much as in a busy city.

Follow these simple guidelines to stay safe in the countryside.

Don't take chances with animals. We don't usually think that cows or pigs are aggressive, but they can hurt you just by being 'playful'. Be specially careful near animals which have young and might feel threatened by you. Cows with calves are the biggest danger.

Stay away from slurry pits. They are deep enough for someone to drown in (and don't smell very nice anyway!).

Survival Out of Doors

If you go walking in quiet parts of the countryside, you must be properly prepared for bad weather or accidents.

- Make sure that you take the right kind of clothes with you. You'll need strong shoes or boots and a waterproof coat. Try not to wear jeans – they are cold and uncomfortable if they get wet.

- Never set off without a map and compass. You should also take a torch in case you get lost in the dark, and a whistle to attract attention.

- Never set off alone in the countryside. It is best to go out in a group of three people or more.

If someone does have an accident, don't move them. One person should go for help, the other should stay with the casualty. Make sure you know exactly where the casualty is. If you think you might not be able to find them again, leave markers such as stones.

MAKE A BASIC SURVIVAL KIT

A very basic survival kit contains:
* Map and compass.
* Torch and whistle.
* Some simple food supplies. You need food which contains plenty of sugar – such as chocolate or glucose sweets. But it's important to have salty foods too. Include a pack of stock cubes.
* A large plastic bag (such as a bin liner). You can climb inside this up to your neck to stay warm and dry if you are lost at night.
* A woolly hat. (Most of your body heat gets out through your head, so you need to keep it covered if you're cold.)
* Pen and paper for messages.
* Basic first-aid kit.

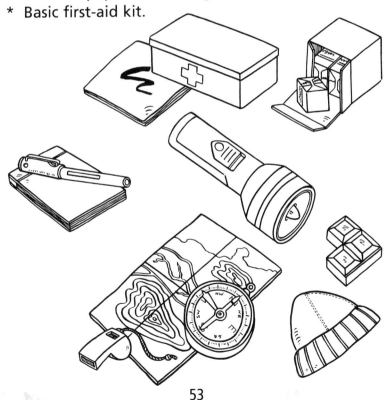

Lightning

Every year about 30 people are struck by lightning in Britain. Some of these are killed by the force of the electricity – there's enough power in just one streak of lightning to cook 4,000 pieces of toast.

Lightning doesn't have to be fatal – if you know what to do in a thunderstorm.

PLACES TO AVOID

- Avoid wide open places and hilltops.
- Never shelter under a tree – trees are one of the most likely objects to be hit.
- Throw away any metal objects you're carrying – golf clubs, umbrellas or fishing rods.

PLACES TO SHELTER

- Inside buildings. If lightning strikes a building it usually leads straight to the ground through gutters or cables. But make sure you unplug your TV and aerial in case that's where the lightning strikes.

- Inside a car. Even if it strikes, the electricity will spread over the metal surface before going into the ground through the tyres.

- If there's nowhere safe to shelter, crouch down low inside a hollow or a ditch.

If anyone is hit by lightning, call an ambulance at once.

Safety in the Sun

Fresh air and sunshine are good for our health, but staying outside in strong sunlight for too long can be dangerous. If you're out of doors in the sun, make sure you take care of yourself.

SUNBURN

Sunburn is caused when our skin is burnt by the heat of the sun. It is painful and looks ugly. It's also dangerous, and can cause skin cancer later in life.

* If you're playing out in the sun, keep as much of your skin covered as you can.

* Wear a sunhat to protect your head and face.

* If you have to be out in the sun, always use a strong sunblock (factor 15 is best). If you can, stay out of the sun altogether between 11 am and 3 pm when it is at its strongest, even in the UK.

HEAT EXHAUSTION AND HEATSTROKE

If someone's body is too hot for too long, they run the risk of heat exhaustion. They lose salt and water from the body through sweating. If they don't drink enough or replace the salt, they may start to have a headache, and feel sick and dizzy.

Heatstroke is a similar illness, but it happens much more quickly and can be serious – especially if the casualty falls unconscious.

If someone has heat exhaustion . . .

- Give them water, mixed with a little salt (put one teaspoon of salt in each litre of water).

- Take off the casualty's outer clothes, lie them down and wrap them in a cool wet sheet. As their temperature falls, swap the wet sheet for a dry one.

- Call a doctor or an ambulance.

Safety near Water

Everyone likes playing in or around water – swimming pools, the sea, canals, boating lakes. But these are all places where accidents can happen. Always take care and remember that it's possible to drown in just a few centimetres of water. Even if you can swim, you still need to watch out for strong currents, or plants and objects hidden beneath the surface.

Don't go into the water yourself unless you really have to, and you are sure that you will be absolutely safe. Even if you're a good swimmer, the shock of cold water will make you weak. Don't try to tow the casualty to the bank unless you're a trained lifesaver.

If you are sure that it's safe to go into the water yourself, try to wade in, not swim.

Every year, people drown when they try rescues that are too difficult for them.

If you see someone who's drowning . . .

- Try to help by reaching out to them from dry land. Use your coat or jumper.

- Is there a lifebelt nearby?

- Can you stretch out a long stick for them to grab hold of?

- Can you find a rope to throw out to them?

Bites and Stings

We're lucky in Britain not to have many dangerous animals – but it's still possible to get a nasty bite from an unfriendly dog or to be stung by bees and wasps. And even small injuries should always be treated properly.

BEE STINGS

- Don't squeeze the sting. That just pushes the poison deeper into the skin. Try to scrape it away with a knife or your fingernail instead.

- Put an ice pack on the sting to stop it swelling up. (You can make an ice pack with ice cubes and a piece of cloth, or even use a pack of frozen peas.)

- If the sting is inside the casualty's mouth, give them an ice cube to suck.

- Most bee stings are painful, but not dangerous. However, some people have a serious allergic reaction to stings. If the casualty shows any signs of shock or has difficulty breathing, call an ambulance at once.

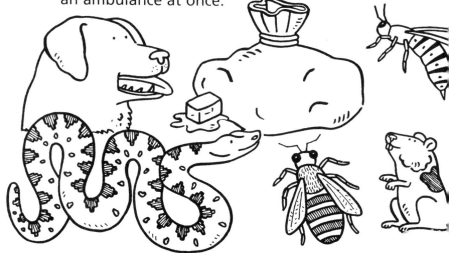

SNAKE BITES

There's only one kind of poisonous snake in Britain, so snake bites are much more of a danger if you're abroad.

- If someone is bitten by a snake, call an ambulance immediately.

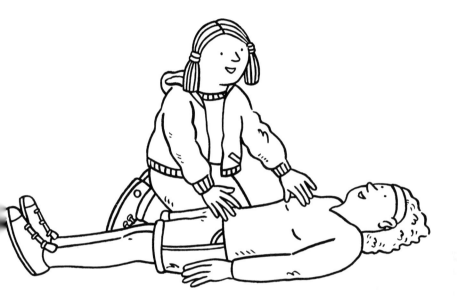

- Lay the casualty down and try to keep them still so that the poison moves through the body more slowly.
- Wash the wound with soap and water if possible.

Even if they aren't poisonous, other animals, such as dogs, can give nasty bites. Always get medical advice if you have been bitten. An anti-tetanus injection will stop the wound from becoming infected.

Acknowledgements

BBC Children's Books would like to thank all the organizations listed below for their help with the preparation of this book.

National Asthma Campaign,
Providence House,
Providence Place,
London N1 0NT

The National Asthma Campaign runs an Asthma Helpline on 0345 010203.

British Epilepsy Association,
Anstey House,
40 Hanover Square,
Leeds LS3 1BE

The British Epilepsy Association telephone helpline is on 0800 309030.

Cancer Research Campaign,
10 Cambridge Terrace,
London NW1 4JL

The Cancer Research Campaign can provide further information on safety in the sun. Please send a SAE.

The Countryside Commission,
Cheltenham,
Gloucestershire.

Advice on fire safety was provided by the Public Relations Branch of the Home Office. For further information on fire safety, please contact your local fire brigade.

For information on firework safety, please contact the Customer Safety Unit of the Department of Trade and Industry on 0171 215 3468.

John Mills and the Medical Department,
St John Ambulance,
1 Grosvenor Crescent,
London SW1X 7EF

The Royal Society for the Prevention of Accidents (RoSPA),
Cannon House,
The Priory Queensway,
Birmingham B4 6BS
Tel: 0121 200 2461

RoSPA is Europe's largest safety organization, specialising in road safety, home safety, safety in and around water and in the play and leisure environments.

Index

allergic reactions   60
anti-tetanus   61
asthma   28
asthma attack   29
attracting attention   7, 19

back injuries   15, 24, 27
bandages   11, 13, 37
bathroom   35
bee stings   60
bites   60-61
bleeding   10-11, 12-13
blisters   45
blood sugar   32-33
breathing   14, 15, 29
broken bones   26-27
burns   41, 42, 45

car accidents   18-19, 22, 23
chemicals   20-21, 45, 51
choking   14
countryside, safety in the   4, 7, 50-51, 52-53
cuts, small   10, 11
cycling   4, 24-25

dangerous substances   20-21, 35, 51
diabetes   32-33
dressings   11, 12-13, 37, 44
drowning   22, 58

electric shocks   45, 46-47, 48-49
electricity   35, 36, 46-47, 48-49
emergency four-point plan   5
epilepsy   30-31
escape routes   41

fire   19, 38-39, 40-41, 42, 46
fireworks   43
first-aid kit   37, 53

gas   36

Green Cross Code   16-17

"hazchem" signs   20
heart attacks   6
heat exhaustion   57
heatstroke   57
help, going for   5, 6-7, 8-9, 19, 29, 31, 36, 41, 55, 57
home, safety at   34-35

insulin   32

lightning   4, 54-55

motorways, safety on   18-19

999 (when to dial)   8, 41

outdoor survival kit   53
oxygen   10

pets   51

recovery position   14, 31
road accident   16, 18-19, 20
road safety   24

seizures   30, 31
skin cancer   56
smoke, danger from   19, 28, 29, 38, 40, 41
snake bites   61
strangers, when to speak to   6, 7

telephone calls   6, 8-9, 19, 36
tetanus   61
traffic   17

unconsciousness   14, 31, 32, 44

water, safety near   22-23, 36, 38, 58-59